ALSO BY MIKE MIGNOLA

Baltimore, or, The Steadfast Tin Soldier and the Vampire
(with Christopher Golden)

The Amazing Screw-On Head and Other Curious Objects (graphic novel)

Hellboy graphic novel series

B.P.R.D. graphic novel series

Witchfinder: In the Service of Angels (graphic novel)

Lobster Johnson Volume 1: Iron Prometheus (graphic novel)

Abe Sapien: The Drowning (graphic novel)

Jenny Finn (graphic novel)

Zombieworld: Champion of the Worms (graphic novel)

Also by Christopher Golden

Baltimore, or, The Steadfast Tin Soldier and the Vampire (with Mike Mignola)

The New Dead (editor)

The Myth Hunters

The Borderkind

The Lost Ones

The Monster's Corner: Stories Through Inhuman Eyes (editor)

Wildwood Road

The Boys Are Back in Town

Of Saints and Shadows

Angel Souls and Devil Hearts

Of Masques and Martyrs

The Gathering Dark

Waking Nightmares

The Ocean Dark (as Jack Rogan)

The Collective (as Jack Rogan)

M

Joe Golem and the Drowning City

an Illustrated Novel

Mike Mignola
& Christopher Golden

St. Martin's Press New York

This is a work of fiction. All of the characters, organizations, and events portrayed in this novel are either products of the authors' imaginations or are used fictitiously.

 For information, address St. Martin's Press, 175 Fifth Avenue, New York, N.Y. 10010.

www.stmartins.com

Library of Congress Cataloging-in-Publication Data

Mignola, Michael.
Joe Golem and the drowning city : an illustrated novel / Mike Mignola, Christopher Golden.
ISBN 978-0-312-64473-4 (hardback)
ISBN 978-1-4299-4079-5 (e-book)
1. Teenage girls—Fiction. 2. Private investigators—Fiction. 3. Paranormal fiction. 4. Steampunk fiction. I. Golden, Christopher. II. Title.
PS3613.I38J64 2012
813'.6—dc23

2011045605

First Edition: April 2012

10 9 8 7 6 5 4 3 2 1

"For my father—who was, at times, a bit of a golem. But I know he meant well."

—Mike Mignola

"For my son, Nicholas, so soon off to college. 'Swiftly fly the years,' and I hate them for it."

—Christopher Golden

Joe Golem
and the Drowning City

M

Chapter One

Orlov the Conjuror dreams he is a ghost. He floats in the corner of a strangely ornate room, a tiny cathedral of Moorish arches and aquarium-glass windows, beyond which are only sea grass and barnacles and a host of fish of various species, all of them aloof and indifferent to the screams and the bloody perversions occurring in that peculiar chamber of horrors.

The ghostly Orlov weeps tears of anguish and futility, for he can do nothing to help the woman splayed grotesquely on the yellow marble altar, its surface cut through with runnels to capture her blood and other fluids. They pour into a pair of downspouts at the lower edges of the altar and run down into a small hole in the dark, and somehow the Conjuror knows that the blood and offal and birthing fluids are sluicing down into the floor to feed something hungry.

The woman has been chained ankle and wrist with rusted iron—incongruous against the clean Numidian marble. The chains are secured to iron rings set into the floor around the altar. An impotent specter, Orlov can only watch as her body betrays itself, jerking and shuddering. The chains bind her not to keep her from escaping but to prevent the eruptions occurring in her flesh from jerking her off of the altar. Her distended belly undulates with movement from within, as three crimson-robed figures hover around her, poking and prodding her flesh and her orifices with clinical interest. They have daubed her skin with ochre paint, inscribing her with sigils whose meanings Orlov cannot deduce. As she bucks against the altar, the ochre paint begins a slow, acidic burn, branding the sigils deeply into her flesh.

Orlov hates them. He clenches his phantom fists as rage fills him, but it is a hopeless, useless fury. Here in this dream, he is nothing. Less than nothing. He can neither move to aid her nor shout curses down upon her tormentors.

Nor can he curse the capering madman orchestrating it all. The occultist's filthy hair is tied back with a rusted metal ring, and two others bind the twin braids of his beard. While his servants work the woman's flesh with calm detachment, his prancing enthusiasm combines childlike glee with almost sexual arousal. As he circles the altar he darts in between the three crimson-robed figures to utter a string of guttural chants, all the while passing a strange object over the woman, inches above her flesh.

Somehow, Orlov knows this object. He wonders if he is dreaming the madman's dream, or if he is merely haunting it, a ghost lingering in the house of the lunatic occultist's unconscious mind. Regardless, the artifact is familiar to him.

It is Lector's Pentajulum, a knot of tubes and small chambers reminiscent of a human heart but made of a colorful, unknown substance with properties akin to both amber and sea glass. The Pentajulum appears inert, and yet a tiny shift in position seems to alter its design—a trick of the light or of the eye, or some queer geometry the human mind cannot perceive.

The occultist gazes into the Pentajulum as if it is his life's only hope, and Orlov understands that it is precisely that. The occultist's wife is dead, crumbling to dust in her tomb, and the madman believes that the Pentajulum is capable of resurrecting her, of allowing them to live a hundred lifetimes together, if only he can make it work. The Pentajulum's arcane science requires something to ignite it. The occultist believes that death is the key, that the agony and pain and surrender as the candle of human life is snuffed out can be channeled into the Pentajulum through the sigils branded on the woman's flesh.

Straining against her chains, the woman screams. The occultist smiles in anticipation. His moment has arrived. He holds the Pentajulum above the center of her chest. But then his brow furrows and he shakes his head. Stubborn, he refuses to retreat, but Orlov can see that his plan has gone awry.

In the shadowy eaves of the room, something stirs. The woman and her tormentors have been joined by some unseen observer, but not a dream-ghost—not a visitor like Orlov himself. The others in the room take no notice. Even the occultist seems not to be aware of the arrival of this presence, and Orlov cannot understand how the massive weight of its attention can go unnoticed. But the occultist's focus remains on the pregnant woman, and his expression turns to panic as his efforts unravel.

Her belly splits. Orlov the Conjuror stares in horror so profound that it makes him wish for the ignorance of the abyss and the darkness of eternity. Her distended flesh has not torn, nor has she pushed forth some monstrous issue. Orlov can think only of flowers blooming as her abdomen unfurls into petals of ridged, purple-veined flesh.

The occultist screams in fury, his anguish echoing off the vaulted ceiling, caught in the arches, ignored by the fish swimming past the windows.

The woman's body continues to blossom, opening up until there is almost nothing recognizably human about her. Then, just as the flower bloomed, it begins to wilt and turn brown. Deteriorating, the woman cries out weakly. Shaken, the ghost of Orlov the Conjuror screams for her, but he makes no sound.

Orlov is certain that he smells something burning.

And he wakes . . .

Stiff and aching, Felix Orlov shifted in his bed and rolled over. He opened his eyes to narrow slits and stared at the dusty gloom of his room, hating the weight of his age-diminished frame and the demanding pressure of his bladder. On another morning he might have sought a more comfortable position and tried to fool his bladder into giving him another hour's sleep, but today sleep held no sanctuary. His dreams were no haven from the mundane, shuffling boredom that his life had become.

Not these dreams.

Unsettled, he lay waiting for the horrible images to crumble and sift out of his mind, the way dreams were meant to in the moments after waking. His eyes widened and a strange panic began to set in. Felix did not want these things inside his head. They were meant to linger as cobwebs and then be dashed away as the morning progressed, yet as he lay there they became, if anything, more vivid.

"Get out," Felix whispered as he rapped his arthritis-swollen knuckles against his forehead, as if somehow that might reset some mental switch.

With a dry, humorless laugh, he peeled back the bedclothes and swung his legs over the edge, sitting up. He pressed his hands against the small of his back and rotated his head, stretching his neck. Pops and clicks reminded him of past injuries and the onset of age. He rose and shuffled toward the bathroom door.

Felix never looked at the details of his bedroom anymore. He chose not to let his gaze linger upon the faded scarlet curtains from Thailand or the posters hanging on the walls in their cracked frames—posters that boasted astonishing feats of magic by Orlov the Conjuror, as well as the astounding performances of those who had inspired him as a boy, Thurston and Fezzini, Blackstone and Houdini. Though Felix no longer liked to look at the posters, or the many mementoes displayed around the room, he could still see them in his mind's eye. He knew that after all this time they were cloaked in a veil of dust, as obscured as his memories of that long ago time when audiences had cheered him, women had bought him drinks, and he could travel from his bed to the toilet without pain.

This morning, however, Felix's only wish was a gauzy veil of dust to obscure the vividness of the dream still lingering in his head. How could he possibly have known the motivations of the man he had thought of as the occultist? The dream had felt like a memory, but he knew it was not his memory. Not at all.

Dreams or memories. The distinction wasn't really important. Felix had some small facility for being able to peer into the dark corners of the human mind, and a certain spiritual sensitivity as well, but nothing like this had ever happened to him before. It felt like he had been sleepwalking in another man's mind.

With a sigh, he stood at the toilet and relieved himself, massaging the small of his back and hating the way even his eyes felt heavy and gritty. As a young man, Felix had taken to repairing clocks almost as a sort of hobby. It kept his fingers limber, an absolute must for a stage magician. How many times had he dismantled clockwork, cleaning and oiling the parts and rebuilding a clock so that it worked smoothly, so that its innards snicked together properly, tight and strong and accurate?

Felix would have given anything to be a clock that some enterprising young man with nimble fingers could dismantle, oil, and rebuild, good as new.

"Damn," he sighed, careful not to fall as he reached down and flushed the toilet.

Normally Felix avoided the mirror, and had done so for years. This morning he shook his head as though he could dislodge his bad dreams and bent over the sink, splashing water on his face. And then he looked at his reflection.

To his surprise, he was not entirely horrified. His nose had grown larger and his cheeks were more sunken, but there were still wisps of white hair on his head, and the corners of his mouth were turned up in a rueful sort of amusement.

Not a cadaver after all, he thought. *And sure as hell not a ghost.*

Stretching again, Felix felt somewhat better, and he managed to walk back into the bedroom without shuffling. Eighty-two years on this earth and he was still able to take care of himself, more or less. It made him stubborn and it made him proud, but not so proud that he wouldn't have admitted that it also made him lonely . . . if there had been anyone who would listen, and give a damn.

There's Molly, he reminded himself. But Molly was a kid, and he wasn't about to dump his old man's woes on her.

Felix took the worn gray trousers off the footboard of the bed, where he had draped them after taking them off the night before, and put them to his nose, inhaling deeply. Not bad. The strangest part of living in this drowning city was that clean clothes tended to carry more of the moldy smell in them than things you'd worn once or twice.

Felix dressed quickly, donning the gray pants and a bone white, starched shirt from his closet. His fingers were still nimble enough to do the buttons without difficulty. He finished with a gray coat that matched the trousers, and a bow tie of deepest red.

He was no longer the dapper man who watched him from the old theatrical posters, but Felix did his best to look sharp. His clothes might be secondhand, frayed, and threadbare, but he took care of them, and he managed to greet each day with a modicum of dignity. In a place steeped in poverty, abandoned by those with more sense and less stubbornness than Felix had, dignity was difficult to come by, and hard-won. If his clothes hung a little loosely on his thinning frame, no matter. He doubted he had many years left to wear them.

As Felix slipped on his shoes, once again perched on the edge of his bed, the dreams at last began to dim a little. That was good. He feared that such nightmares would interfere with his concentration, and he would need to be able to focus later. Though the small notoriety he had gained as Orlov the Conjuror had been as a magician, he had not started out onstage that way. Felix had been a spiritualist, a medium, capable of reading the minds of members of his audience and of communicating with their dead loved ones.

His abilities were real. As a child he had been in a terrible accident that had taken his mother's life and left him with months of painful healing . . . and an unwanted gift. The dead whispered to him. Sometimes they gathered around him in clusters, but such events were rare. Mostly it was only the occasional whisper, a pleading from beyond, a message to be given to someone still living. And every time he made contact, every stage performance or private séance, he had felt the grief of his mother's death ever more keenly, for in what he felt was the cruelest of ironies, she seemed to be the only ghost with whom he could never communicate. In his darkest hours, Felix wondered if she could hear him but refused to answer. He preferred to think that she had passed so fully into the next life that she was out of the reach of his voice. But some nights, the question haunted him still.

For better or worse, Orlov the Conjuror had never been truly famous. He had always struggled, and when he began to travel, he discovered that whenever he was away from New York for more than a few days, he grew ill. Without the ability to play the great theaters of Chicago and Philadelphia and those even farther abroad, in places that had not been so devastated by the rising waters of the early twentieth century, he had never really had any chance at fame. He had settled in the remains of the Crown Theater on Twenty-ninth Street in drowned and sunken New York, like just another prop forgotten backstage, collecting more dust with every passing day. It was like living inside the ghost of his onetime ambitions.

In the years preceding the devastation, the heart of New York City theater had moved slowly north, from the class warfare of the Astor Place Theater in 1849 to Union Square in the 1870s, and on to Madison Square by the turn of the century. Broadway theater had showcased everything from Shakespeare to burlesque, and always there had been magicians, illusionists, and mediums. By the time of the cataclysm in 1925, theaters had proliferated in Times Square, and the curtains were falling permanently on the stages of Lower Manhattan. And then the quakes and the floods came, and there was no longer any such thing as class warfare in that part of the city.

At the dawn of the twentieth century, New York had begun to transform itself into the crossroads of the world, an unmatched center of business, finance, and entertainment. Then plague and superstition had cast a dark curtain across the European continent, ending the First World War before America had sacrificed too many of her own

young men, and New York had seemed poised to become the jewel in the nation's newly forged crown. For a handful of years, the city had become a dream of prosperity.

The first tremors struck in the summer of 1922, but those were mere flirtations with catastrophe, cracking glass and raising dust. The real quakes did not hit until the city had begun to emerge from the winter chill in early 1925. Snow melted, the rains came, and the rivers began to rise, cresting their banks. Years later, Admiral Benjamin Wheeler and his polar expedition would discover changes in the Antarctic ice shelf that led to much speculation about the sea's rise, but in 1925, the people of New York perceived themselves to be victims of God's wrath. They talked of Sodom and Gomorrah, of the sufferings of Job, as buildings fell and the water swept in.

New York became divided between wealthy, glittering Uptown and the struggling poor who remained in the drowning Downtown because they had nowhere else to go. Instead of abandoning their homes, they adapted, closing off the flooded lower floors of structures that were otherwise still habitable and starting a strange, scavenger society in what remained. Most of the people who were left behind fended for themselves, but there were makeshift shops and restaurants and bars, places where those determined to stay—or unable to leave—could pretend that they still lived in America. That they still knew something of civilization.

Years passed. The sunken portion of Manhattan Island evolved. People Downtown tended to ignore the northern view, just as those Uptown liked to pretend the Drowning City did not exist just beyond their reach. Uptown continued to thrive, to flower with new business and gleaming, modern architecture, while Lower Manhattan cannibalized itself, cobbling together a community of canals and bridges, of dangerous shadows and rebellious minds. The Drowning City, some of its older denizens called it. To Felix, it was still New York . . . still home.

There was still theater in Lower Manhattan, but of a crude, makeshift sort, performed in front of audiences who desired distraction from the thinness of their lives, and who often did not understand the meaning of what they saw. Felix had not performed on a stage—had not truly been Orlov the Conjuror—for more than forty years, and he told himself he did not miss it.

Now he donned his spectacles and picked up his pocket watch from the bureau, clicking it open. A quarter to nine. He had slept later than usual, caught in the grip of his awful dream, but he still had time for a bite to eat before this morning's appointment arrived.

Wondering about the weather, he went to the window and pushed aside the scarlet curtains, letting in a flood of gray light. A storm of dust motes swirled before him as Felix bent to look outside. A light rain speckled the glass, but the waves on Twenty-ninth Street were only a light surface ripple. A steam taxi clanked loudly as it ferried its passengers through the canals of the sunken city. Chinese gondoliers often plied the waters in this neighborhood, but Felix could see none of them today.

He glanced in the other direction, bending farther to peer past the ruin of the marquee that had once announced his building in glorious neon as the Crown Theater. Of course the theater itself rotted now under thirty feet of ocean water, the salt eroding stage, sets, and seats and peeling the paper from the walls. Forty years before, Murray Feinberg had closed off the stairwells that led to the theater, blocking them with concrete, which kept the mold and the scavengers from getting in through the theater's remains, but the smell of mold lingered in the walls of most of the sunken city's old buildings. Most days, open windows didn't help much. The ocean breeze was too often fouled by the greasy oil smoke and coal smog given off by the motors that ran the boats, gave the Drowning City electricity, and powered the factories that employed so many of those whose parents and grandparents had refused to evacuate, all those years ago.

New Yorkers. The thought made Felix smile.

Below, he saw the black smoke–belching taxi chugging toward the front of the theater. A bell rope hung there. If Felix had visitors he wanted to see, he could turn a crank that lowered the iron ladder that led up to a well-built wooden catwalk, which in turn ran around to the narrow gap between the theater and its nearest neighbor, where the century-old fire escape still held strong. Felix never worried about scavengers coming at him from that side. Whatever building had been there had only been three stories high, and in this part of the city that was enough for it to have vanished almost completely beneath the water. At low tide, he could see the barnacle-covered roof, half collapsed, and the long, silvery things that swam down there in the dark.

Felix glanced once more along Twenty-ninth Street, at the ladders and rickety walkways that crisscrossed that view, at planks spanning rooftops and hastily constructed bridges of wood, iron, ropes, and cables—the only footpaths the people of Lower Manhattan had known for nearly half a century. Other places had been rebuilt after the devastation of 1925, when one catastrophe after another had razed cities in quakes, eruptions, and tsunamis. Uptown, New York wasn't much different, with its gleaming, modern wealth. But in Lower Manhattan and much of Brooklyn, people had been recovering for all of those years, forging a new, grim, society. *To Hell with Uptown* had been a popular slogan when Felix had been a young man. But even then, he had known it was a joke. The drowning city, that was Hell. The trick was figuring out how to live there.

An urgent knock shook him from his reverie. He had lost sight of the rattling water taxi beneath the catwalk on the front of the building, below the old marquee, but he knew its destination.

Felix smoothed his threadbare coat and went out into the corridor. There were two floors of rooms above the blocked-off, flooded theater, with a set of stairs and a door between them. He lived on the uppermost floor. Once upon a time he had rented out the floor beneath him, but he no longer accepted money from the tenant there.

The rap on the door came again, soft yet urgent.

"I'm coming," he said with a sigh.

He unlocked the door and opened it. On the threshold, fourteen-year-old Molly McHugh beamed at him, all freckles and red hair and youthful vigor that always made him feel more alive.

"Felix—" she began.

"Enough with the knocking," he said. "At what point are you going to realize I'm too old to move as fast as you'd like?"

"Someone's gotta keep you hopping!" Molly said, cocking a hip as if she were the one to keep him in line. And more often than not, she did. "I just wanted to tell you that your breakfast is ready, but I just spotted a taxi outside. Looks like your nine-thirty is here early."

Felix nodded slowly. Molly took so much pride in her role as his assistant—she worked for him in exchange for room and board, taking up the floor beneath him and feeding him breakfast down there each morning—that he didn't want her to know he had also noticed the taxi arriving.

"Nothing to be done about it, I suppose," he said. "Breakfast will have to wait."

Before Molly could reply, bells began to ring throughout the building. Someone had pulled the rope, down by the water. Felix's appointment had arrived.

He could practically hear the ghosts rustling in the eaves already.

Chapter Two

olly didn't like the way Felix looked. She had seen him tired and distracted before, but this was different. His gaze seemed faraway and the lines on his face, already deeply engraved, were thicker. He caught her studying him and feigned a smile that a stranger might accept, but that she, as his friend, refused to honor with a smile of her own.

"What is it, Felix?"

The old conjuror furrowed his brow. He tried to shrug, but it only came off sad and noncommittal.

"Bad dreams, sweetie," he said, both a confession and another feint attempting to parry her away from the subject. Felix Orlov had taught Molly to fence, and she knew when he had gone on the defensive. "I'll be all right."

She knew him too well to be persuaded.

They had met in the darkness of a TriBeCa canal two years before. Molly had been living in the charred ruin of the upper floors of a building that had housed Ray's Smokefish, which had been a greasy fried seafood joint before fire had claimed it. She had never known her father and regretted knowing her mother, who had barely noticed when Molly had run off from the squat full of hookers and puffers where the two of them had lived through one impossibly long winter. Molly didn't like to think about those months, pretended they had been only a nightmare. The time she had spent fending for herself in the burnt wreckage of Ray's Smokefish had been a relief in comparison. She'd been safe there because even the puffers weren't stupid enough to risk their lives in a building that could crumble into the canals any second. It had been the first place she'd ever thought of as her home. No mother. No puffers. No one trying to touch her or get her to smoke up. No one looking at her with eyes that saw her as just like them, fated to die on the nod in a filthy squat.

She'd rather have drowned.

Molly had been perched behind the rooftop sign for Sharkey's Pub, eating what she'd scrounged from the old Korean waitress who always took her smoke breaks on the metal terrace at the back of the building. Laughter, music, and smoke poured out of the pub, four stories above the waterline, the abandoned tribes of Lower Manhattan making a life for themselves in the flooded ruins. A glass shattered and Molly flinched—she could still remember it vividly, that sound, the way she'd twisted around because the breaking glass seemed so close. But it was just the weird acoustics, the sound coming up through the air ducts in the roof.

Then she had heard the clack of wood and a creaking noise bouncing off the walls below, the city canyons creating echo chambers that could amplify little sounds. She had perched at the edge of the roof under the jaws of the shark in the Sharkey's sign and watched the weird gondola make its way through the narrow canal, the two gondoliers banging long poles off the sides of buildings to propel the tiny boat along without sail or motor. They'd had one passenger, an old man, sitting in the back with his hands clasped in front of him and his chin lifted as if he were posing for a portrait.

That had been Molly McHugh's first sight of Felix Orlov.

A few minutes later, as she crossed a decrepit rope-and-plank bridge half a block from the burnt shell of Ray's Smokefish, she heard angry shouts and muffled laughter. A loud crack of breaking wood resounded off of the surrounding buildings like a gunshot. She had clambered across the bridge, ducked through a glassless arched window in the Oracle Publishing building, run through book-filled offices where Uptown missionaries had set up a center for the lost boys and girls of Midtown and Lower Manhattan, and popped out onto the fire escape on the other side of the building. Below her, the gondola was under attack by Water Rats. The four thugs—in their teens and twenties—had already killed one of the gondoliers when Molly slipped soundlessly onto the metal grating above their heads. As she watched, one of the Rats swung a gondola pole at the old man cringing at the back of the little boat. The second gondolier dove into the water and swam, abandoning his boat and his passenger. Two of the Water Rats gave chase, leaving the other two to torment the old man.

Who maybe wasn't so old.

He had stood up, white hair a beacon in the dark, and faced the Rats with his head swaying from side to side, almost like some kind of snake. He spoke to them but kept his voice so low and calm that she couldn't make out the words, and he'd let his left hand drift back and forth in front of him so slowly that Molly thought he must be drunk.

Then Felix had taken a single step forward and thrust his palm at the nearest Water Rat, striking him in the breastbone with such force that the man had fallen out of the little skiff and struck his head on the side of the building before sliding down in the night-black water.

The last Rat pulled a knife.

Molly had cried out almost involuntarily, afraid for the old man and cheering for his courage at the same time. On instinct she rushed to the railing of the fire escape and hit the lever, releasing the ladder, which ratcheted downward so noisily that the knife-wielding Rat paused to look up. He'd uttered some profanity or other, even as Felix grabbed hold of the ladder and began, shakily, to climb.

He would never make it. Molly had known it. The Water Rat was young and strong and would overtake him in swift seconds and stab him in the back or cut his throat, then pick his pockets and let his corpse fall into the water. She had seen the Rats do it before.

She'd ducked back inside the building, seen a box full of old leather-bound hardbacks, and dragged them out onto the fire escape. One of the missionaries, a handsome man with coffee skin and a French accent, came out and began to ask her what she was doing, but Molly ignored him.

Felix climbed. The Water Rat clambered after, having some difficulty because he was too stupid to put away the knife while he gave chase.

Molly shouted down to the old man to watch his head. Felix pressed himself close to the ladder, his thin frame no obstacle at all. The Rat did the opposite, leaning back, sneering up at her, wondering what she was up to.

The first book broke his nose. He sagged on the ladder, shouted in pain, and started dragging himself up faster, but he was still not smart enough to try to press himself closer to the iron rungs. The second book missed entirely, and a frantic tremor went through Molly. As the Rat reached for Felix's leg, she dropped another pair of heavy books.

They crashed into the side of the Rat's face and he lost his footing, barely managing to hang on by one hand as his boots sought purchase.

Molly groaned as she lugged the rest of the box over the railing and let it fall. It scraped Felix's back, knocked him hard against the ladder, and then hit the Rat with terrible force, tearing his fingers off the rung and snapping his head back at a dreadful angle.

He had gone into the water and never come back up.

By the time the other Rats had come back, there were missionaries all over the fire escape, shining lights down at the black water. Molly did not trust them, not even when they insisted she and Felix spend the night at their mission with the lost children of the Drowning City. As much as Felix intrigued her, she had slipped out before dawn and returned to the scorched ruin of Ray's Smokefish.

It had taken Felix two days to track her down so that he could thank her. He needed an assistant, he said. Someone he could depend upon, who could help look after his home and play host to his clients.

No one had ever needed her before.

"You're not all right," she told him.

The bells rang again and once more Felix tried to get away with a wan smile, trying to slip past her and through the door that led to the stairs.

"Felix!" Molly said sharply.

He took a deep breath and all pretense fell away. From the moment she had first seen him, Molly had thought of Felix as an old man, but she had been twelve then. To her, anyone with white hair was *old.* Now, as he let out a long sigh, Felix appeared positively ancient.

"I feel as if I'm fading away," he said.

Molly took his hand. Felix was the closest thing to family she had in the world, and she hated to see him ill. "You should cancel. I'll make excuses for you, send them away."

Felix clucked his tongue. "You'll do no such thing. I don't have many clients left. If we want to continue to be able to afford groceries, I can hardly turn away the ones who still come to me."

Molly squeezed his fingers in hers. Her red hair had fallen across her eyes, but she didn't let it distract her, focused entirely on him.

"I'm supposed to be your assistant, remember? That means I'm responsible for you," she said, a nervous pang in her chest. "You need rest."

"Tomorrow," Felix said, his eyes soft and his smile, at last, genuine. "I'll go out to Brooklyn, and then I'll feel better. I always do."

"You promise?"

"Do I have a choice?"

Molly released his fingers and crossed her arms sternly. "No. You don't."

"Voilà. There you have it. Brooklyn tomorrow. And today, we make a little magic. See what the spirits have to say."

Molly let out a breath, her mind somewhat eased. She nodded, satisfied for the moment, but still concerned for the old man.

"Well, then, young lady," Felix said, gesturing through the door to the stairs. "Lead on."

Something had gone wrong.

Molly stood watching the séance from a shadowed corner of the room, and she did not like the contortions of Felix's face. He looked as though he had found himself stuck in a dream of sorrow and fear from which he could not wake. The Mendehlsons sat on either side of him, the three of them holding hands across the table, the points of an occult pyramid. Mrs. Mendehlson—Sarah—kept her eyes closed as Felix had instructed, features etched with hope and expectation. Felix had managed to make contact many times with the spirit of her son, David, who had been killed in the collapse of one of the crumbling, underwater buildings far Downtown, where fools and adrenaline junkies liked to dive inside the ruins of structures that were completely submerged.

Once, Felix had also found the ghost of Sarah Mendehlson's father, who had died of cancer in his East Twenty-fifth Street apartment after refusing to leave the Drowning City and go Uptown to a hospital. Not that they could have cured him, but they might have given him years more, or at least made him comfortable. Mrs. Mendehlson's father had assured her, through Felix, that he was content with the decision he had made.

Mr. Mendehlson did not share his wife's faith in Felix. No matter how many times the conjuror had given the woman information only her dead loved ones could know, Mr. Mendehlson would never allow himself to be convinced.

When she had first come to live and work here, Molly had also had her doubts. More than doubts, really. She had been certain that Felix was little more than an aging confidence man skilled at parting fools from their money. She had met plenty of scam artists during the years she'd spent on the street. Over time, however, she had found that she had no choice but to accept the truth of Felix's gift, not only because of the things she had seen to convince her, but also because of her growing trust in and love for the man himself.

Now that time had passed, and she had watched Felix at work so many times, Molly's belief in him had become immutable. The truth of his work came in his utter surrender to the spirits who communicated through him. Perhaps Mr. Mendehlson could not accept it because Felix had once been a stage magician, and his work had been an artful deception. Or perhaps it was because it would hurt Mr. Mendehlson too much to acknowledge that his son's ghost still lingered in the ether around the Drowning City, not quite ready to move on.

At first, when Molly had accepted the truth—that Felix could speak to the spirits of the dead—it had unnerved her to think that ghosts might be all around her and she would never know. But in time she had realized that the spirits of the dead were not the things she ought to fear. If ghosts existed side by side with the living . . . if souls lingered after death . . . then she had to admit to herself the probability that other things existed as well. Dark things.

The windows were open only a crack and a light breeze swirled through the room, disturbing the curtains. The painted eyes of dozens of statues and paintings of saints and virgins watched over the proceedings, the one element of Felix's work that actually was a charade. When Molly had begun to understand what it was Felix did here, she had insisted that the religious imagery would give clients more faith in his abilities, and thus make them more open to the spirits they sought to contact. To Felix, his gift was entirely ordinary and a séance could be conducted anywhere, but Molly had persuaded him that others did not view contact with the spirits as so commonplace, and that clients needed assurance that what he did was extraordinary.

Now, standing in the eastern corner of the room, Molly looked around and admired her handiwork in the séance room. Enough morning light seeped in to cast a pleasant, warm glow, but around the table the shadows seemed to shift and eddy like the breeze, or the currents in the street below.

The entire theater creaked and moaned like the timbers of an old sailing ship, a result of the water flowing in and out of the lower floors, so that it felt as if the entire building breathed in and out around them. Normally Molly found it soothing, but today she had sensed something off from the moment the séance had begun.

She might have spoken up, but Felix had always made it clear that hers was a supportive role, and that she was never to interrupt a séance in progress. Her presence there in the corner was meant as a reassurance to clients that Felix did not engage in any chicanery. Had she sat at the table, they might have suspected her of helping him create some illusion or other, but out in the open where they could see her, it was clear she was there precisely for the reason Felix stated—to aid him should he be overcome by effort and require fresh air, or water, or someone to fetch a doctor.

In the time since Molly had come to live with him, nothing of the sort had ever happened, though Felix was often unwell. Now, though, watching him closely, she worried at how pale and drawn he looked, and the way he had stiffened in his chair.

Felix frowned deeply, his lips drooping into sadness for a moment before the muscles in his face twitched into a wince, as though he had inhaled the scent of something that filled him with revulsion. His breathing changed, coming in short sips, almost as if he were sobbing.

Mrs. Mendehlson sensed the disturbance at last, and her expression grew troubled, yet she had such trust in Felix that she kept her eyes firmly shut, the crinkles at their edges telling a long tale of grief and woe.

"What is it, Mr. Orlov?" she asked. "Is something wrong with David?"

Molly wanted to put a stop to it right then. Felix had not made contact with David's spirit, at least not yet.

Though Felix always assured her that there was nothing to fear, every time she watched him conduct a séance, Molly found herself worrying for him. And just as he predicted, every time he made contact with the spirit world he emerged without any worrisome aftereffects, save the lingering sadness that so often accompanied his conversations with the weary dead.

Now, though, she studied his troubled expression and a quiet alarm began to sound inside of her. Felix had seemed uneasy when he dropped into his trance, and Molly had imagined—as she always did—Felix searching a dark room with only his hands to guide his way, listening for the whispers of those who waited there. Today it had been almost as if he were surprised by the contours of that room, like the whole experience was unfamiliar.

"Felix?" she ventured softly, because he hadn't replied to Mrs. Mendehlson, and surely even in his trance, unsettled as he was, he must be able to hear her.

Molly felt a trickle of ice go down her back, the fingers of something that should not be there. She had just broken two of her employer's cardinal rules—not only was she not to interrupt a séance, but she was absolutely never to call Felix by his first name in front of the clients. He ought to have at least shown his irritation, but wherever Felix Orlov was in that moment, he could not hear her.

"Yes, something's wrong with David," Mr. Mendehlson said, his beaklike nose wrinkling in distaste. "He's dead."

Stung, Mrs. Mendehlson flinched and opened her eyes, shooting a stricken, heartbroken look at her husband.

"Alan, you bastard," she hissed. "I know he's dead. But that doesn't mean he's gone. It doesn't mean I can't still love my son!"

Molly barely listened. In the golden light filtering through the room, dust motes swirling, she blinked and tried to focus on Felix. Something had gone wrong, yes, but whatever it was it had not finished. Though the focus of the séance had been shattered, Felix remained closed off from the world, still holding tightly to the Mendehlsons' hands. The old conjuror's face had gone dreadfully pale and sweat beaded on his forehead and cheeks.

Had he touched something besides a departed spirit in that other realm? Had he made contact with something . . . evil?

"Felix?" Molly asked. "Please open your eyes."

The table jerked, legs scraping the floor. Mrs. Mendehlson yelped and her husband uttered curses. Molly took a step forward, wanting to go to Felix but not wanting to break his rules . . . his trust.

It had occurred to her more than once that when he opened himself to the spirits, something else might find its way into him, and as she watched him begin to shake, that fear returned. Had he been invaded? Possessed? If he opened his eyes right now, would it be Felix Orlov looking out at her from inside the shell of his body, or something else?

Her heart fluttered like the wings of a captured bird, and she held her breath as she took two steps nearer and bent to look under the table. It jerked again and the edge struck her forehead. She grunted with pain and blinked to clear her vision. Beneath the table, Molly could see Felix's legs jerking spasmodically again.

"What is it?" Mrs. Mendehlson asked fearfully.

"Not a damn ghost, that's for sure," her husband sneered. "It's all an act. The man's a charlatan."

"Shut up, you stupid man!" Molly screamed, turning on him, tears beginning to burn the corners of her eyes. "Can't you see he needs help?"

Felix began to choke, a wet, glottal sound that turned into words, but they weren't words in any language that Molly had ever heard before. He seemed to cough them up two and three at a time in a harsh, grinding tone that became a chilling chant.

The Mendehlsons shrank away from the conjuror as though whatever had transformed him might be contagious. Spirits spoke through Felix from time to time, and she wondered if this was like that—something speaking through him. But if so, was it a human spirit or something *other,* something demonic?

Again she cried his name, shaking him. She struck his face lightly, but received no response. His eyes had been closed, but now they opened and she saw that they were rolled upward, showing the red-tinged whites. Felix smiled thinly, but it wasn't his smile. Whatever the conjuror had invited in—or whatever had forced its way inside him—uttered a wet, phlegmy laugh.

Molly swung her hand back, ready to strike Felix again, much harder this time, but then he began to shake worse than before, his whole body juddering in the chair. As she watched, his skin began to hiss and wisps of white rose up from his flesh.

Was this ectoplasm? She had heard of it, of course—the strange, gauzy substance said to be excreted from the skin and orifices of some mediums, in which invisible spirits might cloak themselves in order to manifest for the living. Felix had once seen it exude from the skin of another medium but told her it had never happened to him before.

The white wisps grew darker, and Molly smelled something burning. She realized that this was not ectoplasm, but smoke, as if Felix's blood were on fire.

Mrs. Mendehlson screamed and leaped up, knocking her chair over.

Her husband sat and stared. "What is this? What the *hell* is this?"

Felix turned and looked at Molly—truly looked at her. She felt he knew her, that this was Felix, not some outside force—and she saw terror in his eyes. He began to shake his head, trying to tell her something. Staggering, he rose to his feet, crashing into the table and catching himself on its edge, barely able to stay upright. His skin had gone from pale to a soft, sickly green, and under his shirt, his torso seemed to shift.

Shaking, Molly backed away from him and collided with a shelf of books and knickknacks she had hung on the wall. A ceramic sculpture of the Virgin Mary fell and shattered, sending shards across the wooden floorboards.

Felix closed his eyes, and Molly watched as he surrendered to despair.

The tiny echo of breaking crystal erupted into a loud shattering of glass, and Molly turned in time to see a second window explode, glass tearing the curtains. Metal canisters hit the floor and rolled in strange arcs, trailing clouds of hissing yellow gas that ballooned quickly, fogging the room.

Molly tried to call out to Felix but she had begun to choke on the gas. Tears ran down her face, and when she tried to breathe she could only cough and cough. She glanced around, peering through the swirling gas, frantically searching for her friend.

The Mendehlsons were shouting, stumbling away from the table, running for the door, which burst open to reveal a hulking figure silhouetted on the threshold. The multifaceted lenses of his black gas mask gleamed with reflected light, and for a moment Molly could hear him breathing through the air tubes, even over the hissing of the gas canisters.

Two more men in buglike gas masks burst through the broken windows, landing on the floor with a wet squelching noise. Smaller than the first, more the size of an ordinary man, they wore long coats over gleaming black wetsuits that clung to their bodies, and she could smell the ocean on them. Others rushed through the door behind the gasping hulk, who grabbed Mrs. Mendehlson's head with both hands and twisted. The snap of bone echoed off the walls and then she fell, lost in the yellow fog of gas.

Mr. Mendehlson began to scream, but Molly didn't see what happened to him. Felix collided with her, knocking her toward the door that led upstairs. Molly hit the door, her hand snatching at the knob, and she threw it open. Accidently or not, he had reminded her of her only path to escape.

Amidst all the gas, she didn't think the men had noticed her yet, but she paused at the bottom of the stairs, glanced back, and saw two men dragging Felix toward a shattered window. She wanted to scream, to attack them, but Felix had shoved her toward safety, and if she had any hope of helping him, she had to remain free. Still, she only made it halfway up the flight of steps before she hesitated again, frozen by her fear for him. The mist began to creep up the stairs as she stood listening to the shattering of idols and the thump of footfalls below.

There came a creak from the bottom step. Molly stiffened, holding her breath as she stared at the cloud of gas swirling, filling the stairwell. Another creak, and she could just make out the silhouette of the huge gas-man—the one who'd been first through the door—coming up after her. How had he seen her coming up the stairs in the midst of that cloud? She stared for a moment at the strange, clunky mask.

And then she ran.

Molly bolted up the stairs and the hulking man pursued her, his sickly breathing making her wonder what was under that mask, and praying she would never have to see.

Chapter Three

olly flew up the steps, the hulking gas-man chugging after her. A heat of panic rushed through her, and her skin prickled with terror, her heart drumming in her temples. She darted through Felix's door and flung it shut behind her, throwing the bolt, forgoing the chain. The gas-man's steps boomed on the stairs.

She hurtled through the sitting room and into Felix's immaculate bedroom. It took up the corner of the floor, windows facing the side and the rear of the building. At the foot of the back window was a rolled-up pile of metal links, a ladder meant to be some family's fire escape. Felix was deathly afraid of fire and had no access to the building's fire escape from this room.

Out the side window Molly saw two gas-men on the fire escape outside the lower floor. Two others dragged a sickly Felix to the edge and held on to him as they leaped into the water of Twenty-ninth Street, dragging him down with them. She wanted to cry out but heard the hulking gas-man banging on the door to Felix's apartment.

She forced up the back window, wood shrieking in its frame, and then bent to lift the pile of metal, which was precisely as heavy as it looked. She managed to work it up to the opening, fixed the hooks to the frame, and dumped it out the window. The ladder made a terrible clanking as it unfolded.

The apartment door burst inward as she climbed out the window. She descended swiftly, hand over hand, her breathing now ragged and desperate. If the gas-man didn't notice the hooks immediately, she might have twenty or thirty seconds before he realized where she'd gone, and she had to use them. She clambered downward, forcing her limbs to ignore the frenzy of her heart, and then she reached the bottom of the ladder and looked down.

It reached only halfway to the water. Twelve feet or more to go.

She heard the gas-man above her, his breath rattling, snuffling like some kind of beast. Molly did not look up. The Crown Theater backed up to what had been the Sebastian Hotel a lifetime ago, before the flood. Three stories high, only the ruin's rooftop sign jutted from the water at high tide. An alley separated the theater and hotel.

Molly pushed out from the wall and let go of the ladder. She tucked her arms in, closed her eyes, and had a moment when she considered praying before she plunged into the water, tasting salt and fuel and filth but just grateful she hadn't hit the roof of the Sebastian.

Surfacing, she saw the hulking gas-man leap from the window and hurtle toward what he thought was the water below. But the tide had risen to only a couple of feet above the level of the old hotel's roof and she heard a muffled scream from inside his mask as he landed.

Molly took off swimming, climbed on top of the Sebastian Hotel, and stood, up to her knees in water. She expected to hear the roar of boat engines but did not. *What now?* she thought, and a moment later, she had the answer. If the gas-men were taking Felix, then she had to follow them.

She glanced around for a place where she might hide, so she could observe Felix's captors in secret. Out here in the open, they would surely see her, and what then? Would they pursue her? Did they want her, too, or would she end up dead like the Mendehlsons?

As she considered this question, the hulking gas-man rose from shallow water on the rooftop, perhaps twenty yards away. Molly stared with her mouth agape as he rose slowly, seawater sluicing off of his rubbery clothing. His head was tilted at a strange angle, and he seemed to put most of his weight on one leg, but the gas mask had not been dislodged. Molly could only stare at the sunlight gleaming off of the mask's black lenses.

The hulking man was injured, but not nearly as badly as he ought to have been after such an impact. He should have been hurt much worse.

No. He should have been dead. What the hell was this guy?

Stop. It isn't me you want, she thought. They had already taken Felix. Why were they still after her?

Maybe they do want you. Maybe they want you both.

He started lumbering after her, and Molly knew she would not be able to follow Felix's abductors. Right now, she had to run.

She splashed her way across the hotel roof, lifting her knees as she ran. At the east end of the building stood an old stone structure that had contained offices when the city started sinking but had been converted to makeshift apartments in the decades since. The people there were poor but mostly decent folks who had held out against Water Rats and worse for many years. All the windows that could be reached from the hotel roof had been filled with stone or concrete or boarded over, but Molly didn't need to go inside.

She climbed. The carved stone arch around a window gave her enough purchase to scramble out of the water. Standing atop the arch, her soaked shoes slippery on the granite, she reached up and grabbed the ledge that ran around to the front of the building. Hoisting herself up to the wide ledge, she edged out along the side of the hotel and then, carefully, around the front. The fall to the water wouldn't kill her, but if she went into the drink now, the gas-man would catch her for sure.

From her new vantage point Molly had a view of the tangle of bridges that crisscrossed the city for blocks in both directions—some stone, some metal, some nothing more than boards banged together or hung from chains. Unless she wanted to swim for her life, escape meant racing through this multilevel labyrinth of a city. She needed to know every twist and turn by heart.

A narrow metal bridge crossed Twenty-eighth Street from the old apartment house to another building on the other side, a shorter structure whose top two floors were now a shop where old women sold handmade dresses and old men sold cigars. Molly hurried along the ledge to the bridge. Its crosshatched welding and bolted struts made it a kind of cage, impossible to get into or out of except from inside the two buildings it joined. But she didn't need to get inside.

She climbed, using the struts as handholds. Someone shouted from inside the apartment building, a woman crossing the bridge, but Molly did not cry for help. What could they do for her from inside when she was outside?

Hauling herself onto the top of the bridge, she glanced back and saw that the gas-man seemed to be moving faster now, almost as if whatever injuries he had sustained when he struck the roof of the Sebastian were healing already.

Molly ran across the top of the footbridge, the wet soles of her shoes making her slip and nearly fall, which sent her lunging forward with her arms pinwheeling to keep her balance. Then she had reached the other side. Molly let her momentum rocket her toward the cigar and dress shop.

The bridge connected to the building's top floor, and Molly jumped as she reached the end of the metalwork, grabbed hold of a ledge, and dragged herself up. A moment later she rolled onto the roof, the smell of cigar smoke tainting the salt air. She had rolled in layers of gull and pigeon droppings, her wet clothes causing the guano to stick, and she wrinkled her nose in disgust but could not stop to clean herself off.

As Molly angled across the roof, her mind spun with fear and grief and wonderment. The Mendehlsons, parents wrapped up in the pain of their son's death, were now dead themselves, horribly murdered and even now finding the answers they sought about their son's ghost. Mr. Mendehlson would finally learn that Orlov the Conjuror was no charlatan. And what of Felix? The sweating and seizures, that guttural chanting, the smell of smoke from his skin . . . had all of that been some kind of attack from the spirit world, demonic possession, or had it been something to do with the gas-men attacking? Given the timing, she refused to believe the two things were unrelated.

The huge gas-man appeared on the roof behind her, and Molly wondered if he could smell the cigar smoke from the shop through his mask. That was when she knew that her mind had become unhinged. Shock had already begun to work its frenetic madness into her head, and she could not allow that. She had to stay focused.

A fist of ice clutched at her middle. Her sodden clothes clung to her, but she began to sprint. Molly knew these buildings, knew the Drowning City's secret passages and hidden bridges, from years of having little to eat and nowhere to sleep and fending for herself, not to mention running from men who wanted more from a young girl than any man ever should.

At the eastern edge of the cigar and dress shop's roof was an eight-foot span of thick wooden planks. Surefooted now, Molly did not hesitate, but launched herself across the planks, which trembled but did not shift beneath her. The gas-man did not shout after her and his silence gnawed at her bones as she hurled herself through the perpetually open window at the end of the planks. A withered fisherman sat in the corner of the room with a needle in his arm. He nodded to her, but Molly ran out of the room.

In the corridor was a spiral staircase. She grabbed the railing and swung onto the stairs, climbing fast, hurtling upward, legs pumping and feet clanging on the metal steps. Her chest burned with the effort, but she could not allow herself to slow down.

Back in the entry room, the junkie fisherman cried out in fear and Molly knew the gas-man was in the building. A crash came from below and she wondered if the fisherman had gotten in his way somehow. Looking down, she saw the gas-man hurrying toward the spiral staircase, and she thought she could hear his labored breathing. Fear brought bile into the back of her throat, and it tasted like rust.

Molly ducked through a small doorway into what had once been a storage space, or some tiny child's room, closing the door quickly and quietly behind her. The gas-man wouldn't have seen her enter, so if she only stayed silent, she would be safe here. Yet with only a flimsy door—not even locked—between them, she felt too vulnerable. Fortunately, she knew this building well. Once upon a time, it had been an elegant apartment building catering to the privileged from out of town who wished to have a second home in Manhattan.

At the back of the room was an enormous wooden wardrobe, dusty and moldy with age. It had been pulled away from the wall, and behind it was another small door to match the first, only four feet high. Moving as quietly as she was able, Molly slipped through that door as well, listening for the gas-man as she emerged on a landing. There were narrow, carpeted stairs here. The building had been constructed with a warren of corridors and stairways so that servants could move through the building without being seen, like rats in the walls.

Silently, quite like a rat herself, she scurried through those narrow halls. She paused when she heard the crash of the wardrobe being thrown aside, a tremor in her heart. How had the gas-man known which way she had gone? He could not possibly have seen her enter through that small door, and she had made virtually no sound.

Shaken, Molly moved through the warren of old servants' corridors. More than once, she ducked through forgotten doors and up or down small stairways, and yet when she paused to listen, she could still hear the gas-man in pursuit. It should have been impossible.

At last, she crouched in a tiny attic storage space, waiting for him to pass by beneath her. A crack in the attic door let her watch the corridor below, and when she heard him come lumbering down the hall, she remained entirely still. Even her heart stopped in that moment, or so it seemed, fearful of making any sound the gas-man might detect.

He passed by the narrow, almost hidden attic stairway. Molly watched him go past, and her heart gave a small leap of triumph, thinking she had eluded him at last. But then the massive gas-man hesitated and voices cried out in alarm inside her mind. He turned halfway, his massive bulk filling the narrow corridor, and she saw the dim light from the guttering flames in the wall sconces gleaming on the black rubber of his mask. The people who occupied this building now either were out or had heard the crash and terror of the gas-man's pursuit, for no one had emerged to interfere or lend a hand.

Please, no, Molly thought. *I'm not here. Just keep going.*

But he did not. Instead, the gas-man reached up to touch his mask, loosened a strap behind his head, and began to lift it from his face. A hiss of air emitted from within, and a sickly yellow gas jetted from the gap. He raised the mask only a little, and as his features were clouded with gas, Molly could barely make out his face, but what she saw filled her with a horror that stabbed to her marrow and filled her veins with ice.

Then the creature began to sniff at the air, that wet, snuffling sound more disgusting than ever, and she understood.

He was following her *scent.*

Molly stifled a scream. She wanted to cry, but she was fourteen years old and had vowed that all of her tears were behind her. A foolish promise, even if made only to herself, and she knew it. But today wouldn't be the day. Felix needed her. As long as he was alive, she would not abandon him.

She bolted, running the length of the attic room and down the main stairs, where she threw open the door and found herself in a hall only ten feet from the top of the spiral staircase she had used when she had first entered the building. For all of her furtiveness and knowledge of this maze of a building, she had gained only seconds.

To the left, the door to the roof was open and she shot outside, into the sunlight. She climbed a pitted metal ladder, and then she was truly on top of the building, the attic she had just been hiding in now underfoot.

A couple had spread a picnic on the roof, a guy and a girl, maybe twentyish. They were looking Uptown, probably dreaming of a life

beyond the poverty and ruin of the Drowning City, making the best of a faded blanket, a bottle of homemade wine, and some meager sandwiches, until they saw the fear on Molly's face.

"Hey. What are you—"

"Get away," she said, flapping her hands to shoo them like they were gulls. "Hide. Or run. Just don't try to stop him!"

"Stop who?" the girl asked.

But her guy seemed to get it right away, to understand the only part of this that he needed to be concerned about. Someone was coming that could hurt them, and he wouldn't let anything happen to his girlfriend. He broke the wine bottle against a chimney, standing up and brandishing the jagged glass, his eyes full of dark expectation.

Molly raced past him, running to the rear of the building. The one behind it, on Twenty-seventh Street, was only a ten-foot drop below. Wooden stairs had been built decades before, but they were rickety and unreliable, and a heavy cable hung nearby. Molly stripped off her shirt, wrapped it around the cable, and held tight as she rappelled the short drop and kept running, her hair flying behind her, trying to drag her shirt back on without falling.

Back on the last roof, the girl started to scream. Her boyfriend made not a sound, and Molly wondered if he was as dead as the Mendehlsons.

At the edge of the building, she slowed, the width of Twenty-seventh Street stretching out in front of her. A wood and rope bridge hung across the gap, but it had been built recently and she had never crossed it, did not know if it could be trusted. Yet she had come this way knowing that she would have to rely on it, and so she did not stop.

She gathered up the guide ropes on either side in her hands and ran, the ropes burning her palms. The bridge swayed and the boards rattled underfoot, but it was sturdy and well-built. Molly released her grip and reached within herself to find a fresh burst of speed, hurtling toward the opposite roof. If she could reach Twenty-fifth Street she would find one of the busiest parts of the Drowning City, the street a web of bridges, a busy marketplace above the water, taverns in the upper floors of well-preserved buildings.

A crash came from behind her. Startled, Molly began to turn and caught her foot, falling. Throwing out her arms, she landed on her belly and scrabbled to get a grip, praying she wouldn't slide off the bridge. Catching herself, heart thundering, she turned to see the massive gas-man climbing from the wreckage of the ruined steps back on the last roof. His weight had made them give way beneath him.

Could she jump? Swim beneath the waves and find somewhere to hide?

Then he leaped, hurtling through the air above the bridge, and landed ahead of her, on the roof at the end of the bridge. Impossible. Yet there he was.

Molly fell to her knees on the bridge, grabbed one of the guide ropes to which the wooden slats were attached, and dropped over the edge. She weighed barely ninety pounds, but the bridge swayed as she began to swing with all her strength . . . once, twice, a third time, and then she let go, arms flailing, legs tucked up to her chest.

Molly crashed down onto the metal catwalk below the bridge and slammed into the building. From above she could hear the sticky, snuffling breathing of the gas-man. Molly pushed off the wall and bolted along the catwalk, running to the corner of the building and turning into the narrow, shaded alley where the fire escape descended down and into the water.

She had no time to be careful now. Caution would kill her. She threw one leg over the railing, slid down, and searched with her feet for the railing below. There was no time left to take the stairs. Instead she climbed down, agile from a lifetime of surviving in this strange, flooded jungle of stone and iron.

Glancing down, Molly let go and dropped to an ornate wooden walkway built just above the high-tide line. The water washed against the buildings but never reached the bridge, with its Chinese lanterns and little altar shrines spaced at intervals along its length. The walkway led between buildings, from Twenty-seventh Street through to Twenty-sixth, where a small enclave of Chinese lived apart from the much larger community farther Downtown.

At night the walkway would be beautiful, gaslights burning inside the colored-glass lanterns, casting a rainbow of soft hues against the walls on either side. This morning it was just the path to survival.

Something struck the wooden walkway, shaking the boards beneath her feet, and she didn't have to look back to know it was the gas-man. A rush of fury swept through her. For a moment she had let herself believe that she might make it, but once again the hulking man had closed the gap. Molly had let Felix down. Dying, she would let him down yet again.

Tears burned at the corners of her eyes, making her angrier. She would not cry. And yet the tears came despite her refusal.

She glanced back, still running, her footfalls echoing on the wood and off the walls. The gas-man was gaining, only twenty feet behind her now.

Molly collided with a huge man and staggered backward, disoriented, beating at his arms as his powerful hands locked on her shoulders and held her still. The hulking gas-man . . . but it couldn't be; he was right behind her.

She looked up into cold gray eyes, sad but wise, set into a scarred, grizzled face. The newcomer had the solid, imposing build of an old-time boxer, or some back-alley legbreaker. With his huge neck and square jaw, flat nose, and ears that looked too small for his head, he was an ugly man, to be sure. But he had a quiet, inner nobility Molly sensed instantly. Though he had no jacket or tie, his trousers were clean and pressed and his suspenders harkened back to an earlier era. In the first moment, she thought he might be fifty, but then decided he couldn't be much more than thirty. But it had been a rough thirty years, from the look of him.

"I'm sorry, I—"

"You're Molly McHugh?" he said, his voice a low rumble, full of sandpaper grit.

Surprised he knew her name, she flinched away from him. "Who the hell are you?"

"Joe."

He said this like it was the only answer required, then paused a moment, as if memorizing her face. When she opened her mouth to ask for more explanation, he shoved her out of the way. Molly hit the railing, twisting in time to see the hulking gas-man barreling toward them along the Chinese walkway.

The huge man—Joe—slipped out of his long coat, clenching his enormous hands into fists. The gas-man thundered ahead, reaching for him, but Joe only smiled.

Chapter Four

Joe took one step forward and hit the hulking gas-man so hard that yellow mist puffed from the seams of his slick yellow bodysuit with a hiss like a steam engine. As Molly stumbled back against the railing of the bridge, she realized it was the same gas she'd seen escaping from beneath the creature's mask.

Poison. Oh-God-what-if-it's-poison?

She grabbed Joe by the cuff of his rolled-up shirtsleeve and tried to pull him back, but his strength was such that she could not tug him even an inch toward her. She hooked her fingers on his suspenders, but with the flick of a wrist, he shoved her away. Then the gas-man lunged at him, swinging a fist with unnatural speed. The blow struck Joe in the temple with such ferocious power that for a second Molly held her breath, sure he would topple over dead.

Joe shook it off, then waded in, swinging his fists. He took as many blows as he gave, but though the gas-man was staggered by his assault, Joe only seemed more determined every time his opponent landed a punch. The gas-man turned as if to flee, but instead he grabbed hold of one of the posts holding up a Chinese lantern and snapped it off, twisting to swing the lantern.

"Watch out!" Molly shouted, caught between fear for her rescuer and the urge to flee for her life. But the man had intervened to save her—she couldn't just run away.

She needn't have worried. Joe dodged the lantern, then stepped in and punched the gas-man twice more in the abdomen. More yellow mist jetted from the seams of his clothing. The gas-man began to moan, and Molly thought she saw his flesh ripple underneath the rubber casing. He spun around again, with even greater speed, and this time he found his target. The Chinese lantern shattered against Joe's jaw, and the big man stumbled backward, momentarily stunned.

The gas-man clutched the broken lamppost in his gloved hands and charged, aiming for Joe's heart. But Joe sidestepped, and the jagged post never touched him. He grabbed hold of the post and pulled his attacker nearer, stepping inside the gas-man's reach. He caught the gas-man's wrist and twisted it hard enough to snap bone, though no sound issued from within the wet suit. The gas-man let out a kind of shriek, muffled by his mask, and lunged for Joe's throat. Molly watched in horror as Joe tightened his grip on the gas-man's wrist and yanked, moving him as if he were some kind of puppet.

The wetsuit split along the shoulder seam. Blood and sickly yellow mist jetted from the rip in the material, and Joe twisted with such strength that he tore the gas-man's arm off with a wet rip of tendon and fabric.

Molly let out a small cry of revulsion.

As the broken lamppost clattered to the bridge, Joe turned to look at her, holding the severed arm in his hand.

"What did you do?" Molly breathed.

The gas-man collapsed to the planks of the bridge, and they both turned and stared as the huge gas-man deflated, a wilting balloon in the rapidly diminishing shape of a man. Something shuddered inside the wetsuit and then it—and the gas-man's long coat—flopped to the ground, something undulating inside of it.

"Good question," Joe said, staring at the thing flopping inside the wetsuit.

Now that the gas had escaped from within that slick suit, whatever remained bucked and shook inside like an enormous eel. It lunged toward the edge of the bridge, dragging the suit around it. Joe bent to reach for it, muscles straining the threads of his expensive shirt, but he was not fast enough. The thing dropped over the side and into the water below, vanishing into the sea, leaving only its ugly gas mask behind.

"Son of a bitch," the big man rumbled.

Joe stood watching the rippling sea where the strange, eel-like thing had gone into the water, but it did not emerge. Molly tried not to look at the severed arm that he still clutched in his hand. Her thundering heart began slowly to calm, but she could not help remembering the glimpse she had gotten of the face inside the gas-man's mask, and she shuddered

The gas mask lay on the planks of the bridge as if waiting to be picked up.

Joe picked up his discarded jacket and shrugged it back on. His gray eyes turned stormy as he glanced at Molly. When he started toward her, she took a step back, but she didn't run. Despite the limb in its tattered sheath that dangled from Joe's grasp, the worry and kindness in his stony eyes made her feel safe in a way that was entirely foreign to her. Even living with Felix, generous and caring as he'd been, she had always feared the perils of the world. But this man, with his scars and his monstrous size, set her at ease.

"Thank you," she said, wondering what had become of Felix, and if he still lived.

Joe bent to study the gas mask but did not pick it up.

Then the sound of footfalls farther along the bridge drew their attention and they both looked around to see two more gas-men—these the size of ordinary men, apparently having pursued Molly and their larger comrade from the theater—come running toward them, only to jerk to a halt when they saw the empty gas mask on the planks between Joe and Molly, and the severed arm in Joe's hand.

Joe uttered a short, humorless laugh and started to advance on the new arrivals.

"I hit him too hard, huh?" he said. "Maybe I'll try to be gentler with you guys."

Without a word, the gas-men turned and fled the way they'd come, sprinting toward the other end of the Chinese bridge and vanishing around a corner.

Molly felt a spark of hope. Whatever these things were, they had taken Felix. She'd had no chance of finding him, but perhaps that had changed.

She started to run, pursuing the two gas-men, but she made it only three steps before Joe seized her arm.

"No," he said. "You'll never catch them. And if you do, you'll regret it."

Molly tried to yank her arm free, staring at him. "Let me go! You don't understand. They kidnapped my friend. Following them is the only way to find him!"

"It's not the only way," Joe insisted, holding her so firmly that she knew she could never break his grip. "We need to go to Church."

"Church?" she said. "Are you nuts, mister? Prayer's not going to help me track them down. I know every bridge and corner in this part of the city. I can catch them. I can do it without being seen. Just let me go, please!"

Joe shook his head, holding the gas-man's severed arm in one hand and her in the other.

"Sorry, kid. Gotta get this to Church." He narrowed his eyes. "And I better bring you along. No time to argue about it."

Molly shook her head, wondering how she had so badly judged him and why she had felt safe in his presence. He was just another predator. Another kind of monster.

"I'm not going anywhere," she said, gauging her moment, preparing to attack him. If she went for his eyes, he would release her, and then she could bolt. *He's fast,* she thought. *But over the bridges and connectors, I'll be faster.* "Especially not some stupid church."

If she could make it to the Vault on Twenty-third Street, he would never be able to follow her inside—the building had been closed off except for narrow tunnels in and out, much too small for him to pass through.

"I don't want to frighten you," he said, and he almost sounded like he meant it.

Fingers hooked into claws, Molly lashed out at his eyes. But he was too fast for her, twisting away. He dropped the severed arm and spun her around, then shoved her to the ground. His gray eyes had gone from stormy to sad. Towering over her, he produced a small bottle from one pocket of his long coat and a dirty rag from the other.

"I'm sorry," he said.

Molly leaped to her feet and tried to escape him, but he caught her with one hand and clamped the rag over her face with the other. The putrid chemical stink of the rag filled her nostrils. She tried not to breathe it in, but it was too late. She felt her body begin to sag and saw dark shadows moving in at the edges of her vision. She thought of the gas-man and the way he had deflated and wondered if the seams of her skin had split, releasing her spirit in spurts of smoke.

As consciousness left her, she called out to Felix inside her head. He had dreamed he was a ghost. She feared his dreams had come true, and that she might now be joining him.

Then the shadows swallowed her up.

It felt like drowning.

Chapter Five

olly woke with a dull ache in her head, surprised to find herself swaddled in heavy cotton sheets. They were softer than anything she had ever touched, but as her eyes fluttered open, she frowned at the red cloth that hung above her, trying to recall where she was and how she had gotten there.

A wave of memories washed over her and her pulse quickened with alarm. *The gas-men. The Mendehlsons. Felix.* She sat up abruptly, trying to shake the cobwebs of sleep from her mind. The huge man who had saved her—Joe—had put something over her face that had knocked her out. It had to have been him who'd brought her here, but if so, where was he now?

She had to move, to get out of this unfamiliar place. Fear washed through her, yet somehow it forged a grim determination. Felix would never have let anything happen to her, but when the gas-men attacked, she had run away. Molly knew she had to go back to the theater and attempt to figure out what had happened to him, and where the gas-men might have taken him. She thought it was probably hopeless, but she would never forgive herself if she didn't at least try.

Molly dragged the sheet and blanket from the bed, wrapping them warmly around her. She glanced around the room, trying to make sense of her surroundings. She had never been abducted before, but she had known girls to whom that and worse had happened. Girls snatched off the street usually woke up chained to a bed in a cold, damp room that smelled of urine, not in a place like this.

In her entire life, she had never slept in a bed so soft, beneath a blanket that smelled as fresh and clean. Curtains hung from posts at the corners of the bed, a heavy veil of deep red that would have kept her entirely in the dark if the curtains had not been tied back on one side with thick golden cords. Standing beside the huge bed, she stared down at the soft cotton nightgown she wore.

She felt her face flush with anger and embarrassment. Had Joe undressed her while she had been unconscious? Her clothes had been wet, and the nightgown was clean and dry, which was certainly an improvement, but the idea made her skin crawl. Molly had lived in the half-sunken buildings along the canals of New York, survived on her own in squats and deep shadows. She had managed to avoid the worst things that could befall a child on her own in the Drowning City long enough for Felix to find her and take her in. But she had seen terrible things, and heard stories told by other children—boys and girls—of men and women whose behavior suggested that they had broken glass inside them where their conscience should have been.

Calm down, she told herself. *Be smart. Think it through.*

Joe had beaten the gas-man easily. He had monstrous strength. If he had sinister or deviant intentions toward her, Molly had no chance of stopping him. But she felt no ache or discomfort, nothing to indicate that some perversion had been perpetrated upon her while she slept. Though the intimacy of someone having changed her clothes was an intrusion all its own, it was possible that her captor had only kindness in mind. She supposed that she would find out soon enough.

She moved lightly across the room. The door stood open an inch or two and she could hear the murmur of low voices beyond. She needed to get out of here, but she was in no rush to encounter Joe again, so she took a moment to survey her surroundings. The whole room had an antique air about it. A tall wardrobe stood against one wall, with a short bureau beside it. She discovered a bowl of fresh water atop the bureau, and it took her a few moments to understand that it was meant as a washbasin. There was a small bookcase against another wall.

Framed photographs hung on the wall, nearly all of them faded and dulled by time. The people in the pictures wore the clothes of another era, and some of them stood in front of cars not seen in long decades. One shot, in particular, intrigued her. A slender, dapperly dressed man with high cheekbones and round, wireless glasses stood with a second man whose thick mustache might have been meant to add sophistication and cover his otherwise thuglike appearance but failed. His bumpy, slightly skewed nose looked as if it had been broken many times, and his hands were huge. Between these two men was a lovely woman wearing a small hat that must have been pinned to her head and clutching a miniature purse.

Behind them, in the picture, the Flatiron Building was easily recognizable, even though Molly had never seen its lower floors. The photograph had been taken before the city had begun to sink, and showed the Flatiron towering above the south end of Madison Square. The image fascinated her and ignited a curiosity within her. Who still lived in the Drowning City who would care about such things?

She glanced around and noticed other curious objects in the room, on the bookshelf and other, smaller shelves that had been mounted on the wall—figurines carved of dark wood, tiny ornate boxes, several things that might have been strange puzzles, and a blue-tinted crystal ball the size and rough shape of a large apple.

Molly looked at the door again. Whatever her captors' intentions toward her, she could not help Felix while she stood in this elegant room, too embarrassed and afraid to confront her captors. They had not locked her in, or even closed the door all the way—a seeming invitation to attempt escape. Molly had to oblige them.

The hinges complained only a little as she opened the door. She stepped lightly into the corridor and held her breath against the strange chemical smell that assaulted her. To her right, on either side of the

hall, there were doors that seemed to lead into other rooms, as well as an arched opening that must have led into some less private part of the residence. To the left was a set of stairs winding downward, and she started toward them.

From behind her came the creak of hinges and the groan of a heavy footfall on the floorboards. Molly spun just as Joe emerged from a side room. She froze, staring at him, expecting to see something sinister in his eyes or his bearing. But in spite of his size, he only looked kind and slightly amused. The massive man wore a crisp white shirt and brown wool trousers held up by black suspenders. The cuffs of his sleeves were turned up and he had an unlit cigarette tucked behind one ear. His gray eyes were wide with surprise and humor.

"You're not going to get very far in that getup, kid," he said.

A tiny voice in the back of Molly's mind screamed at her not to trust him. Her self-preservation had depended on her learning over the years not to trust anyone. Felix had been the one exception.

"You mean this?" she said, halfway down the corridor and ready to bolt if he made a move toward her. She plucked at her nightgown for emphasis. "Who put this on me? Some kind of freak who gets his kicks changing little girls' clothes?"

Joe blinked, a hurt look crossing his face, so that she almost felt sorry for her accusation.

"You got it wrong, kid. Woke up on the wrong side of the bed, I guess," Joe said. "In the first place, you're not such a little girl. But I prefer my ladies fully grown, and with a little less mouth on 'em."

Molly flinched, then made a fist. "I oughta—"

Joe held up his hands, laughing. "Hang on. I should know better than to poke the hornets' nest. Look, we've got a housekeeper, a sweet old lady who's half-blind. She's the one who took you out of your wet things. They'll be clean and dry by now. Probably folded and in the wardrobe back in your room. Why don't you get dressed, then come in and see us. We don't have a lot of time to waste if we're going to help you get your boss back."

She had a dozen questions to ask, but Joe turned, went back into the side room, and shut the door behind him. For several seconds, Molly stared at the door. She glanced at the stairs, but the idea that her clothes might be clean and dry back in the bedroom was a powerful lure. If they were really there, and she still wanted to escape, she'd rather do so fully dressed.

With a curious look toward the door Joe had just closed, Molly hurried back into the chamber where she'd awoken. When she opened the wardrobe, the first thing she noticed was her small boots, not only clean and dry, but with a small tear at the ankle mended. She found her clothes on the top shelf, neatly folded and smelling of soap and flowers. Pressing them to her face, she smiled as she inhaled deeply, then forced herself to remember that clean clothes were not currency enough to buy her trust.

But they help, she thought, as she stepped out of the nightgown and quickly dressed. *They definitely help.*

Joe had kidnapped her, but he didn't seem inclined to hurt her, and he had saved her life, after all. If he had really wanted to hurt her, she would never have woken up at all, never mind in a warm, comfortable bed. Plus, he'd said he wanted to help her find Felix. The least she could do was hear him out. It wasn't too late to run. She felt sure she could find a window to break, even if all the doors were locked, and jump down into the water. But if she did that, she wouldn't know where to begin to look for Felix.

She had some questions Joe needed to answer. But if he could really help, she owed it to Felix to stay.

Nervously, she stepped out into the hall. She'd been in such a hurry before that details had escaped her, but now she noticed that the wallpaper had begun to yellow and curl at the edges. The candles in the sconces were melted almost to nothing. But what she noticed most was the strong chemical odor she had smelled before. It seemed to have settled into the very walls, and Molly breathed through her mouth, trying not to smell that stink. Instead, she tasted it, and that was almost worse.

She paused outside the opposite door and knocked.

Joe answered. She heard his heavy footfalls before he opened the door.

"Much better," he said. "Come in and meet Mr. Church."

Mister Church. When Joe had first mentioned the word *Church,* before he'd abducted her from the bridge, Molly had thought he meant an actual church, with stained-glass windows and an altar inside. But Church was apparently a man.

As she stepped over the threshold, her eyes went wide. All around the high-ceilinged room were tables laden with strange tubes and other apparatuses, and at last she knew the origin of that chemical

stink. Bunsen burners glowed with blue flames, above which beakers and vials of liquid glowed and bubbled and smoked, and metal pipes at the center of the room vented steam from a softly clanking generator. The steam rose to be collected by a mechanism with a fan inside, which seemed to cycle the heat and moisture back into pipes that ran along the ceiling.

Yet amidst the trappings of what seemed to be scientific inquiry, there were other things as well, objects far more curious than those in the bedchamber across the hall. There were jars of peculiar liquids, bits of things she suspected had once been alive floating suspended within. On one table were pieces of splintered bone and a variety of multicolored powders. Yellowed parchments were piled high in a wooden box that stuck halfway out from beneath another table. Shelves overflowed with books both modern and antique.

The room's sole occupant was a shockingly old man, presumably Mr. Church. Thin and birdlike, his skin furrowed with lines and gray with age, he still retained a remarkable vigor. He wore charcoal gray trousers and a matching vest—two-thirds of a three-piece suit—with a pure white shirt and a red tie tucked into his vest. His glasses perched upon the bridge of his formidable nose as he bent over a gleaming steel table. Upon the table lay a piece of one of the rubbery suits worn by the gas-men. The fabric had been slit and spread on the table, but Mr. Church's focus was clearly the strangely formed limb that Joe had torn off of one of Molly's attackers.

"What the hell is that?" Joe asked.

Mr. Church arched an eyebrow, nodding to Molly in momentary greeting, then turned to Joe.

"It started as a human arm—or something like human," Mr. Church explained. "But over the last few moments it has undergone a metamorphosis."

Fascinated, Molly slipped into the room, moving a few steps toward the steel table. The limb was too small to be human, and oddly jointed. It had a waxy sheen and a rubbery texture that reminded her of the thing inside the hulking gas-man's suit that had slipped away when Joe had defeated it.

"What is it made of?" Joe asked.

"That's difficult to say," Mr. Church said. "There are human cells in its composition, but also cells from a variety of animals, including feline and amphibian, as well as something else that eludes identification. Nature has never produced a creature whose limb would match this abomination."

Molly stared at the twisted limb, an icy chill climbing up the back of her neck. "This came off the man who tried to kill me?"

Even in the few moments since she had first looked at it, the thing seemed to have altered its shape and withered further.

Mr. Church smiled at her, almost pityingly. "My dear Miss McHugh," he said, gesturing toward the table. "I am afraid that the creature to whom this belonged is the very least of our concerns."

Molly glanced away, not wanting to see the awful limb again. Mr. Church bent over the table and took a closer look, perhaps curious to see if the arm still continued to change. Only when Joe cleared his throat did the withered old man turn his attention to her again.

"The girl's got a lot of questions, Mr. Church," Joe said.

Church knitted his brow, then nodded. "Yes, of course she does," he said, his accent unmistakably British. He went to a sink and washed his hands. "I suppose it's time you had some answers."

"I'd say," Molly replied. "You can start by telling me who you are."

Mr. Church smiled, wrinkled face crinkling further. "Who I am is rather a long story, actually. Shall we go into my study?"

Molly shrugged. "If you like."

"Come along, then," he said, guiding her to a door at the far side of the room. He turned the brass knob and pushed it open. "It's time to speak of impossible things."

"Impossible—" she began.

"And yet you'll need to believe them, if we're to help your friend Mr. Orlov."

Molly took a deep breath, filled with trepidation, but when Mr. Church went through the door, she followed.

Chapter Six

"The first story was published in *Beeton's Christmas Annual,*" Mr. Church announced, as he led Molly into his study.

Joe followed but did not enter. Instead, he leaned against the door frame and watched Molly and Mr. Church, arms crossed and a bit of an impatient expression on his face.

Mr. Church gestured for Molly to take a chair in front of the desk, and she did so, watching the old man in fascination. Mr. Church walked along the ornate, floor-to-ceiling bookshelves, trailing his fingers along the gleaming wood. Halfway down, he paused and let his hand come to rest on a tall, thick volume, which he slid from the shelf.

"Of course, the stories became far more popular after the turn of the century, when they began to appear in *The Strand,*" he said, caressing the faded leather of the book with a weary nostalgia.

"I'm sorry," Molly said. "Am I supposed to have any idea what you're talking about?"

Mr. Church returned and set the enormous book on his desk. As he passed close to her, Molly heard a metallic clicking sound, along with a peculiar hiss, like air escaping a balloon. And there was another strange quality to being in his proximity. In the laboratory—for how else could she think of the room they had just departed?—the chemical odors had overpowered all others. But here in his study, with him so near, she realized that Mr. Church had a peculiar aroma all his own. He smelled faintly like the burnt oil from a water taxi.

As he walked around the desk, he smiled at her.

"Go on," he said, choosing a long, smooth pipe from a rack behind the desk. "Have a look. Your answers are waiting."

Molly glanced over at Joe, sharing his impatience but also curious. She slid the heavy book off the desk and onto her lap. The cover was leather, featureless except for the stylized letters *S.C.* that had been imprinted there. As she opened it, she heard a whir and another wheezy hiss, and glanced up to see that the sound had come from Mr. Church as the old man took his seat. As he exhaled, thin plumes of what she at first took to be smoke came from his nose. But when he took a plug of tobacco from a pouch and began to pack it into his pipe, she realized that he had not yet begun to smoke.

"Who are you?" she asked, though really she had wanted to ask him *what* he was.

Mr. Church leaned forward and tapped the first page of the now open book. She glanced down at the page and saw that this was no ordinary book, not a religious tome or an antique novel of the sort that Felix had in his library. Inside the heavy leather cover had been bound many yellowed pages, artifacts of an era long forgotten. They were old magazines, bound together, and the top one was *Beeton's Christmas Annual.* When she saw the date, she frowned deeply.

"Twentieth December, eighteen ninety-six," she read aloud, then glanced up at the old man. "What is this supposed to be?"

Mr. Church puffed his pipe. "Turn to page seventeen, please."

Molly did. An illustration on the page made her blink in surprise and glance up. It featured a tall, thin man in a long coat and gloves, wearing a thin mustache and smoking a pipe not unlike the one in Mr. Church's hands. In his free hand, the man in the illustration held a pistol, down at his side, as though he hoped it would not be noticed. This image accompanied what she quickly saw was a short story, a piece of fiction authored by someone called Dr. Nigel Hawthorne. A quick glimpse of the first two paragraphs was enough for her to realize this was an old-fashioned detective story, about a man named Simon Church.

"So, you've modeled yourself after this detective character, Simon Church?"

Mr. Church pointed at the book with his pipe. "That's only the first story. There were dozens. Several novels as well. Hawthorne had served in Her Majesty's navy as a doctor, but he made his fortune on those stories. Still, he never hesitated to throw himself into the path of danger when called upon. A stalwart friend. A hero, really."

Molly pushed a lock of cinnamon hair behind one ear, waiting to see if Mr. Church would acknowledge all of this as some strange joke. But it seemed that the wrinkled old man was deadly serious.

"I'm not a little kid, y'know," she said, letting her irritation show.

"Perish the thought," Mr. Church said, frowning deeply. He glanced at Joe, who still leaned against the door frame. "Perish the thought, Joe."

"How old are you?" Joe asked. "Thirteen?"

"Fourteen," Molly said sharply, keeping her gaze locked on Mr. Church. "My point is, I'm not stupid. Simon Church is a character in detective stories. He's not real. And even if was, he'd be at least a hundred by now. Probably older. You're not *that* old."

Mr. Church leaned back in his chair, puffing on his pipe. "You're quite certain?"

He coughed, only a little at first, but then more emphatically. A muffled grinding noise came from his chest. Smoke like steam curled from his lips and nostrils, and Molly told herself it had to be from his pipe. When at last the old man caught his breath, there were droplets of blood on his lips and several had sprayed onto the desk. But when he noticed and dabbed at his mouth with a handkerchief, the crisp white fabric came away blotched with black, not red. Oil-black.

Molly stared at the dark spots of liquid on the desk. One had reached as far as the pages of the book open on her lap, and it brought her attention back to the old magazine. The Simon Church story in that Christmas annual had been called "The Case of the Silent Bell." Somewhere in the back of her mind, she thought she had heard of it before. Certainly she'd heard of Simon Church. She had never read any of Nigel Hawthorne's stories about him, but in the time when she had lived in abandoned buildings and foraged along the canals, there had been an old gray-bearded man who had shown flickering movies from a clanking projector. They had been the same dozen or so movies, a box of canisters he had scavenged somewhere, and one of them had been a Simon Church film. The actor who portrayed him had looked nothing like the genuine Mr. Church.

For some reason, she thought of the picture hanging on the wall in the room where she had awoken. One of the men in the photograph had looked quite a bit like she imagined Mr. Church might have appeared in his youth.

"I'm going to ask again," she said. "Who are you, and why did you send this guy to kidnap me?"

Mr. Church lit a match, set it to his pipe, and drew air in through it, trying to get the tobacco burning again. He shook out the match, then fixed her with pale blue eyes that twinkled with some emotion she could not quite discern.

"Nigel was only the first of my associates," Mr. Church went on, as if she hadn't spoken. "I have nearly always worked with a colleague. I find the alternative quite dreary, and the times I have been without someone to act as my second have been the darkest of my long life. Now, as you can see, I am unwell. My efforts at longevity have begun to yield diminishing returns, as was inevitable. Entropy takes hold. Fortunately, I have Joe to carry on in my stead. He has been my colleague and loyal apprentice for years."

Joe gave the old man a nod of thankful recognition, but Molly could see the sadness he felt at the thought of losing his friend.

"Look, I'm sorry you're not well," Molly said. "But I'm not really buying any of this. You're some kind of scientist, fine. And if you say you and Joe are detectives . . . well, I have no idea what you're doing down here in the canals, but okay, I'll go along with that, too. I've seen Joe fight, and I know *he's* not a scientist. But can we get on with how you think you can help me?"

Mr. Church stared a moment, then nodded.

"All right. I only meant to satisfy your curiosity. Let us turn our attention back to you, young lady. Or, more appropriately, let's discuss Orlov the Conjuror, and the peril he now faces."

Molly could almost feel the ticking of the clock.

"All right," she said.

Joe dragged a heavy padded chair over beside Molly with one hand.

"We've been in Lower Manhattan for years," he said as he lowered his bulk into the chair. "The short version is this—we *are* detectives. Though sometimes the things we investigate are unusual."

"The occult," Mr. Church said. "Things of a supernatural bent."

"Only sometimes," Joe said, shooting his friend and employer an irritated look. "It's not always crazy stuff."

"You two are nuts," Molly said.

"Really, Miss McHugh," Mr. Church said crossly. "I'd expected better of you. You can't possibly deny that there is more to Felix Orlov's conjurations than sleight of hand, or that the creatures who invaded your home this morning and escaped with your benefactor were something other than completely human?"

Feeling sick in her gut, Molly flipped a few pages in the book and found herself looking at the cover of an issue of *The Strand* from 1905. The Simon Church story heralded thereupon had been titled "The Scarab of Tarquinia."

She'd been focused only on the fact of Felix's abduction and her determination to get him back. She had not wanted to think about the gas-men, or the strange arm on the examination table in the next room.

"What were they?" she asked, hating the quiet uneasiness in her own voice.

"They were clay," Mr. Church replied. Then he shuddered as if he'd said something offensive.

Molly frowned. "Clay?"

"Something malleable," Mr. Church elaborated. "Something that can be made into whatever you want it to be. I haven't completed my examination, but I believe the things that came after you are the product of terrible experiments, a combination of man and animal that is unnatural, and therefore unstable. The gas inside the suits Joe mentioned stabilizes the flesh, keeping the creatures in human form."

"Is it science or magic?" Molly said.

"Something worse," Mr. Church said. "An exploration of the dangerous shadows between the two."

"We're going off track, here," Joe warned him. "And time is wasting."

"Why were you there, this morning?" Molly asked Joe. "Did someone hire you to investigate us?"

Mr. Church glanced disappointedly into his pipe, which seemed to have gone out.

"No one hired us," he said, letting the pipe dangle from his fingers. "I have been keeping an eye on Felix Orlov for many years. Since before he was born, in fact. It was one of my first cases after I'd moved from London to New York. Hawthorne was long dead and I had yet to meet Joe. My associate at the time was a man by the unlikely name of Morris Sowerberry. It killed him, that case.

"We had been approached by an Uptown architect, a man whose family had been a part of the exodus from Lower Manhattan when the island began to sink and the sea to rise. They had not only survived, they had thrived because their business investments had been sound, and their associates in the city's banks and government felt indebted to them. But it was more than luck and hard work that helped to lift them above the floodwaters and the resulting financial chaos in the city. Many families dabbled in the occult in those days, sacrificing whatever they were asked to primitive powers and shadowy gods in order to come out on top.

"The Orlov family was no different."

Molly gripped the arms of her chair, leaning toward him. "You're talking about Felix's father?"

Mr. Church arched an eyebrow. "Grandfather, actually. Vincent Orlov was not an evil man. In truth, he was an excellent architect who had been only a boy when his parents made an offering to certain ancient entities—"

"What do you mean, 'entities?'" Molly asked.

Mr. Church hesitated, as if searching for words.

"Things that exist in un-dimensioned space, outside of our world. The Orlovs participated in rituals that would safeguard their finances even in the face of the worst disaster this country has ever encountered. When he grew older, Vincent turned his back on the pact his parents had made. He was a good man. When Vincent learned that his daughter, Cynthia, had become romantically entangled with a wealthy lawyer and was now pregnant with his child, he was more concerned for her reputation than his own. Vincent and his wife, Stefania, closed ranks around the girl, keeping her away from her lover and vowing to raise the child as their own."

Intrigued, Molly nodded. "He hired you to find out who the baby's father was?"

"Not at all," Mr. Church said, punctuating his words with the bowl of his pipe. "Vincent knew the identity of Cynthia's lover. The lawyer came from another family whose wealth had been earned through promises made to dark gods. Cynthia resented her parents for forbidding her to see her unborn child's father, and so she contrived to slip out one night, after they had gone to sleep. According to a maid who was her confidante, Cynthia had intended to meet her lover in the bridal suite of the Hotel Talloires, overlooking Washington Square. The square was underwater, of course, as were the first few floors of the Talloires, but the hotel had been renovated so that it could continue to conduct business. Refugees were turned away. Only legitimate guests, mostly Uptown residents trying to determine if they could salvage anything from the flood and devastation, were welcome."

"Spectators and speculators," Joe grumbled, lip curled in disgust.

Mr. Church pointed his pipe. "Precisely," he said, before turning back to Molly.

"When Cynthia had not returned by morning, the maid confessed all to a furious Vincent Orlov. He went to the Hotel Talloires, but when his insistent knocking received no response, he forced the manager to open the door. Inside, they found Cynthia's lover, murdered in grotesque fashion, his entrails removed and draped across the body, ritual symbols painted in his blood. But there was no sign of the young mother-to-be."

Molly let out a breath. Her throat felt dry and her eyes burned from all of the strange odors in this place.

"He hired you to find his daughter," she said.

Mr. Church leaned back in his chair, his pipe held against his chest like some precious pet. "Just so."

The room fell silent, save for the ticking of an ornately carved clock on the fireplace mantel. The noise seemed strangely loud, the room suddenly growing smaller, almost suffocating.

"Did you find her?"

Mr. Church's gaze drifted. He looked past Molly, but not at the books on the shelves behind her. It was as if he were staring into some faraway time and place. His expression bore not a single trace of emotion. The smell of oil had become more pronounced in the last few moments, and she watched as he exhaled, a halo of steam rising around his head.

"I found her. She had been abducted by a dreadful man, an occultist who intended to offer mother and child in sacrifice to a Sumerian death god. He had acquired an arcane source of magic—or of focusing magic—called Lector's Pentajulum. He believed that he could use the Pentajulum to attract the old god's attention and communicate with it, so that he could offer his sacrifice—two lives in one body, an infant growing inside its mother—in exchange for the resurrection of his dead wife."

Molly felt sick. "Did it work?"

"It might have. But I got there first," Mr. Church said. "He intended to murder the pregnant girl, to give her up as an offering. When I kicked through the door, she was bound to a table, surrounded by the occultist's followers, who never stopped chanting his ritual. The occultist turned the Pentajulum toward me, as if he could use it as a weapon. I confess I hesitated for a breath or two, but nothing happened."

Icy dread spread through Molly. All along she had wanted to believe that this was just a story, that there would be some simpler path to the truth, and a reasonable way to find Felix and set him free. Now those hopes had been dashed.

"This is . . ." she said. "I know this. I've heard this story."

Joe looked at her oddly, as if trying to make sense of the words. But Mr. Church was lost in his rumination upon a violent fragment of his past.

"I shot him," Mr. Church said. "The occultist . . . it's been so many years now, I can't remember his name."

"Golnik," Joe supplied.

Mr. Church nodded. "Yes. That was it. Andrew Golnik." He smiled at Molly. "My mind slips sometimes. Like the wind blowing papers off of a pile on my desk, things tend to flutter out of my head."

Molly nodded. "You shot him. He's dead?"

"Oh, yes. Long dead," Mr. Church replied. "I thought I had saved Cynthia Orlov and her baby, but something in her had been tainted by the ritual. After that night, she was confined to an asylum. Shortly after Felix was born, she took her own life."

"That's terrible," Molly said. "I never knew. Felix never said."

Joe tapped the arm of her chair. "You started to say that you'd heard this story before."

Molly hugged herself, feeling a sudden chill in the room. "Felix has a dream like that. A recurring dream, he calls it. He always says that in the dream he feels like a ghost, watching the whole thing happen but not able to help. The details keep changing. Sometimes the baby comes out and it's a monster. Sometimes it's in a church and other times they're outside in a clearing in the woods. The last few times he described the dream to me, they were in an underwater room. He could see fish swimming outside the glass. But every time he has the dream, some parts are the same. The pregnant woman. The chanting. And Lector's Pentajulum."

Mr. Church sat up so quickly that smoke puffed from his nostrils, and she heard something shift heavily inside his chest.

"He called it that?" Mr. Church demanded. "He actually used those words?"

Molly hesitated. She wanted their help finding Felix, but a part of her felt as if, speaking this way, she was betraying him.

"He never knew what it was for," she said. "Its purpose, I mean. But he knew the name of it, yes."

Mr. Church turned to Joe. "He must know more. If anyone can find the Pentajulum, it's Orlov. He's tied to it in some way."

"You don't have it?" Molly asked. "Why didn't you just take it with you that night, after you shot Golnik?"

"Don't you think I searched for it?" Mr. Church said. "An object that dangerous? I would never have left it there, where anyone might lay hands upon it. But with the occultist dead and his followers scattered, there was no sign of the Pentajulum. I assumed one of them must have managed to scurry off with it."

"I don't get it," Joe said. "If Orlov's dreaming about that night, why do parts of the dream keep changing?"

Mr. Church looked troubled, the furrows in his face deepening.

"I don't know."

Molly brushed at her arms, as though the spiders she felt creeping on her skin might be real instead of in imaginary.

"None of that explains why you're still interested in Felix. He's an old man now."

"I have kept watch on Felix throughout his life," Mr. Church said. "The night I stopped Golnik's ritual, I felt something in the room unlike anything I had ever felt before . . . a presence so malign and so enormous that the mere thought of it creates a frisson of fear within me, even to this day."

Molly nodded, a ripple of unease going through her. "Felix talked about it, too."

Joe shook his head. "He couldn't have any memory of the presence in the room. He wasn't even born yet."

"So it's not a memory," Molly said. "But when he has those dreams, he senses it there. He once told me he imagined it would be what a doll felt like, if it could somehow be aware of the world outside the dollhouse."

Mr. Church and Joe exchanged a glance at that, and the old detective gave a thoughtful nod.

"An apt description," Mr. Church said.

"But if all of that happened to Felix's mother, why was he dreaming of it?" Molly asked.

"What Andrew Golnik did to Cynthia Orlov would be enough to traumatize anyone, but drive them insane?" Mr. Church said. "I believe that Miss Orlov's madness, and her eventual suicide, were due more to her exposure to that malignant presence than to any natural trauma. I have kept watch over Felix over the years because I wondered how he might have been affected by exposure to that darkness, and to the arcane power within the Pentajulum."

Joe leaned forward in his chair. "Felix has been a conjuror all his life. Big magic, little magic, talking to the dead. Most people aren't born with that kind of power."

Mr. Church sighed. "Give me honest ghosts, a vampire hungry for blood, boggarts that eat children . . . that's more my area. Not this vast, unknowable cosmic lunacy. These entities are so alien to us, so ancient that we cannot even begin to understand how they think and what motivates them."

"So, why are you involved at all?" Molly asked, strangely hurt by his words, and fearful that he might lose interest and abandon her, despite his long fascination with Felix.

Mr. Church glanced at his pipe, which had gone out. After a moment's hesitation, he set it on a small stand on his desk.

"Why, indeed?" he said, pushing back his chair. "Come with me, Molly. There's something you must see. Joe, if you'll accompany us, please?"

Joe stood as well, returning his chair to its original position. Molly followed Mr. Church into the hall and along the corridor toward the back of the building. She did not want to offend him, but she walked slightly apart from him, the smell of oil and the occasional puff of steam from his nostrils making her decidedly uneasy. A glance at his back showed strange protrusions beneath his clothes, just below his shoulder blades. She did not know how it was possible, but there was no other conclusion: Mr. Church had some kind of mechanism inside of him.

Is that how he has lived so long? she wondered. Only then did she realize how completely she had begun to believe him.

Mr. Church led them to an ornate door. Intricate, gold-filigreed fleur-de-lis had been carved into its wooden panels, and a pair of frosted glass windowpanes allowed for a nearly opaque glimpse of what lay beyond. Joe opened the door to reveal a metal gate, beyond which she saw the internal workings of an old elevator. He pushed the gate aside and held it while Molly and Mr. Church boarded. The big man closed and latched the gate, then worked a lever that brought the elevator lurching to life. It rattled as they began to ascend.

"Tell me, Molly," Mr. Church said. "Joe and I—and several Water Rats in my frequent employ—have spent a great deal of time over the years observing the comings and goings of Felix Orlov. Once upon a time he ranged far afield from his theater, visiting clients and associates. But in the time since you have become a part of his household—"

"I'm not, really," she contended. "I have my own apartment. I'm his assistant."

"Very well," the old detective said as the elevator slowly ground its way upward. "Since you have been his assistant, Orlov the Conjuror has left his theater with diminishing frequency."

"He almost never goes out," Molly agreed.

"Almost," Joe said, running his thumbs beneath his suspenders. "He goes to that cemetery in Brooklyn Heights about every month."

Molly frowned. It disturbed her to know that these people had been watching her and Felix for so long that they knew about Felix's comings and goings from the building. Much of Brooklyn was underwater, and all that remained of Brooklyn Heights was a seven-hundred-acre cemetery. The area above the waterline had once included a park and a small neighborhood, but during the plague that came even before the flooding, the homes on the outskirts of the cemetery had been seized by eminent domain and razed in order to make room for the plague dead. The way Felix told it, the homeowners had been more than happy to go, knowing so many plague victims would be buried nearby. Others were buried in the cemetery from time to time before the city shut it down—madmen and suicides, mostly.

"We know he goes to Brooklyn Heights to visit his mother's grave," Mr. Church said as the elevator began to slow, shaking more ominously, pulley cables crying out in protest. "Have you ever noticed significant changes in his behavior?"

The elevator rattled to a halt. Joe snapped the lever into the off position and unlatched the metal mesh gate, hauling it open.

"Maybe he's gone somewhere and come back acting a little differently?" Joe said, his gruff voice so different from Mr. Church's cultured, melodious tones.

Molly stiffened. "Differently how?"

Joe had stepped off the elevator, and she'd been about to follow, but now he and Mr. Church were studying her intently.

"What is it?" Mr. Church asked. "Something's just occurred to you."

"I don't think it's anything, really."

"Maybe he comes back excited, like he's got a secret," Joe said.

"The cemetery—" Molly began.

Mr. Church shook his head, stepping off the elevator accompanied by the smell of oil and the muffled clank of mechanics. "We've been to his mother's grave."

"I don't think it's only his mother's grave he visits," Molly said softly, feeling somehow as if she were betraying her best and only friend.

Now they were both outside the elevator, staring in at her. She felt trapped.

"Maybe you'd better explain that," Joe said.

Molly shrugged. "You'd have to be with him all the time to notice, but Felix isn't well."

"He's an old man," Mr. Church said, as if the irony were entirely lost on him.

"It isn't just that," Molly said. "He goes through periods where he's very weak and pale. When he's at his worst, he goes out to Brooklyn Heights. He likes to walk the paths there. When he comes home, he's healthy again. Still an old man, but stronger and not so pale. He laughs and tells jokes and tries to teach me card tricks."

As she said this last, her voice cracked with emotion. She bit her lower lip.

"Interesting," Mr. Church said, as though he hadn't noticed her pain and worry. "Something there is replenishing his vitality."

"The Pentajulum?" Joe asked. "But we've searched."

"Near his mother's grave," Mr. Church replied. "The place goes on forever. It could be elsewhere in the cemetery."

"I followed him once," Molly said. "He does visit his mother's grave, but at least half his time is spent at this other spot, under a big old tree. It's like nothing I've ever seen before, and it's growing right out of a grave."

Molly frowned and shook her head. "Look, obviously *you* want this Pentaju-whatever. But you said you would help me find Felix."

"And we will," Mr. Church said. "We're not the only ones trying to find Lector's Pentajulum. There is another force at work in this city—a sinister presence—and I believe that he is the one who sent those creatures to abduct your friend this morning. He wants Felix Orlov because he believes Felix knows where to find the Pentajulum."

Steam pluming from his nostrils, Mr. Church reached a hand into the elevator.

"Come with me."

Molly took Mr. Church's hand and let him guide her. His skin felt rough and dry, but oddly warm, and his grip was gentle as he escorted her a dozen feet down a short corridor to a large wooden door banded with metal straps.

They both stood aside as Joe hauled on the latch, then dragged the creaking door open. A fine, chilly mist billowed out and Molly was ushered through that light mist and into a small, circular stone chamber. She shivered at the sudden, precipitous drop in temperature, and had a moment to wonder how they kept the room so cold before she blinked away the mist and saw the room in its entirety.

"What is this place?" she asked, eyes wide.

Overhead, light shone through a many-paneled dome of darkly tinted glass that reminded Molly of drawings she had seen of a spider's eye. On one side of the chamber pipes jutted up from the floor, then branched off to run in complicated patterns along the curvature of the wall. But her focus was drawn to the opposite wall, where a complex array of machinery sat untended. So many pipes led into and out of the row of bizarre instruments that they reminded Molly of some twisted church organ. Some of the pipes steamed with heat and others were frosted with an icy rime.

Glass and metal gauges festooned the riot of machinery. In the center of the room, a pendulum swung slowly over a map of the city that had been painted on the floor. Pumps sighed and motors clanked. Some of the gauges showed needles pinned dangerously into red warning status, while others seemed to show no stress at all.

Joe took the cigarette from behind his ear and lit it, the orange glow of its tip flaring to life at the touch of a match.

"What is all of this?" Molly asked.

"I spent decades creating these instruments," Mr. Church said. The old detective shuffled to the nearest machine and tapped the glass of a gauge. It hissed steam from a vent, but the needle fell safely back into the green and a second plume jetted from its exhaust pipe. "With them, I monitor the supernatural climate of the city. I am able to track

spikes in occult energy—any changes in the pattern—and often in advance of them occurring."

Molly stepped forward and ran a hand over the smooth glass face of a gauge.

"So this is how you knew the gas-men would go after Felix and me today?"

"Not precisely. My machines predicted a surge of occult activity at his residence this morning. Unnatural energies were coalescing there. I had been expecting something like this for years, and sent Joe right away."

Molly frowned, thinking of the seizure Felix had undergone during the séance.

"Did something attack him?" she asked.

"I don't believe so. Rather, I suspect those energies were generated by Felix himself, or by the occult influence that has tainted him throughout his life. Given your description of what happened to him during the séance with the Mendehlsons—before the attack by the creatures you call 'gas-men'—I believe that during his trance state, he tapped into those energies for the first time, which triggered a kind of . . . evolution, I suppose, of the previously dormant supernatural element of his heritage."

"That makes no sense," Molly replied, studying the gauges more closely. One of them released a jet of cold steam that made her jump back. "Felix sometimes pretended with clients, but only sometimes. Whatever gifts he had, he already had before the séance this morning."

Joe grunted, tapping the glass face of a gauge as if he doubted its reading. "The magic he could do, talking to the dead, all that . . . That was just the tip of the iceberg. If Mr. Church and I are right—"

"And when are we not right?" Mr. Church asked, almost irritably.

"—there's much more to Mr. Orlov than he ever knew himself."

Molly hugged herself against the frigid air of the room. No sunlight came through the opaque windows above. She took some time to make sense of all she had been told. But one question remained.

"If your machines predicted what happened to Felix during the séance," she asked, "if that's why you sent Joe to help, then how is it the gas-men were there at practically the same moment? It can't be a coincidence."

Mr. Church looked as if he had swallowed something sour. His mouth twisted in an almost childish gesture, and then it was gone.

"I don't believe in coincidence," the old detective said. The clank of gears within him grew louder. He sniffed, almost as if he were about to sneeze, and she wondered if oil would come out.

Joe leaned against the pipes lining the far wall, taking a long puff of his cigarette. Neither the cold nor the heat seemed to affect him.

"Mr. Church isn't the only one in the city who can build this stuff," Joe told her, smoke curling from his lips. "Someone else has been monitoring the occult energies in the city, saw the same spike we did, and went there this morning to get their hands on Felix. It's the only explanation that makes any sense."

Molly spun toward Mr. Church.

"This is the guy you mentioned before? You think he sent the gas-men, which means if we find him, then we find Felix. What's his name?"

"Over the past twenty years," Mr. Church began, "I've encountered Dr. Cocteau far too often. Several times I've nearly captured him, and more than once he's returned from seeming death. He is a formidable and elusive opponent. He's a genius, and yet his great mind is a crumbling edifice, turning more and more to ruin with each passing year.

"If anyone else in this city has instruments like these, it can only be Dr. Cocteau. As I am certain he is also seeking Lector's Pentajulum, it is only rational to presume that he has been watching Orlov, just as I have."

Molly threw up her hands. "We should be out there, right now, saving Felix from this Dr. Cocteau!"

Joe gave her an apologetic look. "We would be, if we knew where to look."

"Then how do we find them?" Molly demanded.

"That's precisely what we've been talking about," Mr. Church said, as if lecturing a schoolgirl. "Dr. Cocteau is not going to make it easy to locate him. But we know he wants the Pentajulum. If we can get our hands on it first—and we must, for the alternative is unthinkable—then he will come to us, soon enough, and then we will have him."

The pieces all clicked together in Molly's head at last. Joe and Mr. Church hadn't had a clue where to begin looking for Dr. Cocteau or the Pentajulum before talking to her. Now they suspected the Pentajulum was in Brooklyn Heights, and they had to get to it. Felix was a sweet old man, and he had been brave enough to be her hero once, but if Dr. Cocteau wanted to torture the secret from him, Felix would surrender it. And even if he didn't know what had been restoring him after his cemetery visits, Cocteau might figure it out precisely the way Church and Joe had done.

"We have to go," she said, looking at Mr. Church. "We have to beat him there."

Mr. Church looked troubled. "It's not safe for you. Not at all. Joe will go and do what he can."

"He needs me," Molly said with a tiny shudder. "I can tell you what I remember, but it still might take hours—even days—for him to find the spot you're looking for. But I've been there. I can lead you right to that old tree and the graves around it."

Mr. Church hesitated.

Joe tossed his cigarette on the floor and ground it out with his heel. "She's right," he said. "It'll go much faster. And we can't afford to let Cocteau get there first."

As Joe picked up his cigarette butt, Mr. Church pondered. It was obvious the old detective didn't like the plan, but he valued logic, and he could not deny what made so much sense.

"I only wish I could go with you," he said. "Remember, Molly, that a great deal hinges on this sojourn," he said. "But most importantly, do not put yourself in peril at any cost. I won't have your blood on my hands."

Chapter Seven

Orlov the Conjuror woke screaming. Something covered his face, clamped tightly at his temples and on his cheeks, strapped at the back of his head. He couldn't catch his breath and he thought he would suffocate as he started to thrash his body and legs. His arms were bound behind his back, wrists joined by some kind of restraint. Panic burned through him like a fire of lunacy, and it felt as if he were having some kind of seizure. Eyes wide, he threw himself to one side, and only then did he realize that he was underwater.

Stop. Think. Breathe.

Felix went limp, just letting himself float. Whatever bound his wrists behind his back also kept him anchored so that he would not drift toward the surface of the water. He closed his eyes a moment, trying to conserve air and bring his heart rate down. As he steadied his breathing, he realized that the hard, rubbery thing clamped around his face was some kind of mask, and the strange hiss he heard inside his head—muffled by the water—was the cycling of air into the mask through some kind of tube.

Squinting, Felix tried to see through the murky water. Bleary lights floated somewhere nearby, their illumination stretched and blurred, and he had the momentary thought that they were swimming nearer. But as he drew a long, slow breath and then exhaled, forcing himself to become accustomed to the air mask and the feeling of being suspended in water, anchored in place, he realized that the light had a strangely static quality.

Houdini had made an art form of escaping from seemingly deadly underwater traps, chained and wrapped in a straitjacket. Felix had studied his methods and understood them, but such water escapes had been part of the great magician's act. The immersion and the restraints had been planned in advance, as had the escapes. Waking up underwater and anchored to the bottom, Houdini wouldn't have stood a chance. But whoever had submerged Orlov the Conjuror did not intend for him to drown today, or they wouldn't have given him any air to breathe. He comforted himself with that knowledge and tried to focus.

Closing his eyes again, Felix steadied his breathing and reached backward and down. Though his wrists were bound, it was a simple thing to grab hold of the strange, sinewy tether that anchored him there. Snaking his hands farther along the tether, he hauled himself downward, inch by inch. Felix Orlov was an old man, but in the water, without the weight of his aging body to contend with, he felt twenty or thirty years younger. Legs pointed downward, feet searching for the bottom, he tugged on the tether until his heels hit something solid and smooth. Though he hadn't been deprived of oxygen, his chest ached, and he wondered if his heart could stand the stress of this—whatever this was.

He remembered the Mendehlsons and the men in the strange, balloonlike suits barging into the theater, but not much more than that. They'd hurt him, and he could feel the bruises and wrenched muscles throbbing. He remembered falling and hitting the water and a rush of oil-tainted salty sea flooding his throat, choking him.

And now this.

Blinking, he peered through the water. It seemed clear enough, only murky because there was so little light available. Trying to keep himself sunken, Felix started away from the place where his tether was chained to the smooth, glassy bottom. It wasn't going to work. Felix pushed off, kicking his legs and swimming toward the blurry lights.

His head hit the glass so hard that it jarred the air mask slightly. Disoriented for a moment, he slid his feet forward and touched the barrier that separated him from the lights beyond the water. The dimly glowing lights wavered like lantern flames and he wondered if that was precisely what they were, if the gentle swaying he'd stirred up by moving in the water had caused the illusion.

Felix began to drift upward, the tether beneath him pulling him away from the glass, and he kicked his legs hard enough for the effort to burn his muscles and make his chest ache even worse. But he touched the glass with his elbow and managed to press his mask against it without injuring himself further. Eyes wide inside the mask, he peered out into the room beyond the glass, able to see his surroundings clearly for the first time.

Startled into frantic denial, Felix jerked away from the glass.

It couldn't be. It simply wasn't possible. But he thrashed his legs hard enough to get almost up to the glass again before he floated upward to the extent of the tether's reach. The blurry view was enough to confirm much of what he had seen, and in response he could only float, breath coming in small sips of the air drawn through the tubes into his mask. Felix had been feeling poorly for weeks, the strength draining from him, his age claiming him like the claws of monsters, dragging him into the shadows at the edges of life and then beyond. Sickly as he'd been, he could feel death looming in the slowly breathing darkness of empty rooms.

In his dreams, he had always felt like a ghost, a bodiless specter just observing events unfolding around him. Now, trapped in a bizarre human aquarium, though awake and burdened with flesh and bone, Felix felt again like an apparition, floating there in the water. What he had seen through the glass of his aquarium only enhanced the dreamlike quality of the moment.

Felix wanted his hands free. He could have covered his face, at least pretended to hide from the impossible reality outside the glass. *Go and look again,* he told himself. But the pain in his heart and the weariness in his legs would not allow it. No, he had nowhere to hide and no way to act upon the world around him at all.

Besides, he didn't need to look. He knew what he had seen.

A massive room, a strange sort of chamber with comfortable furniture at one end, including a single, thronelike chair. Nearer to Felix, beyond the glass tank, were several tables that might have been meant for some surgeon's operating theater—complete with raised seating around them so that an audience could observe—if not for the fact that the tops were concave, carved out to eagerly accept an ordinary-sized human. It was as if some Victorian gentleman had bought the furniture, but the surgery tables had been bought from a junkman. The room felt like a dungeon built inside of a palace.

Enormous glass tubes passed through the room in several places, water flowing and bubbling within as though the entire chamber was part of a hydro power system or the heart of some strange experiment. There were huge potted plants, fronds hanging overhead, and he had seen several filthy cats prowling around as though in search of prey.

But what had made the breath catch in his throat were the windows that were set into the walls of that vast chamber. Most were circular, though some were broken down into multiple panes. The largest must have been twenty feet across, at least, and others were as small as nautical portholes. The comparison was apt, for beyond those windows was the sea. The water there was nothing like the aquarium in which Felix drifted. He had seen the creatures swimming beyond the windows, endless schools of small, flitting, silver darts overshadowed by larger fish—some of them gigantic—lazily undulating past the windows, glancing warily into the room. Long eels unfurled and marine vegetation swayed with the ebb and flow of the sea.

Felix had dreamed of a room like this one many times, but it was not this room. Not precisely. Some details were different, but the windows were the same. The plants. The heavy crimson drapes, tied back to reveal the windows, dusty and unnecessary. In the dreams there had been only one table, where now there were three, and the table had been more like the sacrificial altar of some ancient cult instead of a surgeon's operating space. And yet despite the differences, he knew that this room had been a part of his dreams just as much as that other one—the past and the future, this moment, had somehow converged in his subconscious. Ice seemed to crawl through his veins as he wondered how much more of his dreams would come to life in this place.

A painful knot tightened in his gut. He could not stay there. In his dreams, he witnessed events as a ghost, not as a useless lump of flesh imprisoned in some kind of human fish tank. Did his dreams mean he would soon be dead, or only that he felt like a phantom, floating helplessly in the water? Either way, he had to get out of the tank, and the room.

Molly, he thought, and a jolt of guilt lanced through him. What had the bastards done with Molly? The last time he'd seen her, she had been alive. Felix needed to find her, to make sure she was all right.

Breathe, he told himself. *Be calm.*

For nearly anyone else, Felix believed, such a feat would be impossible. But he had trained his body just as he had trained his mind and spirit. When Felix Orlov had first become Orlov the Conjuror, he had studied with other magicians who had taught him that control of his physical self was vital to the performance of everything from sleight of hand to major stage magic, including vanishings and escapes. The first thing these magicians had taught him was how to meditate.

Molly, he thought. And then his fear for her gave way to fear for himself and the memory of his terrifying dreams.

But he knew how to breathe. Felix steadied himself, inhaling and exhaling with deliberate, slow rhythm. He would not be a ghost. And he refused to be a prisoner. Houdini had been a master escape artist, and though Felix knew he was no Houdini, he had studied and trained.

If he had no oxygen, he would have died before extricating himself from the bonds that tethered him to the bottom of the tank. But whoever had taken him prisoner had given him air.

Felix's fingers scuttled downward on his bonds again, exploring the way his wrists were tied. He could not be certain what kind of fabric or rope had been used to restrain him, but there was a small amount of give around his wrists. Not slack, precisely, but *give.* With time, and oxygen, he could work with that.

As he began to work at his bonds, forgetting the water in the aquarium around him and the room around the aquarium, and the sea beyond the windows of the room, a worm of nausea worked its way through his gut. It troubled him enough that he hesitated in his efforts, keeping his breathing steady. Felix swallowed, his throat going abruptly dry, and he realized how itchy he had gotten. It had started in his shoulders and upper arms and then spread to the back of his neck. His legs itched. He used the heels of his shoes to scrape at his legs through his trousers and was able to relieve some of the itching. But then it spread to his forearms and from his neck to his scalp. It felt like there were ants crawling on him. He shook his head, peered around in the water, and knew that there were no insects . . . just the itching.

He twisted and squirmed, trying to use his chin to scratch his shoulders. After a few seconds, the itching subsided a little, but it remained there, a prickling under the skin, the urge to scratch maddening.

Felix's whole body shuddered, and then he convulsed, once, as the ice that had slid through his veins earlier returned. At first he thought something had climbed into the water with him, but after a few seconds of peering into the murk, the blurry lights beyond the glass barely cutting the gloom, he realized that he was still alone in the tank. And yet he could feel the dark weight of the attention of others upon him.

Another presence had entered the room. An awareness.

For a moment Felix thought he had become the focus of the dead, as he had so many times before. So often they chose him to carry their messages, to be their vessel. But he had touched the spirits of hundreds of deceased humans over the decades he had spent as a medium—perhaps even thousands—and he knew what it felt like to be in the presence of a ghost. Whatever presence had entered the room, whatever consciousness observed him, Felix did not recognize as human.

What are you? he thought.

Another convulsion wracked him. The itching returned, swarms of things crawling over his skin, and he screamed into his air mask. His gut seized with a sudden rush of nausea, and he went rigid, taking small, quick breaths and trying not to throw up inside his mask.

He felt the presence there in the aquarium with him, studying him, and his body began to shake. Tears squeezed from the corners of his eyes.

What are you? he pleaded, for once wishing that he were a ghost.

The awareness receded slightly, the way the itching had, leaving a prickling at the back of his mind and the knowledge that it could return at any moment. Felix tried to regain the rhythm of his breathing, needing more than ever to get out of that tank, to breathe the air of the world again. His fingers began to work at his bonds, and after a moment he froze, paralyzed by the realization that his oxygen mask had slipped from his face, but he was still breathing. He no longer needed the mask.

What am I? he thought.

And then he knew that attempting to escape was pointless. Where would he go? He was changing, and the world he had wandered throughout his life would not welcome him any longer. He could feel something waiting for him outside the aquarium—the cold death he had felt lurking in the shadows for so long. Felix Orlov understood, down in his bones, that no sleight of hand would help him now. No amount of conjuring would charm this audience.

Whatever magic might be expected of him, Orlov the Conjuror had performed his last escape.

Chapter Eight

Joe guided the cabin cruiser through the flooded ruin of Lower Manhattan, headed for Brooklyn. He had acquired the craft seven years earlier as a reward from its original owner, an Uptown architect whose son had gotten involved with a gang selling drugs in the Drowning City. Someone had stolen a shipment of heroin, and the gang suspected the architect's son. By finding the actual thieves, Joe had saved the kid's life, then dragged him home to his daddy Uptown.

The cabin cruiser had been a gift to the kid on his eighteenth birthday. The architect had not only paid Joe for his services, but also taken the boat back from his son and given it to the man who had saved the boy's life. Joe would have argued, but the architect's son had been such a mouthy punk that he hadn't minded helping teach the kid a lesson. Mr. Church had helped him find a building with a flooded atrium. They'd replaced the third- and fourth-story windows with tall, shed-style doors that rolled back, and Joe had turned the abandoned structure into his personal boathouse.

He kept the engine running smoothly, clean and well-tuned, instead of belching smoke like half of the motorboats that plied the waters of the Drowning City. His instincts would have been to keep the entire boat immaculate and gleaming, but caution demanded otherwise. With its mahogany and brass polished, the small boat would have been quite a prize, attracting Water Rats and pirates. So he hadn't cleaned the boat properly in nearly twenty years. A layer of filth and grime had built up on the deck and sides, complete with a waterline stain visible any time a wave or a wake gave a glimpse of the hull.

But Joe loved the cabin cruiser, filthy or not.

A light, steady rain fell, and a blanket of gray gloom lay atop the city that afternoon. Though night was still hours away a sickly sort of twilight had descended, and there seemed no hope of it lifting. It surprised Joe that Molly remained on the small deck with him, though he had suggested she take refuge in the small cabin in the bow of the boat. But out of stubbornness or simple determination to search for the man who had made himself her guardian, she sat on the bench at the stern and peered vigilantly at each half-submerged structure they passed. Water Rats would not catch them by surprise.

Not that Joe was afraid of the brutal thugs everyone called Water Rats. He had skirmished with so many of them over all his years in New York that they were like any other vermin to him now, human or otherwise—something to be dealt with and disposed of.

Joe guided the cruiser through the shadow of the sixty-story Woolworth building, which had miraculously withstood the devastation of 1925. There were many shorter buildings that had not fared quite as well, some of them half-collapsed and others entirely swallowed by the tides. This part of the city could be difficult. Various structures jutted from the water or were hidden by it, depending on whether the tide was low or high, and only a fool would try to take any boat through the area without expert knowledge of the ruins, the currents, and the tide.

"Is this safe?"

Joe jerked the wheel to port, startled as the girl soundlessly appeared on his right. Mr. Church had given her a red woolen wrap and an old yellow raincoat, and the colors were startlingly vivid in the gloom and rain. But she had a quiet quickness that surprised him, and he couldn't help smiling at the way he'd jumped when she had suddenly appeared.

"As safe as any other way to get anywhere in this part of the city," Joe replied. But he knew what she meant. They skimmed along the water, keeping well clear of the underside of the Brooklyn Bridge, though they followed its course. Sailing beneath the bridge was inadvisable, as pieces of it—shaken loose by quakes and time—tended to fall at the most inopportune moments. Joe knew of several people who had been killed in such accidents.

"Is this your first time outside Manhattan?" he asked the girl, steering farther away from the bridge, yet maintaining his general heading.

Molly leaned against the cabin door, wet cinnamon hair plastered to her face. She held the raincoat cinched tightly around her throat, determined to keep her clothes dry.

"My first time away from the Drowning City," she corrected him.

Both hands on the wheel, Joe glanced at her. "Brooklyn flooded, too. Once New York was split into five boroughs, and people were proud to be from whatever neighborhood they lived in. Now there are only two parts of the city—flooded or not flooded. There's Uptown, and everywhere else."

She pushed a strand of wet hair away from her face. "You think I don't know that? I've lived here my whole life. Maybe I'm only fourteen, but I've seen enough that I understand this place just as well as you do. Maybe better. I've seen where you live. You wouldn't want to see some of the places I lived before I met Felix."

Joe frowned at the pain on the girl's face. He wanted to ask her to elaborate, to tell him more about the ugliness she'd endured in the years before she came under Felix Orlov's protection. He didn't want to pry, but he wanted to set her at ease and get her to open up. Talking about himself might have broken the silence, but he doubted it would have set her at ease.

They crossed the rain-dappled stretch of sea that people still called the East River. On a clear day they would have had no trouble seeing the building tops and trees of Brooklyn Heights, but in the gloom, Joe had to navigate from memory. Wind-driven waves lapped the hull and the boat rocked hard enough that Molly steadied herself, enduring the storm so that she would not have to be alone down in the cabin. Joe realized that was probably what this was all about—the girl didn't want to be by herself.

"What's your story, kid?"

Molly studied him as if she were ready to be angry with him again. But she smiled hesitantly and shook her head.

"I don't get it. How come when you call me 'kid' I don't feel like punching you?"

"It's a term of endearment. Plus, I'm charming as hell."

"I guess you're okay for a guy with the face of a boxer who's been hit too many times," Molly said, chin high, daring him to argue with her.

Joe laughed. "Are you this much of a smartass with Orlov? I'm guessing not, or he'd have tossed you out on your ass by now."

The mention of the conjuror shattered Molly's carefully constructed bravado, and Joe silently cursed himself for bringing it up. He was trying to distract the girl, not make her more upset. This was exactly why he had hesitated before asking about her past.

"How did you end up living with him, anyway?" Joe ventured, trying to guide her back to safer territory.

Molly pushed her hair away from her face again, and then—quite belatedly—lifted the bright yellow hood of her raincoat. She gazed ahead at the strange horizon of Brooklyn Heights thrusting up out of the water.

"You don't want to hear my story," she said. "If you've been working as a detective or whatever in this city, then you've heard it before. A lot of scary nights and ugly places, and the people who went along with them. The difference for me was Felix. He came along when I needed rescuing, literally at the very moment, and he gave me a reason to believe there were still people out there who weren't one hundred percent bastards."

Joe nudged the wheel a bit, watching the water warily as they drew nearer to Brooklyn. He knew the waters of Manhattan well, but Brooklyn was more of a mystery, and he didn't want to drag the hull across the roof of a short brownstone or some old deli.

"You don't talk like any fourteen-year-old I've run across," Joe said.

"Comes from living with an old man who's used to having an audience, I guess."

Joe nodded. "We have that in common."

"I guess we do," Molly replied, peeking at him from beneath the stiff bill of her raincoat hood. "So what about you? What's your story?"

Joe mulled the question over as he throttled down, turning the wheel so that the cabin cruiser glided past the mostly drowned marquee of a long-forgotten department store. It was one of the landmarks he'd been looking for. A lot of the buildings on the edge of what had been Brooklyn Heights either had crumbled or were low enough that they were entirely underwater. Sometimes they would emerge at low tide, but the department store remained, no matter how high the tide. Only the number of letters visible on the marquee changed.

He guided the cabin cruiser deeper into the eerie remnants of Brooklyn Heights. The flooded neighborhoods of Lower Manhattan were still inhabited, but there wasn't enough left of the Heights to contain any kind of society. There were scavengers and Water Rats and a handful of hermits who didn't want any contact with anyone. Joe spotted boats tied up to roofs and rough bridges connecting buildings in the rare places where there were several in a row that still had useful space above the waterline.

But Molly paid little attention to the ruins around them. Apparently she felt safe with him, and it unnerved Joe a little, as it always did whenever someone depended on him. Who the hell was he, after all? Not Simon Church, that was for sure. He was just a guy with big, heavy fists and the willingness to use them.

"You think your story's too familiar to bother telling me," he said. "And the trouble with me is, I don't really have much of a story to tell."

"What do you mean?" Molly asked, wiping rain from her eyes. "You're a detective. You work with Simon Church. I'd heard of him, but until today I thought he was a character in a book."

Joe smiled. It didn't come naturally or easily, and it always surprised him. It made his jaws ache.

"What's funny?" she asked.

He peered through the rain, approaching the place where he had to turn east in order to make sure they were safe. Navigating carefully, he managed to avoid a half-ruined chimney that barely breached the surface of the water. Something swam by and he glanced over, noting the shape of the harbor seal's head. They'd been showing up more and more, the water temperature sometimes cold enough for them.

"Joe?" Molly prodded.

He shivered and turned up the collar of his coat. He hadn't bothered to wear his hat—the rain would have been terrible for the felt—and now rivulets of water ran down the back of his neck and beneath his clothes. His coat, shirt, and trousers were soaked through, and he felt stiff, his limbs heavy. But, in truth, he always felt that way.

"What's funny is that people think Church is a fictional character, but I feel like that's exactly what *I* am," he said. "It's been more than twenty years since we first met, and pretty much every hour of those years is still in my head. But I have trouble remembering what came before that."

The boat rolled on a series of small waves, and they both had to brace themselves to keep from falling.

"Seriously?" Molly asked. "You lost your memory?"

Joe shrugged, pointing the cabin cruiser between the tops of a pair of telephone poles that jutted from the water.

"Crazy, I know," he said. "I've gotten used to it over time. I used to think my memory would come back. Church has been trying all these years to help me, using every method he can think of, whether it's scientific or occult. But no matter what we do, I can't remember much at all of my life prior to waking up in the same room you woke up in this morning. Apparently, we had both been working the same case—an Uptown banker killing girls from the Drowning City—and I'd fallen into the water and nearly drowned. Church fished me out. He says oxygen deprivation killed part of my brain. Truth is, I have a feeling I knew him before all of that, that he saved me from something he doesn't want to talk about. It's strange, because he's a noble guy, a real straight shooter, which makes him a bad liar. I think he knows more about my past than he's letting on."

"Like what?"

"If I knew that, I could fill in the holes myself."

"You said you don't have much memory of your life before meeting Mr. Church?" Molly asked. "So what do you remember?"

Joe paused. He pushed one hand through his hair, shedding rainwater. Why had he opened himself up to this conversation? He understood why the girl would be curious, but he didn't like to think about the dark abyss of his memory prior to meeting Church, never mind talk about it. Still, he had begun, and he liked the girl too much to simply ignore her.

"I have dreams, sometimes."

The rain seemed to have slowed, but the sky had grown darker.

"Like memories coming back while you're sleeping?" Molly asked.

Joe glanced at her. "You're pretty damn sharp, kid. Yeah, something like that, I guess. I wake up in the middle of these things—sometimes they're dreams and other times they're nightmares—and I feel like I'm standing just outside a door. Behind it is everything I can't remember and all I have to do is open it, and . . ."

He paused. How long had it been since he had spoken this much? Ages, for sure. Church knew him so well that there were days they spoke very little, content in each other's company and intuitive about the next steps that needed to be taken to further whatever case they were working on.

"If I could get that door open, I'd remember everything," Joe went on. "And when I'm sleeping, that seems possible. But when I wake up, the door doesn't even have a knob. There's no getting through it."

He shivered.

"Thing is, there's no way these dreams could be memories," he said.

"Why not?"

Joe gripped the wheel more tightly. His joints felt stiffer than ever, painfully so, and he had to force himself to steady his breathing. Thinking too much about those dreams always put him on the edge of panic, but talking about them was worse. How could he explain to Molly what it was like to be trapped inside such strange nightmares? The dreams were so vivid that, upon waking, it always took him a minute to determine which was the dream world and which reality.

Staring straight ahead into the storm-dark afternoon and the rain, he let his mind drift back to the dream he'd had only the night before. The world seemed to shift beneath him, and he felt a sudden, slippery disorientation. He blinked twice, three times, and then he forced himself to focus on the storm and the water.

But for just a moment, Joe wasn't in the boat with Molly anymore. He was in the dream.

He crashes downhill through a veil of snow, snapping bare branches off of frozen trees. Winter is all around him, and somehow inside of him as well. The snow feels as if it has crept into his heart, a frozen block in his chest.

A scream rises ahead of him, toward the bottom of this hill not ambitious enough to be called a mountain, and he quickens his descent, careening downward. In the darkness he barely notices the barren yew tree in front of him, but its dead trunk snaps on impact, spewing dry rot where the tree has broken open. He barely slows, but in that moment of hesitation another scream tears through the storm, curling on the wind so that its origin is hard to pinpoint. But he knows better than to chase the snow-driven ghost of a scream. His instinct drives him. He knows where the scream will end . . . in the same place the others have.

He bursts from the skeletal trees, crashing over scrub and stone, twenty feet from the edge of the frozen river. Chunks and floes of ice move sluggishly, the river current not entirely stilled by the deepening winter.

Two figures struggle at the riverbank. A girl on the verge of adolescence claws and punches and tries to break the grip of the witch who stole her only an hour before. The witch is tall, her limbs like sticks, as if one of the bare, skeletal trees has shaken off its ice and come to murderous life. Her fingers are as thin as knives and her face is pale and gaunt.

The girl sees him and her eyes widen, and she screams for him.

The witch laughs, a slithering, oddly childlike sound that seems to echo from every snowflake and wind gust. She spins and stares at him, clutching the girl by the hair and around the belly, grinning with putrid yellow eyes, and then she starts into the frozen river, stick-legs punching through the ice and between jagged floes.

He is faster than she thinks. This is the one thing they always do, assuming that his size will make him lumbering and slow. But he is not slow. In half a dozen swift strides he reaches her. She lets out a keening wail that seems to shred the storm around her, trying to elude him, but she has made a dreadful, deadly mistake.

One huge hand closes on the back of her neck. In the peculiar whiteness of the storm, he sees that his fingers are carved from stone, the joints packed with loose soil. Bones crack in his grip, then break, but the witch does not release the girl. Head lolling over his squeezing hand, the witch begins to tear at the girl. Blood spatters his trousers and shoes, and he has had enough. A second or two earlier, he might have freed the girl without her coming to any harm. The time for such hopeful thoughts has come and gone.

With his free hand, he grabs the witch's forearm and crushes it, grinding the bones into jagged pieces like pottery shards. He peels away the witch's grip and grabs the girl by the back of her rough, woolen dress. Turning, he hurls the child one-handed onto the frozen, snow-covered ground.

The witch shrieks, clawing at his hand, twisting in his grasp like a rabid, dying animal. She wants her prey—will do anything to have her hands on the girl again. He walks into the frozen river, his weight crushing through the ice. When he has waded up to his waist, ice grinding at his stone body, he plunges the flailing witch into the frigid water. Bones shatter on the ice, then she is submerged and her screams are silenced by the river.

Quiet spreads its wings across the water and through the bare woods behind him. In the distance to the south, along the bend in the river, he can see the light of lanterns and torches from the village, and as he drowns the witch he thinks of the tears of joy the girl's mother will weep when he carries her home. Yet he does not kill the witches for gratitude or out of some sense of nobility. He kills them because they are witches, and killing them is his purpose . . . the very reason he has been made.

He breaks them and drowns them, or crushes them with stones until their hollow bones are little more than chalk. Their magic has scarred and twisted so many in the village. They have murdered children and stolen their vitality, and sometimes their blood or flesh. They have spoiled crops and snatched infants from their cradles. The witches are monstrous . . . they are fiends . . . and they must be stopped.

If he were flesh and blood his hands would be frozen solid, having held the witch under for so long. But the cold has never troubled him. Now, arms plunged into the river to the elbows, he breaks and snaps her spindly limbs in his hands. At last he crushes her skull, and still he wishes he had stones to weigh her down. Instead, he drags her ice-rimed corpse from the water, punches his fingers through her ribs, and tugs out her black, dripping heart.

He lets the corpse slip away in the grinding, flowing ice, but the heart he keeps. He will bury it beneath an ash tree and hammer an iron spike into the ground above it, and then the witch will be truly dead.

Slipping the black heart of the witch into a deep pocket in his coat, he feels its damp weight and the wretched aura around it. He climbs from the river, the ice dragging at him as he emerges, his trousers quickly freezing in the gusting storm. Through the snow he sees the girl watching him, and he goes to her.

New fear blossoms in her eyes and he hesitates, frowning. She has seen him before. She knows that he hunts the witches, that he serves the village. And yet as he reaches out for her she lets out a cur's whimper and scrambles away from him in the snow.

What is this feeling in his chest? It might be anger, for he usually feels only hatred for the witches. Or perhaps it is pain, with which he is even less acquainted.

"Come," he says, his voice like gravel. "Your mother is waiting."

There is a young woman in the village, a dark beauty whose momentary gaze quiets his heart. She is kind to him, though her eyes are sad, and he feels a warm glow within when she favors him with a glance, or speaks to him, or gives him the gift of her melancholy smile. There is no fear in her eyes, only sorrow and bright wonder and gentle understanding. But now he thinks of her and a new fear struggles to be born within him. Will she one day look at him the way this girl-child does now? The question is a torment, and it has no answer.

He thinks of the old man—the furious, broken-hearted old man—who treats him like a son, and then other faces slip through his mind as if he is in the midst of some fevered dream.

"Come," he says again, and he lifts the girl into his arms. He tells himself it is only the winter that makes her shake so.

Only the winter.

As he trudges back through the storm with the shivering girl in his arms, he listens to the screaming wind and in it he hears the shrieking of witches and other things that have eluded him but will not escape him forever. He knows there are others out there, cloaked in winter and hungering for delicious emotion and withering discontent. There will be other witches.

And he will kill them.

"Joe!"

He blinked, then went rigid in alarm as he saw the brownstone looming out of the rain in front of him. Joe cut the wheel starboard, and the cabin cruiser scraped along the brownstone's topmost story, so close that he could see in through the windows. A pair of aging Water Rats sprang back from the grime-streaked glass and then crept forward. One of them stroked his beard in fascination as he watched the boat grind the stone and then pass by, his tiny black eyes not unlike those of his rodent counterparts.

"That was pretty close, don't you think?" Molly demanded.

He turned to look at her. For a moment he saw the shivering girl from the edge of that frozen river, but then Molly's face came into focus. Raindrops streaked her face. He could see her anger and fear.

"I'm sorry," he said.

"You were heading right for it," she said. "What the hell was that? You were in a trance or something. I tried snapping you out of it, but you were just gone."

"It doesn't happen very often," he said. *But we were talking about it,* he thought. *And my mind started to go there, and with the rain and the river and the gloom . . .*

"What doesn't?" Molly asked.

"A dream."

Molly stared at him. "Wait, you were *dreaming* just now?"

Joe tapped at his coat pockets, felt the outline of his cigarette case and his lighter, and almost pulled them out before he remembered the rain. Now wasn't the time. Instead, he put both hands on the wheel and focused on guiding the cabin cruiser through the wreckage of Brooklyn Heights. He could see the cemetery ahead, for all intents and purposes a huge island covered by graves, and he pointed the bow toward it.

"Seriously," Molly said. "What's with you?"

Joe shrugged. "I don't know."

Then he shot her a look that brought her up short. Whatever she saw in his eyes, it prevented her from saying whatever words she had planned for next.

"Why don't you get that rope ready," he said, gesturing to a line tied to a cleat to the aft of the boat. "We're here."

Chapter Nine

olly tied the rope to one of the above-water posts in the black wrought-iron fence that surrounded the cemetery. Most of the graveyard was hilltop, but the fence ran along the perimeter, so there were places where it was underwater and others where it jutted out. She made sure the knot was tight, afraid to end up here without any way to get back to Manhattan, but she kept glancing at Joe. As kind as he was, with his gentle eyes and his dry humor, a deep sadness clung to him. And when he had gone blank out there on the water and nearly wrecked them against a sunken building, she had nearly leaped over the side and into the river. He didn't frighten her, but he did scare her. She worried about making the trip back across the river.

"All set?" he asked.

"I lived with a stage magician for the past two years," she said, "you think I don't know how to tie a knot?"

Only after the words were out did she realize how sharp they'd sounded. Until she'd snapped at him, she hadn't realized how on edge she really was.

Joe climbed from the cabin cruiser, stepping onto the cracked path that led through the arched, wrought-iron gate. But as he straightened up, he stared at her.

"I didn't say that," he noted. "I just asked if you were set."

Feeling guilty and embarrassed, Molly glanced away. "Sorry. Yeah, we're fine. It'll still be here when we come back, unless some Water Rats get ahold of it and decide it belongs to them."

"Great," Joe said. He nodded toward the entry gate. "Let's go."

Molly hesitated. She was happy to be on dry land—well, as dry as it could be in such a pounding rainstorm—but in the storm, so dark it felt like night, she wasn't thrilled with the idea of wandering the cemetery, even with Joe as her escort.

"I guess this isn't something you can do yourself?" she asked.

Joe gave her a reassuring smile. "I could find Orlov's mother's grave," he said. "But the other one you talked about—with the tree growing out of it—that one I'll need you to lead me to. Besides, you don't want to stay here by yourself, do you?"

She glanced out at the river. The ruined upper branches of trees were visible jutting out of the water nearby. The haunted wreckage of Brooklyn Heights seemed to skim the surface, some buildings entirely underwater and others looming, half-drowned.

"I guess I don't," Molly admitted.

Joe lumbered over to her. The rain had let up a little, and he pushed his fingers through his hair, slicking it back against his skull.

"Wish I'd brought an umbrella," he said, smiling.

Molly laughed softly.

"What's funny?" Joe asked.

"You just don't seem the umbrella type."

Joe shrugged. "Maybe not. But you could've used one. You look like a drowned rat."

Molly had seen too many drowned rats to argue. She pulled her hair back and squeezed some of the rainwater out of it. Despite her yellow raincoat, the water had gotten down inside her jacket and she shivered at the cold dampness against her skin.

"This way," she said, leading Joe beneath the arched iron entryway of the gate. He quickened his pace to follow.

"Don't be like that, kid. I was just teasing," Joe said as he caught up.

"I know," Molly admitted. "I just didn't want to argue. This isn't how I planned for this day to go."

"Me either," Joe agreed.

They trudged up the cracked and broken pavement. Many of the headstones were equally cracked, and some had been knocked over by vandals. Molly didn't like to look at the broken stones. They reminded her that the people buried here were not only dead, but forgotten. Either no one was left alive to mourn them, or no one was still alive who cared.

Vines crawled over the faces of stones and across the doors and roofs of family crypts. In some places, wretched old trees had fallen over, damp moss forming on the bark. The last time Molly had been to the cemetery, at the edge of this peculiar island of the dead, it had been low tide. The water had eroded so much of the soil that broken coffins jutted from the earth, flashing coy glimpses of bone. She was happy the tide was in for this visit.

"Talk to me," she said, glancing around at the seemingly endless graves. "This place gives me the creeps."

"What do you want to talk about?" Joe asked.

"I don't know. Small talk."

"I've never been real good with small talk," he said, as if the fact troubled him.

Molly smiled. "Could've fooled me." She moved nearer to him as they walked. "Tell me more about your dreams. I know Felix thought some of his were . . . what's the word? Prescient. Like they could tell him the future."

She felt Joe stiffen beside her. He kept walking, but he looked around as if he were doing his best to see everything other than Molly herself.

"Look, I just wanted to talk 'cause I'm nervous. I also whistle in the dark," she said. "And I'm used to Felix talking out the things that bother him. I wasn't trying to pry. If you don't want to talk about it—"

"No, it's okay," Joe said, a little too quickly. He frowned, and she could see that the decision to speak was difficult for him. For a second, she thought he would change his mind, and then he forged ahead quickly, as if he wanted to talk before he lost his nerve.

"Mine definitely aren't visions of the future," he said. "Whatever I'm dreaming, it happened a long time ago."

Molly listened in fascination as Joe described his dreams, a kind of story all their own, tracing the history of a man—a creature—sculpted out of the ground itself by the elders of a small village and set to the task of killing the witches who preyed on the town.

"But . . . a man made of dirt and rocks?" Molly asked.

Joe arched an eyebrow and gave her a sidelong glance. "The world is full of weird things. You're a magician's apprentice, kid. You know that better than most. Anyway, Church figures I'm tapping into some kind of ancestral memory. Maybe my lineage goes back to that little Croatian village in the fifteenth century, or whenever the hell it's supposed to be."

"Croatian?"

"Yeah. I know that much. In the dream, I know everything about the river and the village. The river is the Gacka. I've looked it up on modern maps. It's in Croatia. . . ."

He trailed off. Molly shuddered a little and linked her arm with his. Joe glanced away from her but didn't remove his arm. The rain had slowed to a drizzle, but the sky was still cloaked in gray, and the cemetery was all but silent. There were no birds calling, no animals rustling . . . only the wind that shook the branches of the trees.

"Have you thought about going there?" she asked.

"To Croatia?" he said, practically scoffing. "Hell, kid, I'm a New Yorker. Besides, who'd look after Church?"

Molly thought about the smell of oil and the sound of gears coming from inside Mr. Church. She had the unsettling feeling that, despite his age and infirmity, he was more than capable of taking care of himself. But she didn't want to upset Joe by saying so.

"Do you believe this 'ancestral memory' idea?" she asked.

Joe paused, extricating his arm from hers. He pondered the question as he pulled out his cigarette case. He offered her one, but she waved him away. With a shrug, he put a cigarette between his lips, vanished the case inside his sodden jacket, and produced a lighter that clicked as it flared to life.

"I don't know what to believe," Joe said.

He lit the cigarette and then the lighter vanished as well. Molly thought his talent for sleight of hand would have impressed Felix. For a man so huge, Joe continually defied her expectations.

"Ancestral memory," he said. "That basically means I've got memories in my head that've been passed down for hundreds of years, like modern people being afraid of the dark because cavemen knew there were things in the night that wanted to eat them, things they wouldn't see coming. So I'm having dreams that don't belong to me."

Molly ruminated on it, happy to have something to think about besides the eerie moan of the wind in the cemetery's trees. They turned left, climbing a winding, broken path toward a tree-lined hill where many featureless rectangular crypts had been hastily erected when the plague began to hit full force. Generations had passed since then. Molly's parents hadn't even been born yet when the plague hit. But stories still lingered, part of the fabric of culture in the Drowning City. Most of the people who might have remembered were long dead, but the city remembered.

"Maybe it makes sense," she said at last. "If most of your memory is gone, you've got room in there for other stuff."

Joe laughed softly and took a drag of his cigarette. It glowed orange in the gloom.

"Maybe you're right," he said. "I've never thought about it like that before. And it's better than Church's other theory, which is that I've been reincarnated. He thinks maybe I actually lived that life, fighting witches on the banks of some Croatian river, and that I died, but now I'm born again."

"Would that be so bad?" Molly asked, starting to read the names on the headstones they passed—Kontis, Montuori, Charczenko, so many others. "These people . . . they're just dead. If reincarnation means you get a second chance . . ."

"No," Joe said grimly, his expression turning cold. "You die, you're supposed to find peace, right? The kind of life people lead in this part of the world, I figure we've earned a little peace. I've done my bit. Once around the block is enough for me."

Molly had stopped walking. The words had wrought a quiet sadness in her, and she felt strangely close to Joe suddenly. It had been so long since she had made a new friend that she had nearly forgotten what it felt like.

"You okay, kid?" Joe asked. "I'm sorry. I know you're worried about Orlov. I guess I shouldn't be dwelling on this stuff."

She let out a long breath, then hugged herself against the cold and damp, hating the crinkling sound her raincoat made.

"Molly?" Joe prodded. She was happy he hadn't called her *kid*.

"We're here," she said, staring at the marble headstone in front of them. The letters of ORLOV were carved deep. Most of the graves had weeds around them, but Felix had been here often enough to keep the stone mostly clear.

"Right," Joe said.

They had only needed to visit the grave of Cynthia Orlov as a starting point, so Molly would be able to find her way to their actual destination. But Joe took a moment to kneel and run his fingers over the letters on the stone. He looked around, as if he thought someone might be watching.

"What are you doing?" she asked.

"Just making sure it hasn't been disturbed," Joe said, rising to his feet.

Molly pushed her hands into the slick pockets of her raincoat and glanced around. It made no sense to think anyone else would be there. Dr. Cocteau—or whoever had taken Felix—wouldn't have brought him here, or if he had, he wouldn't have lingered. And in this kind of weather, there weren't likely to be any cemetery visitors. From what she knew of the place, Brooklyn Heights didn't get a lot of mourners coming by to pray. Most people were afraid that the plague still lingered in the graves, as if it might grow like flowers from the corpses under the soil.

"Can I ask you something?" Molly said.

Joe gave her a lopsided grin, taking a drag on his cigarette. "Could I stop you if I wanted to?"

"Probably not," Molly said. He didn't have to tell her that she talked a lot. She knew it. Even when she hadn't just witnessed murder and kidnapping and nearly been killed herself, she tended to think out loud.

"This pentagram thing—" she said.

"Lector's Pentajulum," Joe provided.

"Yes," Molly said, pointing at him. "*That.* Mr. Church talked about everyone wanting it, but I still have no idea what it's supposed to do, or be, or whatever."

Joe drew a lungful of smoke from his cigarette, the tip burning brightly. When he exhaled, the smoke curled and drifted from his nostrils, vanishing as if it had never been. He seemed troubled by the question.

"You get that this is really Church's thing, right?" he asked. Cigarette held between two fingers, he tapped the side of his head. "It's not like I'm brainless. I've picked up a lot of occult stuff over the years, and I'm not half bad as a detective. But my detective work is usually about poking the hornet nest with a stick. I keep asking questions until somebody gets mad enough to take a shot at me, and then I know I'm on the right track. But Church is the expert."

Molly pulled back the hood of her raincoat. "Mr. Church isn't here."

Joe gestured with his cigarette. "You want to show me where this other grave is? The one with the tree growing out of it? And I'll tell you what I know."

"This way," Molly said, leading him toward a narrow trail that branched off the main path.

"So, Lector's Pentajulum," Joe started. "Truth is, I don't really know what it is, and I don't think that's just me being dense. People have been after this thing for centuries, wanting to possess it, thinking it's going to give them the power to do miracles or something. And maybe it does. What we think is that it amplifies magic, takes what you can already do and makes it stronger. But there are all kinds of stories about it—that it's a key to parallel worlds; that it's the actual heart of the Sumerian god Enlil or a tool crafted by a race of cosmic architects to create order out of chaos. That it gave birth to the sun, that it swallowed the Arabian city of Ubarra. My favorite is the one where it's supposed to have transformed all of the people on a small Polynesian island into angelic creatures who flew away, leaving their tables set for their evening meal."

Molly stared at him. "It sounds like it can do anything."

Joe nodded. "That's what it sounds like, yeah. But Church has never believed that, and neither do I. Magic doesn't work like that. But whatever power it has is enough that every occultist and mystic through history, all the way back to ancient times, wanted to get their hands on it. According to his writings, John Dee killed to get it. Agrippa had it. Fulcanelli, too. A dozen others. There are records of it down through the ages, but there's no evidence that any of them knew how to control it."

"But if you don't know what it does, why do you want it?" she asked.

"Church and I don't want the Pentajulum so much as we want to keep it out of the hands of maniacs who would do something stupid with it. Lunatics trying to figure out how to unlock its secrets have caused some major disasters over the centuries."

"Disasters?" Molly asked.

Joe shrugged. "Everything you can think of has been blamed on the Pentajulum at some point or another. Pompeii. Atlantis. Even the sinking of New York."

"What do you think Dr. Cocteau wants it for?"

"No idea," Joe said. "But Cocteau is insane. We can't let something as powerful as Lector's Pentajulum fall into his hands. He's figured out there's some connection between your friend Felix and the Pentajulum, and he thinks he can use Felix to find it. We can't let that happen, no matter what."

Joe paused to stub out his cigarette on top of a granite gravestone. He pinched the end to make sure it was out and then dropped the butt into his pocket. Molly waited, wondering if he'd ever lit his coat on fire, and then the two of them walked on again. At one junction, between two family crypts, she thought she might have gotten turned around. Then she saw a stone angel with a cracked face and a broken wing and knew that her memory had led her in the right direction. She had seen that angel before.

She led Joe along a path around the side of the cemetery's hill, beneath the boughs of old, gnarled trees, and then she saw the grave she was looking for. The ugly, misshapen tree had its roots deep in the grave, and its twisted branches and red leaves spread out above it, as if hiding it from the sun. The tree had grown so large that it had cracked the gravestone and tipped it so that it tilted sharply to one side.

"That one," Molly said, slowing a bit to let Joe get ahead of her. She didn't relish the idea of moving any nearer to that tree.

"I figured," he said. "It'd be kind of hard to miss."

Joe walked up to the stone and ran a hand over the smooth black granite.

"The headstone doesn't look old enough to have an adult tree growing out of the grave," he said.

Molly said nothing. She didn't know a lot about how fast trees grew, but it was clear he was right. The tree was tall and rough with age, gnarled and twisted. Four or five feet off the ground, the trunk had split so that it grew in three directions. But as old as the tree looked, it couldn't have been there any longer than the grave.

Joe ducked beneath the branches, but leaves brushed his arms as he worked his way nearer to the trunk and turned to try to read the name engraved on the stone.

"I was afraid of this," he said.

"What is it?" she asked.

He glanced up, his expression even grimmer than usual. In the dark shadow of the grave-tree, his face looked as if it had been carved by some halfhearted sculptor, as if he were one of those crumbling stone angels.

"This is Andrew Golnik's grave," he said.

Molly shivered, the chill and damp finally too much for her. "The occultist? The guy who tried to sacrifice Felix's mother?"

She remembered the dreams Felix had described to her, the dark ritual and the hideous metamorphosis of the pregnant woman.

Mr. Church had been there, and he told the story differently. Nothing like Felix's dreams had happened to his mother. But whatever the occultist had done, it had led to the woman's death and tainted her son with dark magic that would define his life.

"Yeah," Joe said, frowning. "It doesn't make any sense. You said Orlov would come here when he was at his weakest, that it rejuvenates him. But why would visiting Golnik's grave make him feel any better? Church searched his body that night and didn't find the Pentajulum; otherwise I'd think maybe it was buried with him."

"Do you think it's something about the tree that made Felix feel better?" she asked. "Some kind of medicine?"

"It's possible," Joe said. "But the Pentajulum is the thing that connects Golnik to Orlov. Nothing else makes sense to me." He ran a hand over his stubbled chin. "I guess it's possible somebody came afterward—after Golnik's funeral—and buried it down there with him. Some follower of his or something."

Molly shuddered, but this time it wasn't the damp or the cold that troubled her. She glanced around, Joe's confusion forgotten. She had felt a peculiar pressure on the back of her neck, the weight of a presence nearby, as if they were being watched by unseen eyes.

"Did you hear something?" she asked, even though she wasn't sure herself if there had been anything to hear. Had there been an out-of-place noise, perhaps the squelch of boots on the damp cemetery soil?

Joe took a quick look around, but Golnik's grave was his focus.

He studied the headstone and then bent to examine the tree's visible roots where they plunged into the dirt.

Telling herself that the haunting, dour setting had begun to influence her imagination and that there was nothing to fear, Molly pushed a low branch out of the way and slipped inside the reach of the tree. Raindrops showered down from the leaves as the branch snapped back into place. Cold rivulets trickled down the back of her neck. As much as she feared for Felix's life, she wished she could close her eyes and wake up in her bed, warm and dry.

Molly watched as Joe ran his big hands over the thick roots and then started to pick at the grooved and pitted bark.

"What kind of tree is this?" she asked, taking a closer look, peering up into the branches to see if she could spot any sign of buds or berries.

"Nothing I've seen before," Joe said. "At least, nothing I remember. But we don't get a lot of trees in the Downtown canals."

Molly ran her hands over the bark, mimicking Joe. She looked up into the branches as the prickling feeling of being watched grew stronger. Unsettled, she looked around again, even as she started to explore one of the splits in the trunk with her fingers. The bark felt scarred and she frowned as she investigated. At the split, an elliptical wound had formed in the bark, and within it the meaty pulp was rotted and soft. It felt more like the moist fungal tissue of wild mushrooms than wood. Withered, rounded nubs emerged from the rotting wood.

She yanked her hand away, her breath quickening as she stared at the rotting split.

"Joe," she whispered.

But he had noticed her reaction already, and came around the tree to stand beside her.

"What is it?" he asked, even as he investigated for himself, plunging strong fingers into the soft, fungal rot and starting to claw out chunks of the pulp. He'd been at it for only seconds when he hesitated, and Molly knew he had come to the same realization as she had.

The nubs jutting from that rot were the tips of human fingers.

"Stand back," Joe said, and he started to tear away more of the rot.

Molly watched, frozen in disgust as he took a step back and began to kick at the split trunk. On the fourth kick there was a loud crack and the rot-gouged split gave way. One of the three offshoots from the main trunk splintered off and fell to the damp, weedy ground, revealing that much more of the core of the trunk had been infected by that strange, fungal rot.

A human hand jutted up from the center of the rotten core. It had gray, sagging skin and long yellow nails, and the fingers jutted like short, skeletal branches.

"Is it Felix?" Molly asked, hating how tiny her voice sounded.

"I don't see how it could be," Joe replied.

But she noticed he had been careful not to say "no."

Joe started to claw at the soft fungus again, yanking back chunks of healthy tree around that rotten core. Wood cracked and splintered. Molly joined in, putting her weight on one of the remaining offshoots of the trunk. Red leaves quivered above her, showering raindrops down on her head. The tree trunk tore on one side, like a wound opening in flesh, revealing a wrist and partially desiccated arm. Joe leaned on one offshoot of the trunk and Molly on the other, and for a moment the tree trunk gaped open wide enough that she saw the face of the dead man at the core of the rotting tree. She saw the ridged skull and the beard like copper wire and the pits where his eyes should be, and she knew it wasn't Felix.

Molly let go, taking a step back. For a moment, she had felt that unbearable pressure again, the familiar feeling of being watched, and she wondered if what she felt was the focus of those dark pits, the ghost of the rotting man watching her with those empty eyes.

"Andrew Golnik," Joe said. "It's got to be."

He began to kick at one of the two remaining offshoots from the trunk. The wood cracked even more loudly, the split in the trunk running almost to the roots now. Somehow the dead man had grown up out of his grave with the maturing tree. He was a part of it, its rotting core.

"Come on," Joe said. "If we're going to find answers, this is where we'll find them."

He hauled back his foot to launch another kick. The tree shook without any impact, and Molly saw the branches begin to snap and twist as they reached for Joe. One of the roots tugged itself from the rain-sodden soil and whipped toward her, wrapping around her leg.

The trunk began to seal itself back up, trying to hide the corpse of Andrew Golnik, and as the thick root twined around her, crawling up her body, Molly McHugh started to scream.

Chapter Ten

Joe fought against the branches of the tree as they wrapped, serpentine, around his arms and his neck. The bark scraped his throat, drawing blood, and he choked as a branch cut off his air. Black spots danced across his vision almost immediately. He hadn't had time to take a deep breath, and now his chest began to burn with the need for air.

He heard the girl screaming, and the sound of her fear stabbed deeply at him.

Planting his feet, he dug his heels into the earth. Thick, gnarled roots wrapped around his legs, but he would not be moved. Red leaves shook and spilled a fresh shower of raindrops down upon him. A haze of fury and determination began to blur his thoughts, and Joe bared his teeth even as the lack of air made his lungs feel like they were collapsing in upon themselves.

The pointed tip of a branch reached for him, wavering in front of his face, searching for the best spot to strike. Joe tore himself sideways just as the branch thrust forward. It would have speared his left eye if he hadn't moved.

Molly McHugh screamed his name. As he glanced quickly in her direction, he saw something that made his skin crawl with revulsion. The split in the trunk had sealed itself up, but now it reopened, torn wide and glistening with something like sap. Branches and roots twisted around the girl and pushed her toward the maw of the tree.

Inside the tree, the withered, mummified corpse of Andrew Golnik lay revealed, as though it had crawled up from the grave into the trunk of the tree. Frozen in grotesque, grinning death, it did not move, only lay in the peeled interior of the tree, its skin and hair nothing but wisps on the hideous ruin of a man. Rusted metal rings were knotted in the dead man's beard.

As the black spots on his vision spread, the darkness encroached on his thoughts. Images flitted across his mind of other screaming girls; of gnarled, spindly hands dragging them by their hair into trees and dank crypts and into the dark water beneath bridges. Some of those girls he had saved and others he had lost to the witches. But he would not lose Molly McHugh.

Without breath he could not scream, but he roared inside his own mind. The limbs of the tree pulled at him, trying to drag him closer. Where Molly's arm had been drawn inside it, he saw that the tree bark had begun to grow around her wrist and to spread up her arm.

Joe gave in, pressing forward, and for just an instant the branches and roots slackened their grip on him. He twisted his right wrist enough to wrap his hand around the branch and then fought again, digging in, and snapped the branch from the tree. Red leaves withered, died, and fell from the splintered branch as he tossed it down, but his right arm was free.

Golnik's mummy seemed to sneer, the remnants of its lips cracking to dust as they peeled back.

Joe thrashed and fought, and with a crack and a shriek that seemed to sound only inside his own skull, he broke the branch dragging on his left wrist. He reached both hands to his throat and an ancient strength flooded him, a furious power that felt like memory returning, and he ripped the strange branch fingers from his bleeding, abraded throat. Air rushed into his lungs, and he nearly vomited at the putrid, rotting stink that came with his first breath. Death and decay wafted from the hideous gullet of that gaping tree, a fermented, sulfurous odor that made his eyes water and his stomach roil.

Molly's head, right arm, and shoulders had been swallowed by the tree, a pinkish, bloody mucous sap spreading along her clothes as if of its own accord. Bark grew over her in its wake, as if the sap hardened into the skin of the tree. If the girl was still screaming, her terror echoed inside the lower trunk of the tree and he could no longer hear her, but he refused to believe she might be dead.

"Whatever the hell you are, you can't have her," he rasped.

As other branches reached down for him, he batted them aside, splintering wood as he finally managed to reach for his gun. The huge pistol had always weighed heavily in his grip, but now it felt featherlight, an extension of his hand. He shoved the big barrel into the gaping maw of the tree and pressed it against the mummy's chest. The split in the tree began to seal over his wrist and its consuming bark grew instantly along his arm, even as he pulled the trigger.

The boom of the first gunshot was muffled and distant inside the tree, but as he pulled the trigger again and again, the tree began to rot and the split grew wider, the bark crinkling as it withered. Each shot was louder than the last, and as the dying tree peeled open, Joe saw the damage the bullets had done to the corpse of Andrew Golnik. The mummy had been blown apart, its chest a crater of flesh like old papyrus and its yellowed bones shattered into shards like the broken branches of the cursed tree.

Something gleamed inside the dead occultist's chest cavity.

"Stop!" Molly shouted. "Please, stop!"

She had slipped out of the tree as he killed it, and now she lay on the ground, tears streaming from her eyes. Her hands were clapped to her ears and her face contorted with pain. He noticed that the bark that had grown over the skin of her neck, cheeks, and arms had withered and was flaking off, but that observation distracted him for only a moment from the reason for her cries and tears. It wasn't fear that made her shout, but pain. Her head had been inside the trunk of the tree when Joe had fired most of his bullets, and the thunder of those gunshots had hurt her badly.

Joe holstered his gun and dropped to his knees beside her.

"Molly," he said, reaching out to try to take her hands away from her ears.

She jerked away from him, but after a moment she relented. Joe was glad to see there was no blood on her hands or in her ears. He didn't think her eardrums had been popped.

"You're going to be okay," he said.

Molly wiped away her tears and shook her head. "I can't hear you."

Joe took her hand and held it tightly. "Can you hear me at all?" he yelled, hating the way his voice carried through the sprawl of the cemetery.

Her breath hitching, she nodded, calming a little. "Some. But really muffled."

"It'll come back," Joe said loudly, trying a smile.

He wasn't very good at smiling, but Molly nodded again and seemed comforted. She clutched his hand and he helped her to stand. She pressed the heel of one hand against her forehead and he knew she must have a hell of a headache. But a headache and a little temporary hearing loss was a small price to pay for not being absorbed by the evil that had been living inside that tree, and he was sure Molly would agree.

Joe could still feel the taint of the dark magic in that tree. He felt as if it had stained him with its malignance, giving his stomach a sickly twist of nausea, and he longed for a shower. Even a swim in the river would be a relief. He gave the sky a momentary glance, hoping that the heavy, low-hanging clouds would erupt with a fresh downpour instead of the light drizzle that still misted around them.

Molly set about peeling the withered bark-skin off of her face, hands, and arms, her mouth making a little moue of disgust.

In the deepening gloom of the storm-laden afternoon, Joe heard the whistle of a bird off to his left, from a copse of trees near a row of crumbling family crypts. When he glanced back at Molly, she wore a curious expression. He turned to see what had struck her so oddly and realized she was staring at the desiccated remains of the occultist's mummy, which were so much a part of the rotting tree's core that it was impossible to tell where the one ended and the other began.

But it wasn't Golnik's cadaver Molly was looking at.

Joe had been so concerned about the girl that he had forgotten the glimpse he'd caught of something glinting inside the mummy's ruined corpse. Tucked into the bottom of the chest cavity was an object that at first glance resembled nothing so much as an exotic puzzle. Tubes of subtly colored glass—or was it glass?—were knotted together in a strangely organized tangle. It reminded him of a heart.

Joe took a step nearer to the tree, and the design of the knot seemed to shift, all of its turns and angles changing as though it had reconfigured itself.

"I'll be damned," Joe said, reaching for the knot. He plunged his fingers into the rotted corpse and tree and dug the half-buried artifact out, then held it up, studying the way it seemed to defy the eye's attempts to capture its contours.

"What is it?" Molly asked, speaking loudly, having difficulty hearing even her own words.

Joe smiled at her. "It's the Pentajulum."

Her hearing must have been improving, because her face lit up with a grin. Joe didn't blame her. With this shifting bauble, Church would be able to help her track down Felix Orlov.

"But how did it get . . . inside him?" Molly asked, rubbing at her temples to ease the ache in her head. "It's too big for him to have swallowed it."

The Pentajulum pulsed in his hand. Some of the tubes were ice-cold and others emanated a comforting warmth. It almost felt as if it were a part of him, as if it clung to his skin, merging with his flesh . . . as if it wanted him to hold it. The knot had no consistent reality; it seemed quite possible that it also had no consistent size. Golnik might not have been able to swallow it, but another theory presented itself.

"The last time Church saw this thing, it was in Golnik's hand. When Church shot the guy, he fell, and the Pentajulum was nowhere to be found. It had to have been inside already, right then, while he was bleeding out on the floor."

"I don't—"

Joe turned to Molly. "It must have somehow dug its way inside of him."

"That's disgusting. Wouldn't Church have noticed a big hole in the guy?"

"Unless his body absorbed it somehow. Nobody knows enough about this thing to say what it can and can't do," Joe said. "And I gotta tell you, just hanging on to it gives me the shivers. It feels like it's . . . awake. I don't know how to explain it better than that. I'm getting this weird feeling, like it's *aware* of us, and I don't like that at all. Whatever happened with the tree just now . . . yeah, it might've been Golnik's magic, some kind of curse he left behind, infesting that tree, possessing it somehow. But I don't think so. I think it was this. I think it wanted out."

He held the Pentajulum out for her to get a better look, but when she reluctantly reached out for it, he drew it back before her fingers could brush against it. Joe told himself it was out of concern for the girl, that the knot had a weird malignance he didn't want to expose her to, but he wondered if maybe there was more to it than that. Did it exert some influence over him? Now that he had it, did he covet it so much that he did not want anyone else to touch it?

Molly gave her head a little toss, but her ears didn't seem to be bothering her as much. Though Joe imagined they were still ringing.

"So it's just been waiting here for someone to come along?" she asked.

"Not *just* waiting," Joe said. "You saw the way the wood was splitting, the hand reaching up like it was crawling free in slow motion . . . or being born."

Molly looked stricken, her face paler than ever. "You think it made the corpse move, like some kind of puppet?"

"We'll never know," Joe said, staring at the pulsing knot again.

"Put it away," Molly said. "Please. I don't even want to see the thing. Let's just get it back to Mr. Church, so we can find Felix."

Joe glanced at the tree. At least half the leaves had fallen and the rest were turning brown, dying on the branch. The tree looked dead, and the withered remains of Andrew Golnik had decayed further. Whatever had animated the tree and the body—Golnik's dark magic or the Pentajulum—the curse had left them.

"You're right," he said. "Let's—"

"What's that?" Molly interrupted.

Joe frowned, and then he heard the odd sounds that had caught her attention, an odd shush and flap that made him turn and scan the gravestones and the trees around them. When he spotted the figure lurching from between the family crypts off to his left, he swore under his breath.

"Oh, no. Not again," Molly said, backing up toward the withered tree.

Black rubber gas masks glistened in the drizzling rain, goggle-eyes opaque, as three of the thuggish killers Molly called the gas-men broke into a run toward them. Joe shouted and moved in front of the girl, drawing his gun.

"Back off right now. You're not going to get by me."

They didn't slow down.

"Joe!" Molly shouted. "There are more!"

He glanced to the right and saw others running in a crouch, weaving through the headstones and darting from behind trees. Some wore long coats to cover the slick, rubbery clothes that seemed to seal them inside, but others did not. Dark forms surrounded them, some scurrying and others hurtling toward them, and Joe knew he didn't have enough bullets for all of them. But bullets were just the beginning; his fists were just as deadly.

The trio of gas-men who had hidden amongst the crypts closed in, and he could hear their labored breathing inside those monstrous masks. He thought about the way they had come apart in his hands when he had first rescued Molly, and the malleable flesh of the arm Church had examined in his lab, and he wondered if any of the gas-men were actually men. He supposed he would find out.

"Cocteau's going to be very disappointed when you're all dead," Joe said.

He shot the nearest one through the eye-lens of its mask. Air burst out of it like a balloon, and it collapsed, writhing and seeming to shrink. The other two that had been in the first wave caught bullets in the chest, which perforated their suits, and they staggered and fell a dozen feet from where Joe and Molly made their stand in front of the cursed tree.

Molly screamed his name again. He turned to see that she had snapped off a long, sharp length of branch. As Joe took aim at a gas-man lunging for her, Molly speared him through the neck, the splintered end of the branch puncturing flesh and fabric, and a hiss of air burst out with a squirt of inhumanly dark blood.

Joe shifted his aim and shot the next one, but they were moving in faster than he'd expected, swarming around him and Molly. He didn't know how many bullets he had left, and he reached out and pushed Molly behind him again. Courageous as she was, he would not risk her getting hurt.

She stumbled and sprawled onto the grass a few feet away.

As he fired again, he saw a scarecrow-thin gas-man whip a gun from inside his long coat and take aim, and he felt a kind of roar in his heart. They had guns. Why the hell had they taken so long to put them to use?

He shot the scarecrow three times and it fell, skidding into the mud in a tangle of sprawled limbs. But then his trigger clicked on an empty chamber even as, one by one, other gas-men began to draw weapons, and he knew it was over.

Molly started to rise.

"Stay down!" Joe shouted, and even as he did, he understood why the gas-men had waited to draw their weapons. Molly had been in the line of fire until he'd shoved her to the ground. Which meant they wanted her alive but had no such concerns about him.

He grabbed the nearest gas-man, a heavyset thug wearing a filthy fedora with his gas mask, and punched him twice in the head before spinning him around to use as a shield against the gunmen. Bullets punched the air and Joe staggered back as they struck the gas-man in his grasp. One knocked the fedora off of the thug's head and passed straight through, cutting a groove in Joe's left cheek. It seared his skin, and he could smell his own blood as he staggered back, trying to hold on to the gas-man in his arms. But the suit had been perforated, and rank, putrid air hissed out. A moment before, the thing in his arms had had the shape and heft of a man, but now it felt as if he held some kind of writhing animal wrapped in the rubbery fabric. Dying, it thrashed against him and slipped from his grasp, leaving him without protection.

The gas-men kept shooting. Joe lunged toward the nearest one, but a bullet struck him in the chest and he staggered back a step. He looked down to see a hole in his rain-soaked shirt, a starburst of blood growing and spreading through the sodden fabric. He found himself staring at his hands, suddenly wondering why they were not earth and stone.

He heard Molly screaming.

A bullet struck his shoulder, turning him halfway around. Another hit his right leg, and he collapsed to his knees in the graveyard mud. Gas-men loomed out of the rain-streaked gloom around him. He could see the trickles and spatters of rainwater on the lenses of their masks. Two of them had Molly by the arms and were dragging her away as she fought them, but she was alive. That was good.

The gas-men circled him. The stormy sky seemed to darken. The blood soaking his clothing felt warm at first, but then a cold as deep as bone gripped him. Guns were raised, slowly and deliberately, the mouths of their barrels as dark and unfathomable as the goggle-lenses of the gas-men. The last shots were strangely muffled, as if somehow distant, and he fell onto his back and bled into the mud.

Chapter Eleven

olly tried to claw them, but her arms were held apart. She tried to kick them, but her legs were lifted off the ground and they carried her. She thrashed and screamed and spat, and all the fear of her years alone, hiding in the abandoned ruins of the Drowning City from the brutality of the Water Rats, clattered back into her mind. Torment, rape, and pain had haunted her from the shadows the way others believed ghosts wandered the halls of places of death. They were the things she feared at night, but over the years Felix had erased her terror. Now it returned in full, and she remembered all of the horrors she had seen in dank, crumbling buildings and the stories she had heard from broken women and children.

And she fought.

Joe had been so strong, and he had killed so many of them, but now he was dead. She had no one to protect her—only herself. But what could she do against creatures like this? Even if they were only dull, cruel men, they would have easily overpowered her, but they were monsters, things created out of men and magic.

As they carried her through the cemetery, past broken headstones and onto a path that led to the water, she tasted salt on her lips and knew that her tears had mingled with the gentle rain on her face. She screamed again, for Joe and for herself. She cried out for answers, asking the gas-men why they wanted her when they had Felix. She cursed them and promised to kill them. She demanded to know if Dr. Cocteau had sent them and what he meant to do with her.

The gas-men said nothing. She thrashed, and sometimes their wet-gloved grip would slip, but she knew she could not escape them. Still, she fought, and she wept, and she shivered with the cold of the rain that plastered her clothes to her body. As one, the gas-men carrying her let go, and she flailed as she fell to the ground. The breath exploded from her lungs, and she contorted from the pain of the impact. Her head still throbbed and her hearing was still muffled by her nearness to Joe's gun, and now she endured this fresh pain wracking her back.

Molly exhaled, as if surrendering, and then she tried to bolt. She made it a step and a half before they dragged her back and forced her to turn and face the water, and then astonishment halted her. There were two motorboats out a ways, but nearer to the shore was a small submarine, its upper half jutting from the water. She stared at its tiny portholes and the rivets that held its plated hull together.

Though she had seen pictures of submarines, none of them had ever looked like this. Its nose was pointed like that of a swordfish and it had serrated rows of what seemed to be fins on the top and sides. Water trickled from the open tips of the side-fins and smoke slithered from the upper row. It stank of oil, which reminded her of Mr. Church, which made her think of Joe, and she realized that if she let them put her into the strange submarine, she would die. Not tonight, because if they had wanted to kill her right away, she would be lying dead next to Joe. But when Dr. Cocteau had gotten whatever he wanted from her, she would die.

Again she tried to run. One of the gas-men struck her across the face so hard that he knocked her off her feet. She flew backward, tumbling and rolling until she sprawled half in, half out of the river. A pool of oil lay on top of the water, streaking the bank.

Strong hands hoisted her up again, and the gas-men marched into the water, carrying her toward the submarine. Her head rang from the blow she'd received, and all the fight had gone out of her. If she was to survive, she would have to wait for the right moment to fight again, or to run, or to find a way to be clever enough to escape.

They carried her roughly up on top of the submarine, passing her off like she was unwanted garbage. Just before they dragged her down inside, she glanced back toward the sprawling, ugly, overgrown cemetery island and saw the last few gas-men coming down to the river's edge. One of them held something in his hand that shone with dim, shifting colors, and she twisted to get a better look.

Lector's Pentajulum. Of course. If Mr. Church was right, Dr. Cocteau had gotten exactly what he had wanted. It frightened Molly to wonder what he meant to do with it, but she felt dreadfully certain that she would soon find out.

Chapter Twelve

Joe blinked raindrops from his eyes. He stared up at the early-evening clouds, at the blanket of storm, and felt a pang of regret that he would never see the sun again. No more blue-sky mornings. As numbness spread through him, he lolled his head to the side and coughed out the blood that filled his throat. He felt it bubble on his lips, and he wondered—perhaps as deeply as he had ever wondered anything—why he wasn't dead yet. Surely his demise was imminent.

So he waited. With each breath, he felt things tearing inside his chest. The pain clawed at him, the numbness an external shell that did not protect him from the wreckage within. Yet still the spark of his life did not extinguish. He had seen countless impossible things in his years with Simon Church, not least of which was Church's own mechanically and magically provided longevity, but he had been shot more than a dozen times, ruining his ordinary human mechanisms, the parts he needed to keep running. There was impossible, and then there was *impossible.* He could not survive these injuries.

But for the moment, he lived.

Again he blinked the rain away. He had this moment. And beyond that, he suspected he had another. He had no idea how many further moments he would be allowed, but it seemed criminal to waste them numb and bleeding and weeping raindrops in agony. One of the gasmen had reached into his pocket and taken the Penatajulum. It had been this, in fact, that had roused him from unconsciousness. The bizarre thugs had taken Molly and that most powerful of arcane artifacts, and they would bring them to Dr. Cocteau.

"Like hell," Joe rasped, coughing another mouthful of blood into the mud.

Death would come, but as long as the Reaper was tardy, Joe refused to waste the last moments of his life. He rolled onto his side, one hand over his abdomen, covering the worst of his wounds, trying to hold in the things that wanted to seep out. Sodden with blood and rain, his clothes clung to his body, and when he moved, they tugged

at bullet wounds, obliterating the numbness that had been kind to him. Still, he managed to get to his knees, and from there it was a single lurch that drove him to his feet.

Standing in the light, misting rain, Joe felt his blood run down his legs and into his shoes. His feet squelched as he staggered forward, heading downhill after Molly and the gas-men. Broken and torn bits inside him jarred against each other, and he had to bite back a roar of pain. Screaming would be an indulgence and take too much energy. His fingers flexed and he wished for his gun before remembering that he'd run out of bullets.

When the gas-man had taken the Pentajulum from him, he'd gotten a general idea of the direction they were heading. His vision swam in and out, the world flickering along with the candle of his life, but he stayed on course. When he struck the side of a broken headstone and stumbled, he caught himself on the corner of a crypt and managed to stay mostly upright. He took three gasping breaths, swallowing back the blood that burbled up, and pushed himself away from the granite, ignoring the bloody prints his hands left behind.

Long grass dragged at the legs of his trousers, but he slogged on down the hill. He blinked, and there was a large stone angel in front of him, its marble head long since sheared off. He blinked again and found himself on cracked pavement, a path abandoned by mourners who had forgotten this place and left the past behind. He blinked again, and then stood swaying in confusion. Two small boats roared away across the river, belching black smoke, as a long-coated gas-man slid down through the top hatch of a small submarine. Joe shook his head, thinking it must be an illusion, with the strange fin that jutted from the top.

He bit his lip, hard, clearing his vision for just a moment. The submarine did not vanish. Instead, it began to glide along the riverbank, moving slowly south and away, into deeper currents. Steam jetted from the ribbed piping of the topfin, but as the sub dove, water began to spurt from the pipes instead.

Molly, Joe thought. Whether she was on the submarine or one of those boats, they were all going to the same place—Dr. Cocteau's lair. The greater meaning of this fact struck him at last. They had not shot Molly, only handled her roughly, which meant Dr. Cocteau had ordered that she be taken alive. But for what purpose? If he had somehow merged men and beasts into these gas-masked creations, what might he do to the girl?

No. He staggered into the water, wading deep into the river. The water stung his wounds at first, but then soothed them. The urge to float away on the current blossomed within him and he nearly surrendered, but then he thought of Molly, who had trusted him and joked with him. Molly, who had put her faith in him.

Joe charged deeper into the water, following the gliding sub, then dove under, dragging himself hand over hand after it. Eyes open, he saw that the strange transport had the same fin piping on its sides as it had on top, and he swam toward it, tasting the river water and blood that mingled in his mouth. Stretching, reaching, feeling things come unknitted in his chest and gut, he managed to grab hold of the portside fin. The jets of water expelled from the pipes pushed at him, but he held on.

The submarine picked up speed as Joe pulled himself along the curve of the fin until he found himself snug against the hull. From there, he could do nothing but hang on.

Somehow, Joe held his breath as the water rushed over him. He could taste the copper of his blood, even in the water, and the darkness pressed in on him along with the pressure as the submarine slid deeper into the river. His vision waxed and waned, a zoetrope flicker as his body fought against the pull of death, yet he sank just as quickly as the sub. He caught only glimpses of a vast cave opening carved into the schist that made up the bedrock of Manhattan. The submarine slid into the city's hidden underworld. He saw massive iron bars and stone slabs, and a mystery unfurled itself. They were in a centuries-old, sunken sewer system that neither he nor Church had ever known existed. *The Dutch,* he thought. Back in the seventeenth century, New York had been New Amsterdam, and under Dutch rule. *Had to be them, somehow.*

He drifted through the history of the city, beneath centuries of ambition, of building and rebuilding. Yet the sediment of civilization was not as deep here as it was in Europe. Before the United States there had been the British, before the British the Dutch, and before the Dutch there had been the Lenape Indians, the original stewards of the land, who were all but gone from the earth now, and long forgotten. They were a part of the past, and Joe felt himself surrendering to it, floating through it, vanishing inside his own memory.

Joe felt himself sinking, not into the water but into himself, and for long minutes he was lost in the darkness. Yet his grip loosened only slightly, and still he held on. When he became aware again, he started to draw in a breath and gagged on river water. Choking out water and blood, he sealed his lips, but the last of his oxygen was gone. Trapped airless in his own body, he looked around and saw through an open archway to his left an antique, rusted subway train. Glancing down, over the lip of the submarine's fin, he saw the tracks. They had navigated through those ancient sewers and into a drowned remnant of the original Interborough Rapid Transit Company subway line.

They slid past crumbled stations filled with junk and debris that must have been down there since the underground first began to flood. *No wonder we never found Cocteau,* he thought.

He coughed and inhaled water. He fought it, but he had to breathe. He had to scream. The water flowed into him and the darkness returned with it. Too many pieces were broken inside him; too much blood had drained into the mud of Brooklyn Heights and the waters beneath the Drowning City. At the edges of his mind, he saw himself on the bank of another river, a wraithlike witch tearing at the clay of his flesh, but even as all reason fled him, he knew that had been only a dream. Always, just a dream.

Joe felt the candle within him flicker badly, almost extinguished. And then it went out. His fingers loosened as his grip gave way, and he slid away from the submarine, floating in the water. Growing strangely heavy, uncannily so, he began to sink, and came to rest at last beside tracks that no longer led anywhere at all.

Chapter Thirteen

Something clanked loudly inside the strange workings of Simon Church's chest. He tasted smoke instead of steam and smelled burning oil. Pushing his chair back from the desk in his study, he stared down at himself as if his eyes could see what had gone wrong within him.

"No," he said, brows knitted in irritation and discomfort.

This wasn't supposed to happen. The spells were in place, the sigils tattooed into his skin. He drank the tinctures, always used the freshest herbs, and spoke the incantations passed down from priests of Assyrian Arcanum. He had supplemented this ancient medicine by replacing his organs, when they failed, with gears and pumps fueled by modern chemistry and old Arcanum. The mechanisms took little maintenance, and they never simply broke down. Never.

A jolt of pain seized him, and he clutched a hand to his chest. Mr. Church staggered to his feet and beat a fist against the place where his heart ought to have been. He felt something grinding there, and it bent him over in a moment of agony before it abruptly ceased. A cough sputtered out of his mouth, a puff of black smoke. And then the pain abated, and he could breathe evenly again. The steam coated his lips as he exhaled.

The danger seemingly passed, he shuddered as he walked across the room to the cabinet atop which sat a crystal decanter of eighteenth-century brandy. Hands shaking, he poured himself a small amount, and then doubled it. As he raised the glass to his lips, he faltered, and then set the glass down almost hard enough to break it.

Something else had broken inside of him, something neither mechanical nor arcane. A piece of his spirit had crumbled to dust.

Joe had left him. His dearest friend and trusted companion had died, and he had felt it in the severing of the bond they shared, the magical rapport that had been established on the day they had first met. In the moment of Joe's death, something had quite literally broken inside Simon Church, and though whatever mechanism had given way was now working again, he knew that it would not last forever. Chemistry, medicine, arcanum, and mechanics had kept his body

working, but it was his soul that had powered it all, his sense of purpose, his sheer force of will. Joe's dying had just carved away a piece of that. His will now faltered. His heart—not the mechanism he'd invented but the part that still kept him alive, his investment in the world around him—had been broken.

Entropy had taken hold. He would begin to deteriorate now. And perhaps that was for the best.

"Oh, my friend. My dearest friend," he whispered.

Only then did he realize that he had begun to cry. His breath hitched, and he swiped almost angrily at his tears. They left an oily streak on the back of his hand. Mr. Church raised the brandy snifter again and took a deep swallow. The liquor felt like silk and fire as it slid down his throat, and he stood for several seconds before he took another swallow, and then a third, finishing the glass.

Steadied, he took the decanter and the glass with him and returned to his desk. The leather creaked as he settled into his chair and laid his head back. As if they had been waiting for him, the tears returned in a single, wracking sob that filled the study, echoing from the spines of a thousand books.

"I'm so sorry," he whispered, closing his eyes.

Hawthorne had been his first investigative partner, but it was only right that Joe should be his last. After all, without Joe, he would have succumbed to the weight of the years on his soul long ago. A terrible melancholy had seized him in those dark days, and Joe's arrival in his life—his friendship—had made him want to continue to engage with the world.

How had Joe died? the great detective wondered. It took precious little deduction to know that the journey to Brooklyn Heights had led to his demise, and no great leap of logic to realize that Joe's death must have resulted from an encounter with Dr. Cocteau and his thuggish creations. Other possibilities existed. The mysterious grave that seemed to help heal Felix Orlov's frequent malaise might have contained some unknown danger. Contact with Lector's Pentajulum—if Joe and Molly had indeed found it—might have destroyed them both, although what little the world knew of the Pentajulum made that seem unlikely.

No, he thought. *It had to be Dr. Cocteau.* Joe would not have been easy to kill.

Mr. Church's eyes opened. He stared for a moment at his desk, then bent forward and poured himself another finger of brandy. Draining it quickly, he set both glass and decanter aside and reached instead for his pipe. He tapped it out and cleaned it rapidly, his spiderlike fingers moving of their own accord, so often had he performed this task. Then he filled and lit the pipe, sucking in the aromatic smoke, and it soothed him as much as he would ever now be soothed.

In the curls of smoke that began to rise, he saw the silhouette of a figure in the darkest corner of the room. He jerked back in his chair, startled. He fumbled those spider-fingers into the top desk drawer, grasping for the pistol he kept there, but then the silhouette coalesced from the shadows—made from shadows, and made from memory—and he knew the stout form so well that his jaw went slack and his burning pipe fell into his lap. He snatched the pipe up and held it, ignoring the ash and tobacco that had spilled out to ruin his trousers.

"Hawthorne?" he breathed.

The gossamer thing in the shadows nodded ominously, but then it smiled kindly, and a bit sadly, and the dread he'd felt at the sight of the specter vanished. Again Church's hands began to shake, and he watched the ghost drift closer to the desk. He saw that there were others behind it, the shades of other men who had filled the same role Hawthorne had had in his life—friend and companion and confessor, partner in the solving of crime after crime. One by one he had let them into his life, and one by one they had died, and Simon Church had found a way to keep himself alive.

Hawthorne's ghost tilted its head and regarded him with love and sympathy, and Mr. Church felt something grind inside his chest again. The mechanism clanked several times, and the spasms made him jerk against the leather chair—once, twice, a third time. His left arm did not seem to want to respond to his brain's commands. It would not reach to put the fallen pipe onto the desk. His right hand shook badly as he tried to move it from the open drawer, jerking side to side.

"Not yet," Mr. Church whispered. "Not yet, my old friends."

Warm tears touched his lips, and this time, when he tasted them, they were pure oil. He imagined his face must be streaked with black, and though he could not seem to look down, he knew the oil would be staining his jacket even now.

Mr. Church forced himself to stand, hearing the grinding inside the way he heard his own voice when he spoke. A part of him.

He averted his gaze from the gray specters looming in the shadowed corners. If he looked into their eyes, he feared he would know why they had come, and the answer to that question held terror for him.

"I see you," he whispered. "And I'm sorry, old friends, but you frighten me. Spiritual hands have stepped in to alter the course of my life more than once, to offer guidance and even gifts, but both blood and oil run cold in me this evening. I believe I know why you've come, for better or for worse, and there is something I must do."

Church, whispered the ghost of Dr. Nigel Hawthorne. *You have given Death an admirable fight.*

"Hush!" Mr. Church said, his hands shaking. He gritted his teeth against the pain in his chest as he staggered across the room toward the bookshelves that held his rarest and most precious volumes.

Church, whispered dead Thomas Cranham, the third man who had performed Hawthorne's functions after the doctor's death. *Do you remember this?*

"No," Mr. Church said as his knees buckled. He slammed into the shelves, and books tumbled out. The yellowed skull of an ancient Chaldean chemist hit the floor and shattered to dust.

Simon, please, look at it, Cranham's ghost pleaded.

Mr. Church closed his eyes, sorrow filling up all of the empty places that his long years had left inside of him. He had never realized how hollow he had allowed himself to become until now, as anguish filled him up.

"Not yet, damn you," he rasped.

Immediately, he regretted it. He had loved these men while they lived, each and every one of them. During the time when they had been his companions, not one of them had ever betrayed him. Some had been better detectives than others, smarter and more diligent, and some had simply been better company, quicker to laugh, with a gift for lightening his haunted heart.

He chuckled to himself at the thought, but even the chuckle made his chest clench with fresh pain. The grinding inside him grew louder in his ears.

Please, Simon, for your own sake, whispered another voice that he knew so well. This time he could not help glancing over at the ephemeral figure standing in the shadows. Arthur Kenneally had been forcibly drowned in the Thames by a brutal killer in the filthy Shadwell district of London—a killer who would have spared his life if Kenneally had just told him where to find Simon Church.

Mr. Church closed his eyes and leaned against the bookshelf, his forehead pressed against the smooth leather bindings of his most precious books. Grief and terror bubbled inside of him like a scream he would not be able to hold inside forever. In his century as a detective, he had seen ghosts before, spirits lurking in dark houses and on rocky ocean bluffs, places of regret and disappointment and forlorn love. But only once had he seen the shade of someone he had known in his own life.

Yet now they were all here, all of the men who had stepped into the role of best friend and confidant, who had faced danger with him and endured his arrogance and his intensity, the cold focus that he often employed to the dismissal of all else. Hawthorne, who had known him best of all, and known the best of him, when the vigor of youth still inspired him . . . and Kenneally, who had given his own life rather than betray and endanger the great detective Simon Church.

And he would not face them?

Grimacing against his pain, against the screaming clutch of muscle and the grind of broken gears inside him, Mr. Church forced himself upright. Lifting his chin, he turned toward the specters of his past who had come from the shadows—who had perhaps always lurked nearby, just out of reach—and opened his eyes. He stared at the ghosts and wished for his pipe.

Do you remember this? Hawthorne asked, though now Mr. Church saw that his lips did not move, that the ghost's voice sounded like the whisper of the breeze fluttering long drapes. His phantom figure fading in and out, Hawthorne pointed at a small rosewood box that sat unobtrusively on a waist-level shelf.

Mr. Church swallowed hard, tasting oil. His mouth felt dry.

"Of course I do," he said.

Inside the box was a single opal, a red stone shot through with veins of black. If he were to test the box, he knew he would find that its contents also included detritus from a hundred-year-old bay leaf that had once been wrapped around the stone.

"How could I forget?" he said, though now he spoke in a whisper meant only for himself.

Old guilt slipped its arms around him like an illicit lover, comfortable and shameful all at once. He had kept the box as a reminder, but as the decades had passed, it had become just one more souvenir in a home filled with them. As he glanced around the study, he knew what he would see—a broken calabash pipe, a fountain pen, a sikh's dagger, a tiny runic tablet, a silent bell, a cracked goblet, and dozens of other artifacts from the crimes he had solved and the tragedies he had averted throughout his life.

Morris knew the risks, Thomas Cranham's ghost said.

Mr. Church nodded, flinching at a new knot of pain in his side. He searched the diaphanous faces of the spirits who gathered in his study, but he already knew that he would not see Morris Sowerberry among them. Guilt clutched at his failing heart that he had not noticed immediately. Sowerberry had not been the most stalwart or the most amiable or the most competent of his associates through the years, nor had he been the only one to die during the course of an investigation. But his death had certainly been the most unsettling . . . if one could even call it "death."

Tasked by Scotland Yard with helping them track down the Knightsbridge Strangler, Mr. Church had solved the puzzle of the killer's identity, only to be captured by the Strangler himself. The killer had known he had reached the end game and intended to work out his frustrations over the course of long days of brutality, making Church's pain linger before snuffing out his life. Sowerberry had known of Church's conclusions but had no evidence to present to Scotland Yard. More than once, he had tried to follow the killer without being noticed, but somehow the man always seemed to sense and elude him, until at last Sowerberry had decided that the only way he could trail the killer back to where Church was being held would be if he himself were invisible.

Amongst Mr. Church's collection of arcane artifacts and lore had been the Pasha's Opal, a souvenir from a previous case. Wrapped in a fresh bay leaf, it was purported to render whoever held it in his hand invisible. For Sowerberry, it had worked all too well. Invisible to the naked eye, he had followed the killer until, at last, the man had led him to the old tailor shop where Mr. Church had been imprisoned in the basement. He had assaulted the killer, still invisible, and grappled with him, but during the struggle he had dropped the opal and it had slipped from its bay leaf wrapping.

Though already invisible, in that moment Sowerberry had vanished. The Knightsbridge Strangler had already been knocked unconscious and Mr. Church had managed to work himself free of his bonds in time, but of Sowerberry there was never any sign. Never able to become visible again, he had slipped away from the world, flesh and bone, and his spirit would never rest. He could not have been here among the other ghosts, for he was neither physical nor spiritual, no longer alive but never entirely dead.

Simon, the ghost of Nigel Hawthorne said. His voice seemed a chill breath whispering in Mr. Church's ear, though the spirit still lurked in the gloomy recesses of the room with the rest. *Cranham is right. Sowerberry knew the risk he took. He had read the file on the Pasha's Opal and the warnings therein.*

"I know," Mr. Church said, staring for the first time at the translucent eyes of the first partner he had ever taken on in his investigations, dead for more than sixty-five years. "But he took the risk, Hawthorne. In this line of work, we hurl ourselves into danger over and over, without reservation, knowing that we do so for the greater good."

But Morris did it for you, Cranham observed, his voice so faraway, a sound like rustling paper.

"I know that!" Mr. Church said, instantly regretting that he had snapped at Cranham. He was not entirely certain why the specters had come, but he felt sure it had not been so that they could be upbraided by him.

At last, Hawthorne's gray shade slipped from the shadows. In the deep gloom streaming through the window, a mix of oncoming evening and ominous storm outside, he was little more than a silhouette formed of smoke.

Morris Sowerberry earned his rest, Hawthorne whispered. *His parents await him for eternity. The woman he loved and never married wonders when his spirit will finally slip the bonds of the physical world and join hers. But that is simply not to be. Sowerberry will never have his rest, Simon. This is no fault of yours, despite the guilt you carry in your heart, but if you could step back through time, armed with the knowledge of events before they occur, wouldn't you stop him from taking the opal? Wouldn't you want Sowerberry to have the rest he had earned?*

Mr. Church leaned against the bookcase. A dreadful weight had formed in his chest and grew heavier by the moment, all of the oil and blood pooling there, and the slowing mechanisms no longer able to provide enough strength for him to bear their burden. He smelled the smoke from inside him and tasted oily tears on his lips again.

"Of course," he rasped, his voice no louder than the whispers of the ghosts. "You know that I would."

In his long years, he had seen terrifying specters, bloodthirsty ghosts of madmen, and hate-filled apparitions. He had seen lost, mournful phantoms, bare echoes of lonely lives, afraid to enter what they feared would be an even lonelier afterlife. Though it chilled him, now, to be surrounded by the spirits of long-dead friends, he felt no fear. If anything, he felt safe. Certainly, he did not feel alone, and for that his own ghost would be grateful forever and beyond.

But he wished they had not come, for it made what he had to do next all the harder.

You must leave Joe as he is, Cranham's ghost said. *Let his spirit rest. He's earned that.*

Church knew that he owed Hawthorne and the others his attention. For all of the times he had been so focused on some riddle or enigma, distracted by a case, that he had ignored the input they offered, he would not ignore them now. The pain crippled him. His breath came in thin, reedy sips, and his left hand had begun to tremble uncontrollably, but he listened to every word. He only wished he could comply.

"I'm sorry," he said, hearing the slur in his voice. Not a single part of him worked properly anymore. "There is more to be done."

Mr. Church caught a look of disappointment on the face of Hawthorne's ghost. Despite the gossamer insubstantiality of the spirit, the way even the wan light in the room passed through, and the hollow void of his eyes, still the specter's gaze held all the nuances of emotion. Flickering in and out, the ghost of Nigel Hawthorne loomed closer, vanishing and reappearing several times until they were near enough to each other to whisper secrets without the others hearing.

I don't like seeing you in pain, Simon, Hawthorne's ghost said, his features more the hint of a face in coalescing smoke now. *I will ease your burden, if I can. But you must listen.*

"I told you—" Mr. Church began.

You must, Hawthorne's ghost said, even more firmly.

The specter reached out a wispy, transparent hand and pressed it to Mr. Church's chest. The pain seemed to abate, and Mr. Church exhaled. And yet he knew that this was no cure, only a brief respite. The spark of some strange vitality ignited inside him, and he understood that Hawthorne had given part of his own spirit, part of himself, to offer blessed relief.

"Thank you," Mr. Church rasped.

But the ghost did not withdraw his hand from Mr. Church's chest. Instead, he spoke a single word. *Remember.*

Chapter Fourteen

It is another era, years past. Church sits at the desk in his study. A jazz record plays, its soft notes dancing through the room. The drapes are tied back and moonlight streams in, splashing across the faded, once-lovely carpet. Dust motes swirl, a languid storm of neglect floating in the pale yellow light. If not for Church's presence, one might think the room had been abandoned for months or more. He remains so entirely still that he might as well be part of the furnishings.

Church takes a deep, hitching breath, disturbing some of the dust that floats around him. He stares at the peculiar mechanism on the desk before him, its once-gleaming metal now dingy with oil and imbued with magic. It looks like something he has taken from among the mechanical organs he has built for himself, but this apparatus of tiny iron pumps and sealed iron chambers is so much more than that.

Once the implantation is completed, and his useless, dying organ has been removed, this will be his heart.

It weighs very little, considering the metal involved, and yet his desk seems to sag under its burden. Mr. Church massages his temples, staring at the mechanism staining the desktop. In no mood for his pipe, he draws a Turkish cigarette from a mahogany box and lights it with a wooden match, which he blows out and drops into an ashtray. Thin wisps of smoke, the ghosts of the extinguished flame, rise from the dead match, and he watches then dissipate.

The record's music fills the room, but Mr. Church cannot feel it within him. It does nothing to lift his spirits, seeming instead to speak to the part of him that longs for an end to all music. An end to blood and oil and cigarettes and the life he has spent accumulating the things in his study, the remnants of times past, the markers on his road. He smokes awhile, feeling the tightness in his chest. He can feel the gears moving in there, hear the workings of the other mechanisms he installed over time so that he could hold on to life. The mad contraption he has made, this new and impossible heart, will give him many years still, even decades, if he wants them.

But is that the purpose of a heart? he wonders. Often in his long life he has thought that perhaps the purpose of the human heart is to break. He has found and lost love many times. He has embraced friends who were profoundly loyal and loved them almost as deeply. One by one they died, some violently or tragically, and others merely succumbing to the slow unraveling of age. Church has been alone often in his life, but he has never felt so alone as this.

He smokes and he spins the heart apparatus in idle circles on the desk. In time he lifts it and holds it in his palm, testing its weight, and he thinks of the crimes that he has solved and the lives he has saved. He remembers the ghosts he has banished and the curses he has broken. His work keeps people safe, and it has been his passion since boyhood, but all of the loss and loneliness wear on him now, and he thinks perhaps the time has come to stop putting himself back together when his body wants to give in to nature and fall apart.

Someday he will have to die. Why not today? The world will spin without him, until one day it doesn't. How many people will really notice if he is gone?

Church gazes at the shaft of moonlight that touches the edge of his desktop. He takes a puff of his cigarette and blows it toward the light, watching the smoke mix with the motes of dust and then drift upward into the dark. His chest has ached for days, but he has lived long enough to construct a new heart and to perform the incantations that will make the impossible possible. Yet now that it is done, he no longer wants it. No longer needs it.

No more, he thinks.

The cigarette has burned nearly to his fingers now, but Church takes another deep pull of its spicy sweet smoke into his lungs and leans back in the creaking leather chair, closing his eyes. He holds the smoke inside, letting it languish, and only when he must breathe—when the apparatus that replaced his lungs years ago demands air—does he breathe the smoke out.

His eyes remain closed. He can feel the edges of the cigarette begin to burn between his fingers.

Is this enough? he asks without speaking, and without knowing precisely who it is that he is asking.

He hears a sound as if in answer, a kind of sifting, sprinkling noise. Church frowns, wondering if he has heard correctly, or if he has rats in his walls again and it is the scratch of their claws he's heard. But after a moment there comes a louder noise from the same direction, just off to his right.

He opens his eyes and turns in search of the source of that sound. Nothing seems out of place. The books are on their shelves along with the artifacts of his career, both occult and mundane. A large globe rests on its stand. The most prominent thing in that corner of the room is the huge stone figure of the golem that watches him with a statue's eyes.

Just at the edge of the moonlight's reach, Church can see a half-crumbled piece of stone on the floor at the golem's feet, surrounded by a sprinkle of clay. Curious, he puts down the heart apparatus and stubs out his cigarette, only then noticing how badly he'd allowed his fingers to burn. They sting, and he blows warm breath between his fingers, cooling the burns, as he rises from his chair and walks over to get a better look at the debris that seems to have fallen from the golem. He cocks his head, regarding the stone figure carefully.

Church had acquired the golem from a museum in Dubrovnik. In a town on a river in northern Dalmatia, the people believed that once the area had been overrun by witches who tormented, murdered, and enslaved people, who ate babies and defiled innocents. The people were afraid to go out at night, travel far from home, or be caught abroad after dark. According to the legend, the town elders had created a golem out of stone and river clay and brought it to life. The golem hunted and killed the witches for years, finally driving the last of them to the river's mouth and into the sea. Its job completed, it was allowed to rest, becoming inert, nothing more than a statue.

A construction team had discovered the golem buried in the river-bank while preparing to build the foundation for a new bridge. It had been claimed by the museum, where most of the curators had treated it like nothing more than native sculpture, a curiosity for display. That had changed when a series of murders in Dubrovnik led investigators to the museum, and the golem. The mayor of Dubrovnik himself had contacted Church and requested his involvement, and in three days' time, the entire twisted affair had come to light. A local woman descended from the witches that had plagued the river town had used the golem as a puppet to kill her enemies, thinking herself clever and her perversion of the golem deliciously ironic. Afterward, the museum curators had intended to destroy the golem, fearful of it being manipulated by witchcraft again, but Simon had learned a great deal of its sad and noble history, and it pained him to see it destroyed. After some argument and certain financial considerations, he persuaded the museum to let him crate the golem up and ship it home.

And here it has sat for many years since, a silent companion, observing all, or so he had imagined. Church drops to a crouch and runs his fingers over the fine grains of dry clay that have fallen to the floor. He rubs them between his fingers and finds them slightly damp, holds them to his nose and smells the river.

Impossible, he thinks. But he has thought the same thing many times and been proven wrong.

Alarmed, he rises again, glancing about the room, studying every corner and the interplay of moonlight and shadow. Has it happened again? Has some witch managed to wrest control of the golem? His failing heart pains him and he holds one hand to his chest, glancing at his desk and the replacement he has forged for himself.

Turning back, Church steps closer to the stone figure, studying it carefully. Moon-shadows fall upon its craggy features, making it hard to tell, but he thinks perhaps its expression has changed. But something else is different. Church stares in fascination at the cracks in its chest. They have always been there, the fissures that open in dry clay, but they are different now.

They are bleeding.

Astonished, Church begins to pick at the edge of one fissure. He notices a spot to one side and lower where the sliver of rock on the floor had fallen off. Working his fingers at the edges of the crack, he feels it give way. There are pieces of stone surrounded by soft clay and loose dirt, and he begins to peel and brush it away.

He catches his breath when he sees human flesh beneath.

Staggering back, he can only stand and stare as the golem begins to shift and the stone and earth crumble and break away. Its gray eyes regard Church for a moment, a kind of elated panic gleaming in them. They are human eyes, and beneath the crumbling clay and stone is a human countenance. The golem staggers forward, more of its earthen shell flaking away, and Church can only stare in wonderment as clay and stone crack and fall to the wooden floorboards in shards and clumps and sifting grains.

The man takes another step toward Church and collapses into the pile of earth that has crumbled off of him. Huge and powerful, yet weak in his moment of rebirth, he falls to the floor in front of Church, unconscious but alive.

Church wants to revive him, to speak with him, to learn his secrets, but as he reaches down to rouse the man, a sharp pain shoots through his heart. Frantic now, he glances around and sees the iron and copper mechanism on his desk, and he starts toward it.

He isn't meant to die now. This is a sign that he must go on. Someone must show this remarkable creature the world.

Mr. Church came back to the present abruptly, as if waking from a nightmare. He found himself still leaning against the bookcase, the smell of burning oil in his nostrils and the pain of grinding gears and seizing muscles sharp in his chest. He let out a breath that was more oil smoke than steam, and he forced himself to stand straighter, and to look into the sorrowful eyes of Nigel Hawthorne's ghost.

"Thank you," he rasped, his voice coated with rust. "That is one of my most precious memories. To live it again so vividly . . . was a gift."

Hawthorne's ghost frowned.

He did so much for so many, the specter said. *He scoured the earth of an evil none of us could have survived. And then his spirit lingered for centuries before the Maker gave him human life. He was your last partner, and doubtless the best of us. But now he is truly dead, Simon. He was rewarded for his service, given a man's life to live, and a man's death at the end. He has earned the peace of the hereafter.*

Church gave a rasping chuckle, then looked at the ghost of Cranham, who had been the most loyal of all. "You know, when I first saw you all . . . I thought you had come . . . to comfort me as I died."

That is precisely why we've come, Cranham said, fading somewhat, more of a shadow than ever. *We wanted to ease your mind, Simon. You have fought so hard for so long to hang on to your life. It is so precious to you that we knew how frightened you would be to let it finally slip through your fingers. But we know better than any others how your mind works, and we know what you intend to do.*

"What must be done," Mr. Church sighed. "And Joe would say the same, if he could."

But he cannot, Hawthorne said, insubstantial and yet somehow more present in the room now than Mr. Church himself. *So you must choose for him, and bear the burden of that choice. He was given life so that you would not be so alone—*

"Not just for me," Mr. Church said.

But on your terms, the ghost of Gavin Thompson whispered, far in the back of the collection of spirits, this strange jury that had gathered. *As always, like the rest of us, once he came to work with you, he lived on your terms. Flesh and blood might have been a gift for him, but his being brought to life was a gift for you. You cannot deny it.*

Something began to clank loudly in Mr. Church's chest, and the smell of smoke grew worse. He managed to raise his right hand and wipe away his tears. He wanted to argue with Thompson. None of them had been there, that night when Joe had opened his eyes, right here in this room. But they were right, of course. Joe's awakening had been a gift for them both.

"You believe that if I bring him back, Joe's spirit will never rest. But you don't know that."

The spirits regarded him in silence, a pause heavy with their disapproval. Mr. Church shuddered. He did not fear these apparitions, for they were his friends, but they were still the dead, and death had ever been his nemesis.

Please, Simon— Cranham began.

"Joe is unique," Mr. Church said, forging ahead. "We can't know what his fate will be, because the world has never known anything like him. I fear death, old friends, but I know it comes for me, and I cannot resist it any longer."

He glanced around at the faces of the ghosts.

"But someone must be here to fight," he insisted. "During your lives, and in your work with me, we encountered evil over and over. But I tell you, this is something more. I first felt it the night that I interrupted the ritual Andrew Golnik performed on Cythnia Orlov, and the memory still chills me. It unsettles me so deeply that I worry not only for the world I will leave behind as I breathe my last, but for our souls in the hereafter, for I do not know the reach of the unnatural presence that I felt that night, peering into our world as if through a gap in a curtain.

"This is not something supernatural. It is entirely *unnatural,* and it does not belong to the fabric of our reality. It is alien and malign, and Dr. Cocteau wishes to pay obeisance to this hideous sentience. He wants to open himself to it, and thus the world, to see what power he might gain from it, and he thinks the Pentajulum will do that for him. I don't know what the Pentajulum will do. Cocteau could destroy the world or hand it over to this presence that lurks beyond the veil separating its reality from our own. And all that stands between Cocteau and what he wants, or worse, whatever *it* wants, is ninety clever pounds of redheaded waif named Molly McHugh.

"Molly is going to need help, and I cannot be here for her. My time is done. But Joe . . . Joe was first brought to life to fight things that the world didn't understand, to save people from strange evils. If you are right and Joe's spirit is lost forever, then I will spend eternity in a damnation of my own making, but still this must be done, and you—all of you—know it."

While he'd been speaking, his anguish and certainty had given him the strength to go on. Now that he'd had his say, Mr. Church felt a tightening in his throat and it became harder to draw breath. His left hand shook and slipped from the shelf he had been propping himself against, and he began to slide to the floor. Panic surged through him at the thought that he had run out of time.

On his knees, he turned to fix the ghosts of Hawthorne and Cranham in a grim stare.

"My time is fleeting. This must be done. I'm sorry."

Hawthorne glanced around at the other ghosts, looking last at Cranham, who nodded once, gravely. The two apparitions came closer, vanishing and reappearing, flickering in and out of existence. He stared into the wispy nothing that was Nigel Hawthorne's face, the pain in his chest growing. The grinding inside of him had stopped, but somehow that worried him more.

We'll stay with you, Simon. Until the end.

Mr. Church felt himself welling with emotion, an awful anguish for his own fate, and for Joe's, and gratitude for the kindness of old friends. With a monstrous effort that resulted in the rasp of metal scraping metal and a coughing jag that produced thick, dark fluid that leaked from his mouth and nose, Mr. Church hauled himself to his feet using the bookshelves for balance.

It took him only moments to lay hands upon the journal in which he had recorded all that he had learned about the witches of Obrovac, on the river Zrmanja, and the ritual the townspeople had used to breathe life into the golem. He flipped dry, yellowed pages with his dry, yellowed fingers, and ignored the droplets of black fluid that fell onto the open book.

Chapter Fifteen

Joe could feel the water flowing over his face. It cradled him, gently rocking his head. This seemed strange, and at first he thought he must be awakening in a place of spirits, floating in the beautiful cloud of peace that the hereafter represented to him. But when he tried to move, he felt a terrible weight pressing down on him, as if he'd been buried alive, and the first flicker of panic sparked inside him.

He opened his eyes to unfocused darkness, but the cold rush of water over them was unmistakable, and he realized he must be drowning.

Thrashing against the weight that bore down on him, Joe forced himself upward, one hand finding the metal smoothness of a railroad track. He pulled himself upright, holding his breath, wondering what awful weight encased him, making it impossible to swim. How could he find his way in this dark, flooded tunnel, with only vague outlines of distant objects to guide him? He needed to breathe! He needed to . . .

Joe stood stiffly on rotting subway tracks, one foot on the metal rail, and he wondered why his lungs did not burn. He wanted to breathe, but it didn't really feel like he needed to do so. How long had he been lying there, dead or close to dead? Had he held his breath the whole time, or had he inhaled and exhaled the salty, almost metallic river water?

He breathed in, the river rushing into his lungs. He breathed out, feeling it flow from his lips. After a moment he closed his lips and stopped breathing completely, finding little difference. He didn't need to breathe.

How? he wondered, his thoughts muddled. Had he been killed and brought back to some shambling mockery of life? His mind felt sluggish and he banged a palm against his skull, frustrated that his recent memories seemed so fragmentary. There was a girl, Molly. They had been in a cemetery. The killers had come in their gas masks and taken the girl. He frowned, trying to remember. They had taken something else, as well. Something important.

A dark hostility coalesced inside him as he thought about the gasmen and the brutal way they'd handled the girl. *And they killed me,* he thought, remembering the guns and bullets. *They killed me.*

His hands flew to his body, probing the places where the bullets had struck him. But the dreadful weight that dragged at his every move slowed him. His fingers scraped something hard and rough, and the feeling of contact seemed distant, as if he were only dreaming this gruesome attempt to re-create his shooting.

In the encompassing dark of the flooded tunnel, somehow he still managed to see, though dimly. He held out one hand in front of him, drawing it close for a better look, and he stared in horror at the ruin of his fingers. The flesh was torn and ragged. In places it hung off of his fingers and his palm in tiny strips. It looked shriveled from the time he'd been in the water, and yet, despite the mangling of his flesh, he felt no pain in his hand. Only a heaviness, and a startling strength.

Curiously, he prodded his right hand with the fingers of his left, and saw that both hands were ruined. A whole patch of skin had been scoured away from the back of his left hand, revealing dark, rough skin beneath. *What the hell?* he asked himself. Probing the ruined skin, fear blossoming larger inside him, he found that the dead skin came away easily, and soon—unable to stop himself—he had stripped most of the old skin away, revealing the gray hands underneath, rough and hard-edged. He recognized them from his dreams. Huge and powerful, sculpted from rock and clay, they had murdered a hundred witches and more.

No, no, he thought, stumbling backward as though he could escape his own hands. *It can't be.*

His right foot clanged on the railing, the sound muffled by the water, but audible. Stone against metal, reverberating. Joe shook his head, feeling the weight of it. He hadn't been buried alive. The stone and earth that weighed him down was inside of him. He could feel it now, the strange, useless sheath that his skin had become. He reached up and felt the dead skin stretched over his stone face.

What am I? he wondered. But he thought he knew. *Golem.* He stared again at his stone hands. Was he a man transformed into a golem, or a golem who had once masqueraded as a man?

For several long minutes Joe let the current eddy around him, holding his hands close so that he could make out every crack and fissure in the dark water, where no human eyes could ever have seen. Emotions drifted through him, grief for the man he had been and a strange elation as fragments of far more ancient memory appeared in his mind.

He tried to sort through his memories. An image rose in his thoughts of a man with a long nose and thin, wispy hair, smoking a pipe. His eyes were intense, alight with both humor and purpose.

Church, Joe thought. For a second, the name had escaped him, and he chided himself. The man had been his greatest friend, and yet Joe had trouble summoning a clear picture of his face. Memories of his life as a man were fading, splintering, and slipping away like the cobwebs of a dream upon waking.

Yet still he thought of the girl screaming as the men in the masks carried her away, and he knew something had to be done. He could feel a strange tentativeness in the world, even in the water around him, as if the entire city had tensed against an assault from which it had no protection. A powerful wrongness emanated from a place off to his left, along the tunnel—a blemish on reality—as if a kind of sickness had intruded. An infection.

Joe turned that way and marched through the deep water at the bottom of the tunnel, searching for the source of that infection, and a girl whose name he no longer remembered.

* * *

Mr. Church's eyes fluttered open and he found himself on the floor of his study amidst the detritus of the ritual. The candles had burned down and gone out, wicks drowned in their own melted wax. The book lay where it had fallen when he collapsed, pages bent and torn. His mortar and pestle and the vials of herbs he had sprinkled over the candle flames were scattered on the floorboards.

"Is it . . . done?" he croaked, the enormity of the question filling him with grief like he had never known.

Night had fallen. Very little light remained in the study, but in the dark there were shadows within shadows, and the silhouettes of his old friends manifested themselves again, one by one.

Hawthorne's ghost wavered in and out of sight, though it might have been Mr. Church's vision—the flutter of his life and not the inconsistency of the specter.

It is, the specter said solemnly.

Mr. Church nodded, his breath hitching. His insides felt as cold as ice, with no more steam to warm him. The mechanisms within him had fallen silent, and now the last of the chemistry and magic that had sustained him had run out. But it was best that he die now. For all the crimes he had solved, in the end he had committed the greatest crime of all. He had doomed his best and most loyal friend to wander the earth as a golem again . . . perhaps forever.

He couldn't breathe. Not a trace of air remained to him. It felt as if his chest were caving in upon itself. All the parts of him that were still just a man, the boy he had been so long ago, cried out for breath, but he had none. He wondered if Joe would hate him for what he had done.

Simon, Cranham's ghost said. *It will be all right.*

Mr. Church felt something release within him. With a breath that was not at all like breathing, he seemed to expand, and all the tension fled from him. All of his fear vanished, and yet a deep melancholy remained.

Come, Simon, Hawthorne said. *Take my hand.*

The great detective opened his eyes and reached out for his friends.

A moment later, all was quiet in the study. Even the crumpled, withered body of the old man, sprawled on the floor, was completely still. All of the ghosts had departed Simon Church's study.

Even his own.

Chapter Sixteen

olly wanted to go home. The problem was that she didn't know if she had one anymore. She lay on a narrow bunk along the gangway, her ankles tightly bound and her wrists cuffed behind her back. The submarine's interior was so cramped and narrow that she had felt smothered by claustrophobia from the moment the gas-men had dragged her down the hatch. She doubted the gas-men had the same emotions and sensitivities as ordinary people, but she didn't know how human beings could stand to be submerged beneath the water in the cramped machine.

Not that she felt like asking, or thought the humans on board the submarine would answer her. The gas-men had dragged her on board, but they were just passengers, like she was. The submarine had its own captain and crew, men in drab gray uniforms with strange military insignia she imagined must belong to the navy of some Eastern European nation, based on their guttural speech and olive complexions.

She wondered how the grizzled men had come to be in Dr. Cocteau's employ. Had they deserted their own nation and hired themselves out as some kind of pirate crew, or had Cocteau somehow persuaded their government to loan him a crew? After the day she'd had, nothing seemed too impossible to her.

For the moment, she had only her own thoughts and her imagination for company. The berths on board the submarine were tiny bunks that could be folded up out of the way, and she had been unceremoniously dumped onto one of them. Anyone trying to pass through the compartment on the way fore or aft would have to squeeze past her or lift the bunk out of the way, causing her to roll into the hull because she didn't have her hands free to catch herself.

No one looked at her—not the gas-men, and certainly not the pale officers with their clammy-looking flesh and heavily lidded eyes. Molly had seen men with drug problems before, and the little beads of sweat that stood out on their skin were darkly familiar.

Lying on the rough bunk, she shivered with the chill that emanated from the metal hull behind her. The river depths were frigid, and Molly had been growing colder by the moment. Gas-men and grim, pale submariners passed by but she refused to ask for a blanket, knowing she would be ignored. They barely looked at her, not even to make sure she did not attempt to escape. And they were right to dismiss such a possibility. She was bound hand and foot, in a submarine at the bottom of the icy cold river, surrounded by creatures whose humanity had been perverted by magic and men who seemed as hollow as the dead.

Where would she run?

A scream had been building up pressure inside of her since they had dragged her down into the sub and the hatch had closed. She thought of Joe, who had been kind to her, and warm in his quiet, funny way, and who must be dead by now, back in the cemetery by the occultist's grave. There had been so many bullets, and so much blood.

Poor Joe, she thought. *I'm sorry.*

And yet, with every passing moment aboard the sub, Molly's grief for Joe was gradually being eclipsed by the blossoming terror of what might happen to her once this ominously quiet crew reached its destination. Molly lay on her side on the bunk, listening for voices, for any communication that might give her a clue about what awaited her. Were they taking her to Felix? If so, then she had hope. Once she saw him, once they'd had a chance to talk, she felt sure they would find a way out of all of this. He was Orlov the Conjuror, after all.

Shaking from the cold, teeth chattering, she nursed that spark of hope.

Molly forced herself to breathe and to wait. She tried to control her shivering at first, then chose instead to ignore it. She could not stop herself from feeling the cold, but she could get a handle on her fear. In her life—particularly in the time before Felix had befriended her—she had been afraid more often than not. When the gas-men paused in the gangway and regarded her, the black lenses of their masks reflecting the dim running lights inside the sub, she only stared back, forcing her face to become its own sort of mask. When a tall, thin officer with bruise-dark circles under his eyes paused to let his gaze wander along her body, a vulture's hunger in his eyes, she boldly returned his stare and made sure he knew that she would not submit easily to the things his dark eyes suggested. He lingered uncertainly, and then a small, stooped gas-man came ambling along the gangway and he had to move to make way. The vulture did not return.

But the strangely hunched gas-man had not gone far. In a crouch he scuttled toward her, less than half the size of the next largest of them, no bigger than a prepubescent child. The temptation to close her eyes and feign sleep was great, but Molly would not be daunted. Her shoulder hurt and the cuffs were too tight on her wrists, but she lay there, rocking with the rumble of the submarine's steam engines, and she set her jaw in defiance as the hunched little gas-man crept nearer.

Dread trickled along her spine and spread through her. The gas-man pushed his face nearer and she wanted so much to look away. His breathing was the worst—a damp, sucking noise coming from within the mask. Molly looked at her reflection in the buglike lenses of his mask and for a moment a memory flashed through her mind of the huge gas-man—the one Joe had killed to save her—stalking her across rooftops and bridges. He had tracked her by smell. When he had paused to get a clearer scent, lifting his mask, she had gotten a glimpse of his true face . . . of damp, rippling lips pulsing like the maw of some bizarre marine animal, or the flower of an undersea plant, with teeth like thorns. Molly didn't know if they were all the same, but she felt tainted somehow as the little gas-man crouched by her, knowing that the wet snuffling noise inside his mask was him enjoying her scent. It made her want to vomit, and she forced herself to take shallow breaths, trying to stave off her nausea.

The hunched creature lifted a hand and she froze, rigid on the bunk. Would he try to touch her, or did he plan to take off his mask? Frantic, not knowing which answer would be worse, she tensed to attack.

His hand reached for the edge of his mask.

Molly twisted on the bunk, pushed her back against the hull, and drew up her knees, ready to piston her legs into a punishing kick. A jarring impact made her roll toward the nose of the sub, onto her face on the bunk, and she slid off into the gangway, still bound. A loud scrape and clank echoed through the submarine, and it came to a juddering halt.

She heard the hunched gas-man right behind her, his wet breathing muffled by his mask, so close to her ear. The entire submarine creaked and settled, and a hiss of air went through, just the slightest breeze, as though the internal pressure was being vented. Molly slid across the floor and pushed her back against the hatch into the next section, using the leverage to stand despite the restrictions of her bonds. She stared at her bunk, where it blocked so much of the gangway, and found that she was alone. The little gas-man was gone.

As Molly glanced around the gangway for something she might use to try to cut through the leather strap around her ankles, the submarine began to rise, jarring her. She leaned against the arched hatchway frame for balance. Frowning in surprise, she realized that the sub wasn't surfacing . . . it was being lifted. It didn't even feel as if they were in the water anymore. As she tried to puzzle out their location, the hatch at the other end of the gangway opened and a wan, shaky-looking submariner entered.

He arched an eyebrow, studying her with a strange combination of amusement and disdain, and then he said something in that guttural language she did not understand. Molly raised her chin defiantly, ready to fight if she had to, but then the hatch behind her opened and she tumbled through, landing hard. The back of her skull bounced on the floor and fresh pain bloomed.

Two gas-men stood above her, the black lenses of their masks hiding any semblance of humanity, if they had any. Silent save for their breathing, they cocked their heads to the left in unison, as if sharing a thought. The hunched little gas-man scuttled up behind them, chest heaving with his sickly, wheezing breath.

Her resolve cracked.

"What are you going to do with me?" she asked, a plea for mercy in her tone.

They hoisted her off the floor and carried her along the gangway, back the way they had come when they brought her aboard. Wherever they had been headed, they had arrived.

The gas-men passed Molly up through the hatch, hand over hand, as if she were someone's old, battered luggage. On the deck of the sub she blinked in surprise at the glare of bright lights that illuminated a long, tubular chamber that appeared to have once been part of a subway tunnel. The ends had been capped with granite and mortar walls, which somehow had been made watertight, for as she looked around, she was astonished to find the submarine high and dry. A tall, broad-shouldered gas-man threw her over his shoulder—she could feel the edge of his mask jabbing her in the side but had zero temptation to try to rip the mask off. Exposing what was inside the gas-men's rubbery outfits released the strange yellow gas from inside, and it might have given her an opportunity to flee, but she had nowhere left to run, and certainly no one to run to. Felix would be here, if he was still alive. Whatever her future held, the answers were here.

A company of gas-men and submarine officers crossed a metal footbridge that had been rolled into place, connecting the deck of the sub with a broad ledge that ran along one side of the chamber like a balcony. Molly jounced along on the gas-man's shoulder, giving her a perfect downward view. A small stream of water ran along subway tracks far below. Giant metal clamps held the submarine in place on either side, and a kind of platform supported it from below. It took her a moment to work out how it was possible, and then she realized that the sub had not surfaced. Instead, it had entered this chamber through some kind of door, now closed, and once the clamps and support were in place, all of the water had been somehow vented from the place. The stream below was the trickle that made it through the seal, or what remained after the room had been drained.

They were still underwater. Still deep beneath the Drowning City.

The grizzled, uniformed crewmen stopped on the platform and let the gas-men pass by, their job complete. They had made her nervous with their unsavory appearance and salacious glances, but at least she could see their faces and knew they were human. As she was carried through an arched metal door, she watched them filing back across the footbridge onto their sub, and wondered if she had left the last of ordinary humanity behind.

Before the door clanged shut, the bright lights in the submarine drydock winked out, throwing them all into darkness, and yet not one of the officers cried out. She imagined them scurrying like rats back into their hole, and realized that her last glimpse of ordinary humanity had been that of the burly detective, Joe, sprawled in the graveyard in Brooklyn Heights in the rain. Whatever happened from here on, she would not mistake it for ordinary or human again.

The gas-man carried her up an iron spiral staircase that seemed to have been sunk into the bedrock, perhaps originally installed for the workers on the early New York subway. Lightbulbs burned in metal mesh cages overhead and the walls wept moisture. Molly twisted around, trying to get a better look at her surroundings, just in case she and Felix had to come this way while escaping.

Once she found Felix, once they were in the same room, then her first goal would have been accomplished, and she could start work on the second one—setting him free and somehow getting back to the surface.

If he's alive, she thought. *If he's still in his right mind.* Images of the last moments of the séance with the Mendehlsons forced their way into her mind. What had gone wrong with Felix just before the gas-men had burst in? Had it killed him? If not, had it damaged his brain, incapacitated him somehow?

Shush, she admonished herself. *You'll know when you see him.* She only hoped that would be soon.

The gas-men trooped up the spiral staircase, their clothes rustling and flapping. As Molly twisted to look upward, she saw the little hunched one almost scampering up the steps, two ahead of the gas-man who carried her, and revulsion rippled through her. The rest of them inspired a kind of primal fear in her, a natural response to things that were fundamentally *un*natural. But that skulking creature bothered her all the more because there seemed something so primitive about it.

A loud clanking came from above, followed by the squeal of hinges. They reached a landing in the staircase and the gas-men filed through a small doorway that was more of a hatch. Glancing back, upside down, she saw that the iron stairs continued to circle upward. Then the gas-man who carried her ducked through the doorway and the hatch clanged shut behind them. One of them spun the wheel that sealed the door closed, and then the one who'd been lugging her put her down roughly, and others moved in to remove her handcuffs and the leather strap around her ankles. Her wrists were sore and her ankles chafed, but her hands and feet prickled with newly unrestricted blood flow and the rust left behind by disuse.

On the bridges and along the canals of the Drowning City, living amongst Water Rats and hardened survivors, Molly had learned to be an actress, to project an air of weary indifference and callous disregard. She had also learned the value of a sharp tongue. But as the gas-men gathered in a strange half-moon cluster to regard her, she found all of those skills useless. What acerbic remark would benefit her here? None.

With the hatch closed behind her, only one path remained open. Molly forged ahead, rubbing the circulation back into her hands and wrists as she marched along the corridor and around a corner, only to find another hatch awaiting her, guarded by a single gas-man. At the sight of her, the door guard spun the hatch wheel and hauled it open with a screech of hinges, holding it for her as if he were a queen's footman. Molly hesitated only a moment before stepping through.

On the other side of the door, she froze.

The room on the other side seemed impossibly vast for something underwater. The concave ceiling rose to a height of forty feet or more, and she could not clearly see the far side of the chamber. Huge pipes entered and exited the walls and ceiling at odd angles, reminding her of the piping in the submarine. They branched and twisted, sometimes meeting in seemingly senseless knots where their paths joined and then separated again, as though the entire chamber was some strange, vast musical instrument. Pipe joints and seams were rimmed with bolts and rust and glistened with condensation. Dim lights gleamed at intervals like distant campfires along the walls and amidst the various pieces of machinery, throwing the whole chamber into a cascade of strange shadows that suggested more details than the lights illuminated.

The walls seemed to sweat. Loud machines breathed hissing steam and thumped like giant beating hearts. And yet what astounded Molly most was not the room's machinery or the overall feeling of grime and neglect. What had caused her to hesitate and stare was the dreamlike contrast of the massive chamber's decorative touches. Beams and posts had been arrayed in places throughout the room, and someone had hung curtains, intricate tapestries, and heavy velvet drapes from them, giving the whole room the impression of a traveling gypsy theater troupe attempting to portray a royal court on a makeshift stage.

Only when the little, hunched thing in its eerie mask scampered out from behind the nearest set of curtains did Molly realize that he had somehow gotten ahead of them. He stared at her, cocking his head for a moment, and then pushed back through the curtains. After a moment, he stuck his head out again, watching her with whatever eyes lurked behind those darkly glinting lenses. The gas-man wanted her to follow, but Molly could not get her feet to move.

Another gas-man nudged her from behind and got her started,

and then they were marching her forward again as the skulking little gas-man led the way. She followed him through the curtains and, once within the confines of that makeshift room, she had another surprise. There were stained rugs on the floor and old paintings hung from chains, displayed against the curtains and drapes. Ornate furniture had been arranged as if in a sitting room, and Molly realized that the various chambers created by the posts, beams, and fabric hangings were meant to mimic the rooms of a palace. Yet the decorations felt false, like a flimsy set built for a theatrical production, ready to be whisked off backstage the next time the curtain closed.

With the pipes dripping high above and the machinery still chugging nearby, behind the curtains, she followed the skulker through several rooms and along one corridor of this strange, false home with the gas-men trooping behind her.

When at last they emerged in a much larger room, Molly faltered once again. With all of the pumps, pipes, and drapes blocking her view, she hadn't had any idea what awaited her. Now she held her breath as she glanced quickly around, trying to take in the mad panorama without being overcome by its pervasive bizarreness. She saw a dais with an ornate chair that could only have been intended as some kind of throne, a long dining table with a single chair, and a trio of what appeared to be dingy surgical tables with weathered leather restraints dangling from the sides. Shelves and standing counters nearby were piled haphazardly with surgical supplies and things floating in jars.

And yet none of these peculiar trappings startled her as much as the object that seemed to be the room's centerpiece—an enormous glass sphere, twenty feet in diameter, which sat atop a metal base replete with levers, wheels, and valves whose purpose was not at all apparent. The first thing the sphere made her think of was the cracked crystal ball Felix had given her to use when she was decorating the séance room in the old theatre. He swore it had once belonged to a Gypsy fortune-teller, but when she asked if it actually worked, he would only reply that it depended entirely upon what one wanted to see in the crystal.

After a moment, though, Molly realized that the sphere reminded her less of the crystal ball than it did of the array of glass snow globes the old man had kept on a shelf in his kitchen. There had been only four of them—not quite enough to constitute a collection, but enough that it seemed right to display them together. Once, while dusting, she had broken the antique Coney Island snow globe, only then discovering that it had also been a wind-up musical snow globe, which played an old tune called "Ain't She Sweet" when one turned the key on the bottom . . . or dropped and broke it while dusting.

Something moved in the murky water inside the sphere, making her think a third thing—that it reminded her of a fish tank—but with that heavy metal base and the fact that there was no opening on top, the snow globe comparison seemed more apt.

Only as she walked deeper into the room did she see beyond the throne platform, the surgical tables, and the huge sphere. The curtains that facilitated the illusion of room-ness around the disparate elements in the chamber were only a half-circle, and beyond them stood an actual wall, towering and foreboding, rising high into the darkness above.

Molly caught her breath, staring at the wall, for it comprised in large part windows of various shapes and sizes, all of which looked out into the depths of the Drowning City. The view might have been of some other subterranean chamber, flooded with river water, or of the river bottom itself. Fish swam past outside, some of them unsettlingly large, as if the window had been cast from warped funhouse glass.

Felix's dream, she thought. A glance at the surgical tables made her shudder. This couldn't be the place where Andrew Golnik had nearly killed Felix's mother while she had carried him in her womb. There had been some kind of sacrificial altar there, not a surgical table. Mr. Church had been clear about that. But there could be no doubt that Felix had somehow mixed the past and future in his dreams, a past he could never have remembered and a future only a clairvoyant could have foreseen.

The broad-shouldered gas-man nudged her forward. Molly felt her skin prickle with fear and with the cold, damp air that seemed to embrace her.

The skulker came out from behind the water globe, cocked his head expectantly and impatiently, and then scuttled back out of sight. With the gas-men pressing behind her, she had no choice but to move forward. A part of her wanted to drag her feet, to fight and run, to refuse to see what awaited her after this haunting odyssey. But then she remembered Felix, and the sight of the gas-men dragging him over the edge of the walkway in front of the theater and down into the water of Twenty-ninth Street. She steeled herself and marched forward, circling around the back of the sphere. Something stirred in the water, and she thought for a moment that she saw a chain near the bottom, before it was dragged back into the murk.

The gas-men had been trooping behind her, their breathing loud inside their masks, but now they slowed and lowered their heads like well-trained dogs. Then the wet, sickly breathing of the skulker grew louder, and she came around the back of the sphere. She saw the hunched little gas-man crouched obediently at the foot of a round-bellied old man with a thick beard the same snow white as his hair. He wore a long, burgundy wool coat with a wide velvet lapel of a darker shade. She had seen old photographs in one of Felix's books and thought this was called a smoking jacket. His shirt collar was open and he wore no tie. The old man turned to regard her through small spectacles that sat on the bridge of his thick nose, making his eyes seem larger than they were.

He looked kindly, this old man, and despite the strange dichotomy of the vast chamber, with its finery unable to mask the dingy truth of its rust and age, his clothes were impeccably clean and neat, not at all the frayed, threadbare sorts of things that Felix had been forced to wear. In this way, the man reminded her more of Mr. Church, both of them antiquated figures from another era, and she wondered how long they had been clashing with each other.

Molly stared at him in astonishment. He looked so gentle and ordinary, if wealthy, that she refused to believe the old grandfatherly fellow was the madman that Mr. Church had warned her about.

He laughed softly. "Oh, Miss McHugh, I can practically read your mind."

A ripple of alarm went through her, and he must have seen it on her face.

"No, no," he said quickly, as if chiding himself for worrying her. "It's only an expression. I only meant that, well, one look at you and I knew what you were thinking. And I must inform you that, yes, I am he."

She shook her head, which had been filled with too much insanity for a lifetime, never mind a single day.

"Dr. Cocteau?" she said.

Amused, he gave a little apologetic shrug in reply. "At your service."

Molly stiffened, refusing to be charmed by the old man in his fine clothes and little spectacles. "What have you done with Felix Orlov?"

Dr. Cocteau nodded sadly. "Of course you deserve to know. I'm afraid you won't like the answer. But, yes, your father is here with us."

"What?" Molly said, confused. "Felix isn't my father."

"Not by birth. I know that. But the father of your heart, surely? I'm only sorry that in his absence, you've looked to men like Simon Church and his brutish lackey for some kind of paternal substitute."

Anger rushed through her, and a flicker of recognition. "I haven't been—"

"It's only natural, Molly," Dr. Cocteau said gently. "Perfectly understandable. But it's for the best that you've joined us, not only for Felix's sake and my own, but for yours as well. You've spent enough time among madmen, don't you think?"

She stood there, fearful and confused, trying to hide all of her thoughts from this man who seemed able to see right through her. Simon Church had seemed so confident that, despite the wildness of his claims and the strange mix of science and magic that kept him alive, she had put her faith in him.

No, she thought. *You put your faith in Joe.* And to a certain extent, that was true. Though he didn't talk nearly as much as Mr. Church, it had been the quiet goodness she sensed in Joe, and his own faith in Mr. Church, that had made her believe in them both. But here was Dr. Cocteau, a man who—despite his surroundings—hardly seemed as evil, unnatural, and insane as Mr. Church had painted him.

"Please," she said. "Where's Felix?"

Dr. Cocteau gave her a look of such heartbreaking sympathy that for a moment she thought he was about to tell her that Felix was dead. Instead, he nodded regretfully toward the glass sphere.

"He's in there."

Molly stared at him, feeling all of the blood drain from her face. Panicked, she rushed to the sphere and pressed her face against it, palms on the glass, trying to see through the murky water. As before, she saw something moving inside, swishing and jerking as if struggling . . . or drowning. If Cocteau was serious . . .

"You have to let him out!" she shouted, glancing at him before staring back into the dark water. "He'll drown!"

"No, he won't," Dr. Cocteau replied. "On the contrary, he would not survive if we took him out of the tank. I need your help, Molly. Felix needs your help. That's why I had you brought here."

The utter reasonableness of his tone and rationale began to sink in for a moment, and then she remembered the gas-men, and the way they had gunned Joe down in the island cemetery of Brooklyn Heights. But what if Cocteau was telling the truth?

"And what do I have to do, exactly?" she asked, turning a suspicious eye toward the portly, white-bearded old man.

"Just be here with him," Dr. Cocteau replied. "Keep him calm."

Molly frowned. "What is he *doing* in there?"

A joyful smile spread across his face and he gazed adoringly at the water globe. "Felix is fulfilling his destiny. He's becoming his father's son."

Frustrated and even more profoundly confused, Molly started to shake her head. From the corner of her eye, she saw a rush of movement within the sphere, and she turned in time to see a face through the murky water. Felix's face . . . but not the face she had known so well. Now it was something else entirely—strangely, hideously altered.

Molly backed away from the glass and began to scream.

Chapter Seventeen

In Simon Church's apartment, things began to break down. A shelf gave way, spilling antique books with fold-out maps of impossible places and ancient empires to the floor. A porcelain mask from the Venetian Carnevale remained hanging on the wall, but it yellowed in no time at all and began to crack and flake, its colors fading.

Clocks stopped. The last to fall silent was the grandfather clock Church had brought from England so many years ago. It had once belonged to his parents. His young son, Nathaniel, had loved the clock, sometimes climbing inside to hide and making tick-tock noises until his father had found him. The boy had grown sickly and died at the age of seven, leaving behind a void of such dark, morbid gravity that it had drawn in Nathaniel's mother—Church's only wife, and only love—soon after.

In the last seventy years of his life, Simon Church had never spoken her name. There were sinister forces at work in the universe that could do abominable things with the name of one's beloved dead, and he would not give them that power. But he dreamed about her often. Only Hawthorne had known that he had ever been married, that he had ever had a son, a boy who might have grown, in time, to be a detective himself, if only he had lived long enough for Church to teach him.

In Church's apartment, plants began to brown and the leaves to fall off. The tobacco in his tins grew moldy. The chemicals in his lab were rendered inert. Parchment yellowed and curled. Had anyone attempted to take the elevator, it might have worked at first, but the gears would have ground together and begun to smoke, trapping the intruder inside. In the bedroom where Joe had tucked Molly under the covers and where she had awoken in fear and confusion, and yet in warmth and comfort, old photographs from a time before the water swallowed Lower Manhattan fell off the wall, glass shattering.

When the housekeeper arrived in the morning, she would find the body of Simon Church on the floor in the study where he had fallen, but she would only recognize him because she knew of no one else who had peculiar machinery inside them. His remains had begun to yellow and curl like the parchment, to give way like the shelves and pictures. The years Mr. Church had staved off for so long had caught up with him at last, and the withering hand of time put its touch upon his belongings as well.

Paint peeled. Wallpaper drooped. Ink dried in its well. Soon it would be as if it had been decades since anyone had set foot in those rooms, instead of hours.

And yet upstairs, in the domed room on the top floor, machines continued to hum, clank, and run on without interruption. Valves hissed with steam. The needles on gauges jittered dangerously as they slid into red danger zones. The only thing that had ceased functioning properly in that room was the massive pendulum, which had stopped swinging.

The pendulum had not broken down, however. It had ceased moving, but it hung at an angle now, pointing to a single location, not far from the place near the southern tip of the Drowning City where New York's city hall had been located a hundred years before. The pendulum indicated this location with a rigidity that suggested a powerful magnet might have exerted its influence, but there was no magnet. The pendulum, like the rest of Mr. Church's occult-sensing apparatus, was only doing its job.

The needles on the gauges continued to climb.

In the tunnel, Joe trudged along the subway tracks, swaying with the ebb and flow of the current. Fish swam around him in the dark water and sometimes he paused to watch them, his thoughts drifting. He flexed his fingers, opening and closing his hands, and then he held them up to stare at them, thinking of hideous, gleeful witches who stole children and cursed the harvest.

An ordinary bluefish darted toward his chest and then away, but not before he flinched, remembering bullets.

Joe frowned, stone brow knitting behind the mask of skin that hung partway off of his face. Bullets in his chest, mud in his mouth, rain falling on his eyes. He'd been shot, hadn't he? Slowly he nodded. Yes, he had. And the bastards who'd shot him had taken the girl. Was her name Molly? *Yes, Molly.*

With renewed purpose, he began walking again. Fish nibbled at the dead flesh peeling from his stone body, but he ignored them, thinking of rivers, deciding that all rivers were really one river, including time and fate, and that he was glad the current was on his side.

Chapter Eighteen

olly pushed back from the tank so hard that she went sprawling onto a faded Persian rug. She stared at the glass sphere but glimpsed only a dark shape in motion within. The face she had seen, however, had burned itself into her mind, and she knew she would never be able to erase it.

"That's not . . . that can't be Felix," she said under her breath.

Gas-men watched from a distance, some from between the curtains that created the false impression that this room was separate from the huge chamber. Others stood blocking her avenue of retreat, still and silent, the dark lenses of their masks hiding any hint of personality.

Feeling sick, Molly pressed the heels of her hands over her eyes and tried to steady her breathing. She shook her head, still covering her eyes. The thing in the tank could not be Felix Orlov for many reasons, not least of which was that it was easily twice the size of a man. She had caught a glimpse of one hand, and it had only three long, many-jointed fingers that looked more like the claws of a crab. Its arm had the same kind of spiked carapace, like an insect or a crustacean, but worst of all was the face, which had become a writhing mass of twisted flesh. Dr. Cocteau was insane or lying or both. Whatever he had captive in that tank, it wasn't Felix.

And yet it was. Staring into that hideous face, she could still see something of her friend within it, could still sense a familiar aura around it.

She twisted to the right and vomited onto the rug beneath her, one of so many Cocteau had arranged at haphazard intervals around the vast chamber. Her stomach convulsed and she nearly retched again, but managed to prevent it, breathing through her mouth and turning away from the stink of her own vomit.

For the first time she noticed that water had leaked from the globe and soaked into the carpet. She could feel its damp chill settling into the seat of her pants and now her knees, so she scrambled backward farther until she found herself on the dusty tiles of the original flooring installed in this enormous subway station three-quarters of a century before. For that was what it had to be, some downtown equivalent of Grand Central Station's main terminal, built and then abandoned to time. She'd heard tales of such expensive failures in the history of the New York underground during her years living with squatters and scavengers, but nothing on this scale. Cocteau had claimed it for himself and sealed it off from the river.

And I'm trapped down here with him, Molly thought. She turned to look at the water globe again, but found that she no longer wanted a closer look. Her lower lip trembled and she had to force herself not to cry. Cocteau had called Felix her father, and he'd been wrong about that. He had raised her like a father, she supposed, and she loved him

as if he were, but now they took care of each other. He was her best friend. Her only real friend.

"Oh, God," she whispered, pressing her hands against her temples, breathing now not to keep from throwing up but to keep from screaming.

Unsteady, she staggered to her feet and turned, looking around for Dr. Cocteau, who had gone strangely silent. She saw the gas-men arrayed around the room, at the foot of the dais by Cocteau's throne—of course it had to be his—and blocking any chance of escape. They reminded her of crows sitting in a line on the edge of a building or in the branches of a tree in the Brooklyn Heights cemetery. The black birds would sit in silence, ominously watching the world go by, as though they had some insidious plan in progress and were just waiting for the word to put it into action. What did they call it, a flock of those birds? Felix had taught her. *Yes, that's it,* she thought. *A murder of crows.*

A murder.

Dr. Cocteau had retreated to the shadows in front of the towering row of windows that curved up to the ceiling. The skulker had climbed up onto a high-backed chair and stood on the upholstered arm, his head bent toward Cocteau's ear. The small, hunched gas-man had lifted his mask up just slightly and yellow gas seeped from the gap. Dr. Cocteau nodded, as though the creature whispered secrets of grave import, and then he noticed her staring at him and for a moment his eyes narrowed. Then a broad smile spread across his almost cherubic features. He patted the skulker's shoulder and the creature lowered his mask again. Dr. Cocteau came toward her, but the skulker remained standing on the floral upholstery as though that chair was his own little throne.

"Change him back," Molly said, a flicker of rage blazing quickly larger and burning away her fear.

"You misunderstand," Dr. Cocteau began. "This is not my doing. Not at all. You've watched Mr. Orlov go through periods of what you thought of as illness through all of your years with him. This is simply the culmination of—"

Molly slapped him so hard that his spectacles flew off and landed on the damp rug. Dr. Cocteau stared at her, standing as if paralyzed, his mouth hanging open in shock. A momentary lapse of his kindly demeanor revealed his anger in the twitching of an eye and the flaring of his nostrils, but then he took a deep breath and gazed at the rug beneath his feet.

The skulker hopped off of his mini-throne beneath the windows and scurried over to fetch his master's glasses. Cocteau didn't even look at the creature as he received the spectacles and returned them to the bridge of his nose, settling the arms behind his ears.

"Molly, I understand that you're upset," Dr. Cocteau said, smoothing the velvet lapels of his jacket before fixing her with a look of those empathetic eyes. "But that can't happen again or this simply won't work."

"Really?" Molly asked, angrily meeting his gaze. She ignored the skulker and the rest of the gas-men and the water globe inside of which Felix was no longer Felix, and focused all her frustration and fear on Dr. Cocteau. "Maybe you should tell me exactly what *this* is, then, because it sure looks like you turned my best friend into a . . . a monster."

Cocteau shook his head, smiling sadly. "Oh, my dear. Nothing could be further from the truth." He walked to the sphere and put one palm against it, gazing lovingly through the glass before turning back to her. "Come here."

Reluctantly, she approached the tank again, but she did her best not to look too deeply into the murky water. It had horrified and disgusted her to see what Felix had become, but worse than that, it had broken her heart. Here he was, still alive but no longer human, no longer Felix. She wanted to mourn for him, but he wasn't even dead.

"That's right," Dr. Cocteau said, reaching out to pat her head as if she were a stranger's puppy he wanted to set at ease. "We'll talk, but while we do, you just stay here. He needs you. Needs to see you and know that you're here. It's the only way to help him."

Cocteau turned toward the skulker and a flicker of that hidden anger crossed his face again. "Now I hope you'll give me just a moment to take care of unfinished business, and I will be able to give you my full attention and answer all of your questions."

Molly stared at him, but this close to the glass—to Felix—she could only shudder and try not to cry in grief and frustration. She wanted to attack Cocteau, to scream and hurl herself at him, but that would do no good. She wanted to save Felix, and if this man, with his peculiar manner and his twisted science, could tell her how, then she had to remain in control.

Stroking his white beard, Cocteau studied the skulker a moment and then turned to a pair of gas-men standing beside the throne platform.

"You two, come here," the old man said, beckoning the gas-men to him.

They hurried to his side, strangely fast despite the odd, unsteady gait she now noticed was characteristic of all of them. All except the skulker.

Dr. Cocteau glanced at her. "You're not going to like this, I suspect," he said. "But I want to show you that there are no secrets here. I'll hide nothing from you. It's the only way for you to realize my sincerity. You see, you went to Simon Church, a man who has been surrogate father to countless apprentices and colleagues in his life, and cost each of them their lives with his mad pursuits. His current aide, the man you know as Joe, has been almost as irritating a thorn in my side as Church himself. These are dangerous men whose only desire is to harness and control energies they do not understand, so that they can deprive others of those same energies . . . even if the fate of the world is at stake."

"What are you *talking* about?" Molly asked, shaking her head. And yet, though it sounded half like babble, she could see how it might be possible to view Church and Joe that way.

"Joe is a danger to everything I have planned. He's a danger to your friend Felix especially."

Molly shook her head, a bitter taste in her mouth. Mr. Church might be odd, and she might have believed unpleasant things about him because of it, especially after seeing the crazy apparatuses in the dome room at the top of his apartment. But she had felt so at ease with Joe, as if they could have been friends. Good friends. She had never had a brother to look out for her but had always wished for one.

"Joe's not a danger to anyone," she said. "He's dead."

Dr. Cocteau removed his glasses and cleaned them with the cuff of his jacket, a smirk on his face.

"That's what my servants tell me, as well," he said, returning his spectacles to their perch. "You'll forgive me if I hesitate to take your word for it, or theirs. I have crossed paths with Joe before and have found him very difficult to kill. And I've certainly tried."

He said this last with his usual warmth, but a chill went up the back of Molly's neck and settled there.

"Excuse me a moment," Dr. Cocteau said with a little bow of his head.

He beckoned for the two gas-men to follow him and then led them through the gap between heavy green theatrical curtains, the fabric rippling and closing behind them. Molly glanced around at the other gas-men, but they seemed almost inert, now, awaiting instructions from their master. She had no doubt that they would stop her if she tried to escape, but they did not seem interested in interfering with her otherwise.

She started toward the gap in the green curtains.

On the floral, high-backed chair where he seemed to mimic his master's imperial nature, the skulker stood up on the seat. As she moved, his head turned to track her. She imagined she could hear the wet, sickly sounds of his breathing from here, but he was at least thirty feet away, in front of the aquarium wall, and the vast chamber swallowed sounds. It had to be all in her head.

What are you? she wondered as she glanced at the skulker. Mr. Church had said the gas-men were the result of some kind of experiment involving humans, magic, and animals, that their flesh had been made malleable, but the gas inside their suits kept their flesh stabilized in a human form. But the skulker didn't behave like a man, and his size and gait seemed almost apelike. Was that it, she wondered? Had something gone wrong with this one, or had it been a different sort of experiment? Was the skulker some kind of orangutan or chimpanzee?

Whatever it was, its mask lenses tracked her as she glided toward the opening in the curtain. She reached it, reached out to touch the curtain, and the skulker jumped down from his chair and took a few steps toward her. Her heart raced and her throat felt dry. The other gas-men still did not seem troubled by her, but the skulker watched her with his entire body tensed, as if ready to attack her. She told herself he was only making sure she didn't try to flee, or maybe he thought he was protecting Dr. Cocteau from her like some kind of watchdog.

She pulled the curtain open a couple of inches, heart pounding.

She could feel her pulse throbbing in her temples. The skulker took two more steps and paused again, as still as a statue, like a predator in the jungle, ready to pounce.

But Molly did not need to open the curtain any further. She had a view of the next makeshift room. Chains and ropes on pulleys hung down from the ceiling, dangling over an oval pool bounded by a rim of badly poured concrete. It was yet another absurd element of Dr. Cocteau's strange lair. Cocteau stood with the two gas-men he had commanded to accompany him, and as Molly watched, he helped them slip off their masks, yellow gas spilling out.

She flinched and glanced away, but after a moment she forced herself to look back. The gas-men were stripping off their suits, and she saw glistening, green-black skin and strange ridges, but the gas from within their suits billowed around them in a yellow fog that obscured most of the details of their nakedness. One of them dove into the pool, but the other hesitated, and then turned as if he had sensed her gaze upon it. He had jaundiced eyes spread too far apart, only nostril slits where his nose ought to have been, and a mouth full of rows of needle teeth.

He tried to dive into the pool, but his hesitation had allowed more of the gas to disperse. As he slipped over the uneven concrete lip, his limbs fused together and his torso narrowed, so that what hit the water had become a horrifying, twisted merger of man and eel.

Dr. Cocteau went to a small metal shelf in the corner and picked up something from a pile of tools arrayed there. On the floor next to the shelf was a row of air tanks and masks used for breathing underwater. While living on her own, Molly had befriended a small family of salvage divers who traded what they retrieved from the submerged city for the things they needed to survive. The son, Damien, had even taken Molly diving once, showing her how to use the tanks, but she had not liked the cold, murky water and the abandoned cemetery the city had become below the waterline.

The air tanks were a curiosity, though. The gas-men would not need them. But then she remembered Cocteau's human servants in the submarine crew and thought that perhaps the tanks were meant for them. Molly's gaze lingered on those air tanks for a moment, but then Dr. Cocteau drew her attention again as he walked over to the jagged concrete pool and reached into his jacket pocket to withdraw a leather pouch.

The gas-men's dark shapes swam in the pool, circling around each other, and it looked as if they were growing. Dr. Cocteau retrieved small, yellow, chalky things from the pouch that might have been odd mushrooms or chunks of bone. The tool he had taken from the shelf turned out to be a small mallet, with which he pounded the chalky bits to dust.

Brushing the remnants into his hands, he raised them over the pool and waited until dark, pointed heads flashed above the water, and then he rubbed his palms together, sprinkling the dust and grit down onto the things swimming there.

"Go and hunt," Dr. Cocteau said. "And don't return until you've got him rotting in your bellies."

The dark shapes vanished deeper into the pool and the water stopped swirling. Only then did Molly realize that this oval was not just a pool, but somehow an exit. The eel things the gas-men had become must be able to access the river and the flooded subway tunnels from there.

For a fleeting moment, Molly glanced back at the air tanks and wondered if she might use the pool as an exit herself. She had seen pirates and Water Rats using such tanks and masks, as well as professors and archaeologists from Uptown who had shown a rare interest in what had become of old New York. It couldn't be that difficult to figure out how to operate one, she reasoned.

Dr. Cocteau put the mallet back on the tool shelf and began to turn. Molly let the curtain fall back into place and hurried back to her spot near the water globe. The skulker did not move, only watched her, but she could feel the disapproving glare beneath his gas mask. She wondered if he had fur under his suit, or some kind of amphibian scales. When she had first entered the room, Dr. Cocteau's appearance and warmth had confused her, but this was the man who had created these monstrosities, had taken human beings and twisted them into monstrous slaves. He was a monster himself. And that meant that any doubt she might have had about Mr. Church had to be pushed aside. She knew who the good guys were, and she regretted ever having doubted them, even for a moment.

She put a hand on the glass sphere. For the first time, she wanted Felix to feel her there, to surge forward, testing his chains, so that she could look into his eyes. His transformation filled her with grief and horror, but she would not abandon him. She wanted him to know that he wasn't alone. Whatever happened to him, she wanted him to know she loved him.

"Now then. Where were we?" Dr. Cocteau said from behind her.

Molly bit her lip and wiped a tear from her eye. She peered into the murky water again but could see only a dark shape floating inside. After a moment she turned to face her captor, taking a deep breath, wondering if Mr. Church knew where she was, and if he did, whether there was anything the old detective could do to help her now that Joe was dead.

"You were going to answer my questions," she said.

"Yes, of course," Dr. Cocteau said, as if he had needed reminding, which of course he hadn't. His kindly grandfather act was all pretense and seemed obscene to her now. "Go on. But do forgive me if I need to rest a moment. I'm an old man, you see, and I have a great deal to do before the night is through."

He turned and walked to the dais, went up the steps on the side, and settled himself imperiously into his throne. She glanced around, wondering if there was somewhere for her to sit or if she was meant just to stand there and gaze adoringly up at him, as his one human subject. The only chair she could see was the one over by the aquarium wall, and the skulker had retreated to his place in front of the array of oddly shaped windows. Tired as she was, Molly did not want to sit like some obedient child on the floor in front of the dais, so she stood with her arms crossed defiantly and stared at Dr. Cocteau on his weathered throne. Now that she had a better look at it, Molly thought the chair itself ridiculous and sad. It looked more like a stage prop that ought to be collecting dust behind the curtain in Felix's theater than an actual throne.

"Try to imagine the entire universe is your friend Mr. Orlov's tank," Dr. Cocteau said. "A sphere full of stars. Or a square or a cylinder. It doesn't really matter what shape it takes, but for the sake of argument, we'll say a sphere."

He gazed at her expectantly, as if trying to teach his dog to speak.

"The universe is a sphere," she echoed.

Dr. Cocteau brightened proudly. "Precisely. Now, from Mr. Orlov's perspective, well . . . we are outside the sphere, aren't we? As are my servants, and the rest of my home, the river and tunnels, and above us the ruins of the city, and beyond that a world and another universe. But if our entire universe is inside a sphere, have you ever wondered, Molly, what is outside the glass? If you travel to the outskirts of the universe, what awaits at its perimeter?"

Molly shook her head. "Not really."

"There are other universes," Dr. Cocteau said solemnly. "Some are beyond the limits of our own, and others are here beside us, as close as the room on the other side of the curtains where you spied on me moments ago."

Molly felt her face flush. She had thought she had been so stealthy.

"But the curtain isn't easily parted," he continued. "Even just a glimpse into other realms is impossible for most. And to do so . . . the risk is enormous."

His tone made her skin crawl. She did not want to allow such possibilities into her imagination.

"Mr. Church already told me all of this," she said.

Dr. Cocteau's smile vanished. One corner of his mouth lifted in a sneer. "Simon Church is a fool. He monitors the ebb and flow of occult powers . . . the supernatural . . . but he has never understood that what he thinks of as supernatural is still a part of the fabric of our reality. Natural and supernatural are no different than night and day. They both belong to the order of things.

"Church has been willfully blind, calling me a madman for my experiments, but I have spent more than ninety years studying the energies that bleed back and forth between our dimension and the dark void where the old gods retreated when they left our world, before time as we understand it began—"

"You're not making any sense," Molly said.

Dr. Cocteau froze, his eyes narrowing. For all but a moment earlier, he had hidden his rage so well she thought she had imagined it.

Now the mask slipped. He gripped the arms of his throne with white-knuckled tension and sneered at her with undisguised malice.

"I'm not . . ." he began. He shook his head. "Has it occurred to you that you're simply too stupid to understand?"

Molly held her breath, too scared to reply. But her silence only infuriated him more. Dr. Cocteau stood and leaped from the dais, landing in a spidery crouch only a few feet from her, and Molly cried out and retreated toward the glass sphere, staring in horror.

A man of his age should not be capable of such things.

As Cocteau approached her, he dug a hand into his pocket and came out with a fistful of pink, flaky powder. Molly pressed against the glass, looked around for somewhere to run, but the gas-men watched impassively and the skulker had begun to jump up and down in glee. A squeal came from inside his mask and she knew that she had been right—once he had been some kind of ape or monkey.

"Felix!" Molly cried, turning to pound on the glass. She screamed his name and saw the dark shape twisting in the murk. An arm reached toward the glass, a long, jointed arm with three long, crab-like fingers. Then another, and a third, and finally a fourth. She caught only a momentary glimpse of his face, but this time she did not scream. Her heart filled with sorrow for him.

Then Dr. Cocteau spun her around.

"Look!" he said, glaring at her from behind his spectacles, his smile almost hungry.

He threw the handful of pinkish dust into the air and it spread into a cloud that began to drift immediately. Some of it got into Molly's eyes and she felt a strange, giddy rush in her veins. Her skin seemed to prickle with the contact, but she was staring up at the drifting cloud of dust and she realized it had begun to glitter. She tried to wipe at her eyes as the dust became a thin, obscure layer of fog that rose higher above them, spreading out, the glitter effect expanding.

The rest of the room grew dark all at once, as if at Cocteau's command. Molly could hear the rustle and squeak of the gas-men's rubber suits and the heavy, wet breathing of the skulker. She could hear the burble of water in the sphere behind her. But darkness swam in everywhere, obscuring even the aquarium wall and the skulker in his little throne, and soon the only light came from above.

"It's beautiful," Molly said, her lips numb, her voice coming as if from a great distance. For a moment, she felt as if she couldn't breathe.

"The universe," Dr. Cocteau whispered into her ear.

Where the ceiling had been, up so high, Molly now saw only stars. Once, the power Uptown had failed and she had stood with Felix on the roof of the theater and looked at the night sky. Without the lights of the city, she had seen that the universe was an endless field of stars, so many more than she had ever imagined. And now she saw them again, as if she stood atop a building and stared at the stars and the night sky in utter darkness, just her and the lunatic Dr. Cocteau.

No. There are others, she thought. *We're not alone.*

And they weren't. She could feel the others watching them from between stars and from the depths of darkness, and yet close enough to breathe in her ear, near enough for her skin to crawl from the presence of their malign intelligence. She saw nothing of them, but she felt them there, watching and waiting, voracious and full of hatred. So close that if they wanted to, they could reach between the curtains of the universe and put their hands on her.

Molly began to scream, falling to the floor and thrashing. When Dr. Cocteau tried to grab her, she fought him and attempted to crawl away. After a few seconds, as his big hands held her arms tight to her body, she blacked out.

Chapter Nineteen

Joe marches forward, looking for witches.

This is a part of the river he has never seen, which should be impossible. He thought he had explored every part of it, both along the banks and under the water. But the tracks beneath him are the work of hammer and forge, not of magic, of that he is certain. No witch would take the time to construct something so orderly.

He peers through the dark water, eyes narrowed as he watches the fish swim by, and he wonders about the purpose of this tunnel. It must either lie beneath the main river, or be some sort of underground tributary. But the walls and ceiling were laid by masons, not eroded by time. Who would build such a thing? It confuses him, and he realizes that he cannot remember how far he has come from the village, or how he came to be in the rushing current of this subterranean river tunnel.

His fingers flex and close into fists. In near complete darkness, he bends against the current and marches on. The wooden blocks that lay crossways beneath him are a path, and though he is not certain what he will find at its end, he knows that he is pointed in the right direction.

Witches, he thinks. *There are witches ahead.* He can sense the dark power that radiates from them. His hands long to snap their bones. He will crush their evil hearts and make the people of the village safe, keep both day and night free of fear, as he has done since the day he awakened to this life. He has seen women sickened by curses and men murdered and flayed. He has hunted witches along the river and in the woods, only to discover the bloody bones of infants they have eaten, cracked open so they could get to the marrow. Killing witches is his duty, but it is also a pleasure.

He decides that they have done something to cloud his mind. Perhaps they have found a way to reverse the ritual the villagers used to create him, and now the magic that binds him together will unravel, and the river current will pull him apart and what is left will sink into the silt. Perhaps. But for now, his hands will still make fists, and so he strides onward.

The witches must be near now. He can feel their sinister presence ahead. There are tributaries off of this tunnel, the river rushing out to fill other passages and chambers, and for the first time, it occurs to him that this warren of tunnels is like some kind of underwater city. It makes no sense. There are no cities near the village. But his questions will wait for later. He will indulge them after the witches are dead. Once the girl is safe.

He falters slightly, frowning. The river rushes against him but he fights the current even as he wonders where that thought came from. What girl? This must be part of the confusion the witches have inflicted upon him. A girl from the village, no doubt. They have taken a child again.

He nods to himself. This must be right. Thoughts of the girl managed to slip through whatever walls they had erected in his mind. Now that he thinks of her, he can see a face in his mind, a wry smile and fierce eyes beneath a cascade of coppery red hair. He vows to himself that she will not die at the hands of witches.

Never, he says, the sound a gentle rumble against his ears under the water. *No more children.*

The tracks beneath his feet curve slightly leftward. He follows, but as he comes around the turn, he feels a disturbance in the water ahead, feels the pressure of something enormous rushing through the dark river toward him. No, *two* somethings, enormous children of a leviathan churning along the tunnel, monsters sent by the witches.

In the dim glow from light set into the tunnel roof, he sees only darkness, save for the glint of a thousand fangs.

Chapter Twenty

When Molly came to, the lights were dim in the vast chamber of Dr. Cocteau's home, but the ceiling was only the ceiling. Whatever the old man had done to her eyes, to her perception, it had passed. She lay on a smooth, hard surface, her head lolled to one side, and it was cold against her cheek. With a rush of fear, she bolted upright, her heart clenching when she realized where she was—on one of Cocteau's surgical tables. She wrapped her arms around herself and tried to rub the cold away, grateful at least that he had not strapped her into the leather restraints.

"You must listen closely now, if you want your answers," Dr. Cocteau said.

Molly spun around and saw that he had been standing in the shadows at the head of the table all along, just behind her, perhaps watching her while she lay unconscious. The skulker had climbed up into his arms and he held the creature like a child, his wet, sticky breathing more disgusting than ever. The image of the two of them together, like father and son, made her shudder.

"You felt it," Dr. Cocteau said.

"In the stars," Molly whispered, drawing her knees up to her chin and wrapping her arms around them. She glanced at the new shadows that had gathered in the room now that the lights had been turned lower, at the gas-men lurking there.

"No," he said sharply. "Not *in* the stars. Between the stars. Behind anything your eyes can see."

Molly nodded. "Mr. Church called it 'un-dimensioned space.'"

"Yes!" Dr. Cocteau replied, excitement lighting his eyes. He hugged the skulker and nuzzled his nose against his gas mask. "That's exactly right. But they did not always live in that space. These old gods roamed our world during its infancy, a first, hidden incarnation that science will never understand. The old ones found the solidifying world too confining, and they abandoned it, sliding into another reality, one infinitely more vast."

Deeply unnerved, Molly glanced toward the curtained area where the pool awaited, still wishing she could make a break for those air tanks. She also considered making a rush for the spiral staircase the gas-men had brought her up, but even if it went to the surface, she would never reach it without Cocteau or the gas-men getting to her first. An image flashed in her mind of the way Cocteau had leaped down from the dais, and she got a queasy feeling in her gut. Whatever dark energies he had dabbled with over the years, they had taken their toll on him.

"Now, pay attention," Dr. Cocteau said, hugging the skulker tightly before putting him down. He came and sat on the edge of the surgical table. She wanted to scream, kick him, and run. Felix still swam inside that bizarre tank, but she needed Mr. Church and Joe. Whatever was happening to him, she couldn't help him on her own.

"Help Felix," she said.

Dr. Cocteau frowned irritably. "Hush, girl, and I will."

She nodded for him to continue.

"I am a seer," Dr. Cocteau said. "A scrier, a prognosticator. I would even flatter myself by going so far as to say I am a prophet. I roll the bones, girl. I read the stars. I search for signs in the dregs of my teacup or the entrails of the rats we kill in the tunnels. The very existence of the old gods who live in this strange realm influences our world in ways one cannot possibly understand if one is not searching for such omens. Some have said that this century is cursed, that the plagues and the wars and the convulsions of the Earth are the result of that curse. They are fools.

"For many years, all signs have pointed to an approaching cataclysm, an event so terrible that this world and the human race will never recover. Only recently have I begun to understand that all signs point to myself as the originator of this cataclysm."

Molly's breath caught in her chest. "You want to destroy the world?"

Dr. Cocteau looked shocked. "Not at all," he said, hugging the skulker close to him. The sight made Molly shudder. "I love this world, despite its many flaws. If there was any way that I could fulfill my ambitions—dare I say, my destiny—and still avert this catastrophe, of course I would do so. But I am a traveler, my dear. I am an *explorer,* not some kind of scientific tourist. I am the one human being willing to leave this reality and take the next step, no matter what the cost. When there are lands to discover that are just out of reach, that human eyes have never seen, then I will find a way to cross that breach."

Molly stared at him, hugging her knees closer against her chest. She was afraid that she *did* see.

"There were two elements I needed in order to make my journey," Dr. Cocteau said, his gaze no longer on her but peering into some distant shadow, some sideways world she could not see. "First, I had to find a way to part the curtain that separates our world from their realm. I presume you have, by now, learned the details of your friend Mr. Orlov's strange birth."

When Molly nodded, he smiled, but his gaze remained distant.

"Church was there when the grief-stricken Andrew Golnik attempted to offer Orlov's mother—with him yet in her womb—as a sacrifice to some deity or other. Golnik thought Lector's Pentajulum would force the Sumerian death god to pay attention to him, but he did not understand the Pentajulum. Not at all. He *did* get the attention of something ancient, but it had never been worshipped by human beings . . . never even shared this world with humanity. Using the Pentajulum gave it a window through which it could peer, and when it understood that Golnik intended his offering as some kind of invitation, it began to part the curtain . . . to slide through.

"If Mr. Church hadn't arrived when he did, and shot Golnik, there is no telling what would have happened. Cataclysm, possibly. Or perhaps some deathless entity from that un-dimensioned space would have

worn Golnik or the woman like a suit of flesh and wandered our world. Perhaps that old god would have proven to be an explorer, like me. No matter, of course, because that isn't what happened. Church shot Golnik and the Pentajulum was lost, but the presence of the old god had touched Mrs. Orlov and her unborn son. The woman died screaming in an asylum, but her son was born and survived, never quite able to adjust to his life. He sensed the other worlds around him, just out of reach, and he felt the way his body would change . . . *wanted* to change, to become the thing he was destined to be."

"His father's son," Molly whispered in horror.

Dr. Cocteau grinned, turning to the skulker, whose wet, ragged breathing had grown quieter with his rapt attention. "*Now* she's getting it."

The skulker turned to stare at her with his black lens eyes.

"You're as crazy as Mr. Church said," Molly said.

"You don't believe that," Dr. Cocteau replied. "You want all of this to be the babbling of a madman because you fear the alternative, just as Church always has. And, truthfully, if I were you, I would be just as frightened. At best, my journey beyond our dimension will draw the attention of beings to whom you and the rest of humanity are less than ants, and it may be to their amusement to destroy you. At worst, the cataclysm I have prophesied will occur, and the bleeding of their dimension into ours *will* destroy you. Destroy everything."

Molly felt a cold, numb hollow opening within her. Once again, Dr. Cocteau had read her perfectly.

"Even if you get through and survive it, there may be no home for you to come back to."

Dr. Cocteau smiled the way adults often did at the naïve innocence of children. It made her want to hurt him.

"I won't be coming back," he said. "And I may not survive very long. But, oh, the sights I'll see. I will commune with the old gods in a way that no human ever has, and I will see the source of their power and be imbued with their majesty. I alone will represent man in the next step of human evolution, unlocking the possibility of elevation to godhood."

Molly blinked, staring at him. "Godhood? You can't be serious."

Dr. Cocteau twitched, his lips pursing as if he'd tasted something sour. "You wanted answers, girl. If you'd rather we begin—"

"I think I've got the basics," Molly said sharply. "But I still don't understand why you need Felix if the Pentajulum is enough to get their attention."

The madman pushed his fingers through his bushy white beard as if neatening it, but managed only to make it bristle. He was growing visibly more irritated, and Molly took half a step back from him, wondering if he would try to attack her himself, if she would have to run.

"I said I needed two elements," Dr. Cocteau huffed. "This is only one of them."

He reached into his jacket pocket—which seemed to have infinite space inside it, and might have been magic—and pulled out Lector's Pentajulum. Its weird colors and shifting design seemed to absorb the light in the room and reflect it back with a dully colorful glow. Dr. Cocteau studied it, smiling as if he wanted to stroke it or lay his cheek against it the way a child might a favorite stuffed animal.

"I have spent years gathering all of the extant writings on the subject of the Pentajulum. I am as close to an expert as this world has ever produced, and I believe it will protect me as I travel through the dimensional barrier and allow me to communicate with the old gods. They will perceive me as their equal."

He gestured at the glass sphere, its murk darker than ever.

"When my research into the Pentajulum led to my discovering the story of Orlov's birth, I felt certain I had the other element I needed. I knew that, in time, his true nature would reveal itself, that the passage of time and his repeated contact with the etheric plane would eventually trigger a transformation. Had I realized that exposure to the Pentajulum when he went to pray at his mother's grave was delaying his maturity, I would have put a stop to it years ago."

"Wait," Molly said. "You knew the Pentajulum was there?"

Dr. Cocteau smirked. "I deduced its location years ago, but decided it would be safer where it was than in my possession, where an arrogant fool like Simon Church might have stolen it. As long as I knew where it was, I would always be able retrieve it when Felix reached his true maturity. When my servants reported that you and Joe were also headed to the cemetery, the timing seemed serendipitous."

Molly glared at him. "Because you need my help."

"Indeed. The time has come. Felix could not hold off his metamorphosis forever. The stars aligned this morning and I rolled the bones to confirm my interpretation. I sent my servants to fetch your father because I knew that he would begin his ascendance today, and once again, my foresight has proven accurate."

Molly thought of the séance with the Mendehlsons. She thought something had gone wrong with Felix's communication with the dead, but was it possible that his seizures and his illness and the way his face had begun to change had less to do with evil spirits and more to do with his own birthright? She wanted to think not, but the timing of the gas-men's arrival was too accurate for it to be mere coincidence. Dr. Cocteau had known what was about to happen.

She turned and stared at the glass sphere, wishing she could see Felix in that dark water . . . wishing he were still Felix. Cocteau had called him her father again, and this time she hadn't argued. If Dr. Cocteau's predictions had come true, did that mean the rest of his madness was also true?

"Once Felix has transformed, he will look up at me and see an equal, a brother. He will be able to part the curtain between this di-

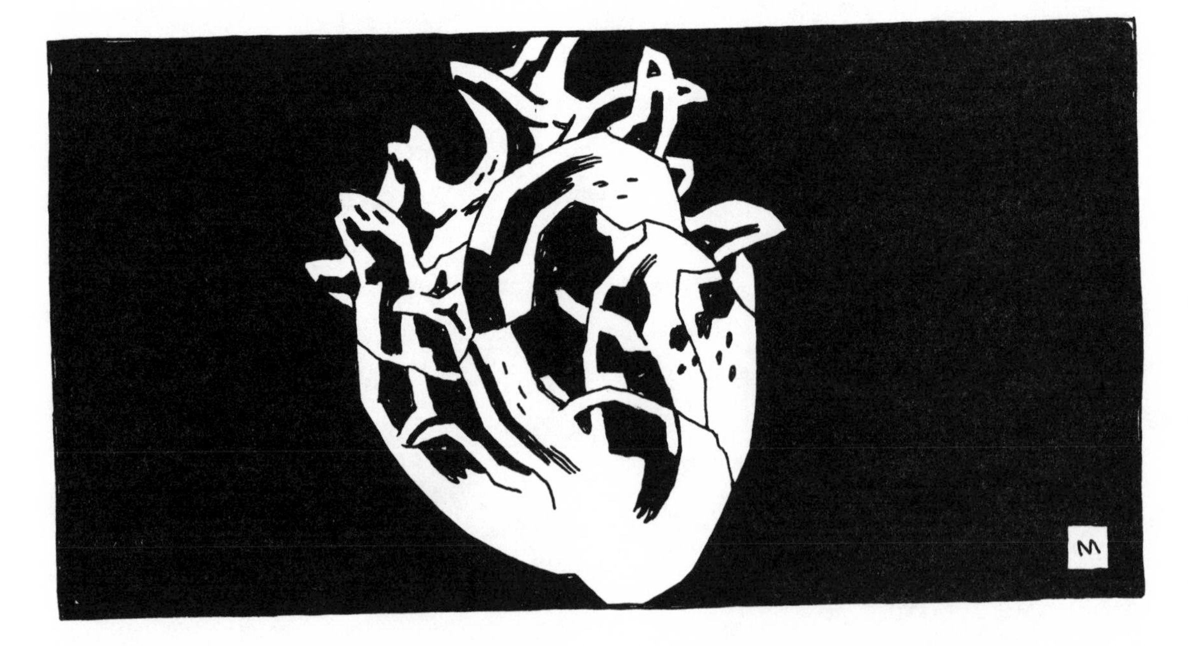

mension and the limbo space beside it and slip through. When Felix ascends through the veil of time-space to the realm of the ancient ones, we will be together as brothers."

Molly hugged herself, her throat growing dry. "You still haven't said why you need *me* here."

Dr. Cocteau hesitated, and Molly felt a fresh surge of fear. She had wondered if he had been talking in circles simply because that was his nature, or if he had been purposely avoiding the central question. Now she knew for certain that he had been, and that the answer to it troubled him.

"Felix's transformation is happening faster than I anticipated," he said. "I wanted you here because he loves you. You are a daughter to him. I believe that your presence will slow the metamorphosis, that seeing you will make him struggle to hold on to his humanity. It won't work for long, but I only need a little time to work out how to activate the Pentajulum, so that when he awakens to his new, godlike power, I can communicate with him. Otherwise, this opportunity will be lost forever."

Molly stared at him openmouthed, filled with a horror unlike any she had felt thus far.

"You don't know how it works," she said in a hushed voice. "You said you knew everything about the Pentajulum, but you're just like everyone else who's tried to use it."

"Nonsense!" Dr. Cocteau barked. "I know precisely how to wield it. I only need to activate its power."

Molly glanced at the water globe and shook her head in cold sorrow. "You're going to get us all killed. You, me, Felix . . . probably a lot more. If half of what you're saying is true, you're going to roll the dice on the fate of the human race on an occult gadget you have no idea how to turn on."

Dr. Cocteau dropped the skulker—who landed in a crouch and then stood, staring—and strode toward her. He seemed as if he might strike her, his hand beginning to reach for her, but then he glanced at the water tank as if he thought perhaps that might not go over well with the being he hoped would be his cosmic brother.

"It would be better if you understood," he said. "It would be better if you believed. That is why I've taken the time to explain all of this to you. But in the end the only thing that truly matters is that you obey. And you will."

Dr. Cocteau bent over to glare at her, his considerable bulk looming ominously, seething with menace. The dim lamplight reflected on the lenses of his spectacles.

Perfect.

Molly punched him so hard she broke both his nose and his glasses. Pain shot through her knuckles as he staggered backward, clutching at his face, blood sluicing between his fingers.

The gas-men were taken off guard. She'd counted on that. She had a few seconds at best before they really came after her, and she intended to use them. Bolting for the part in the curtains, she glanced once over her shoulder at the glass sphere and the figure in the murky water within. It might have been a trick of the light, but she thought the thing that had once been Felix Orlov looked even larger.

Then she focused her full attention on escape. She grabbed the curtain and yanked, tearing it partway down, and threw it over a standing lantern nearby. The weight of the heavy velvet pulled the lamp over and it crashed to the ground, burning oil igniting the curtain and spreading in an instant with a hungry roar.

"So much for obedience," she said as she darted through into the next makeshift room, where the concrete pool waited.

Surviving in the Drowning City, she had learned to run for her life.

She sprinted toward the row of air tanks, the canisters glittering with the orange glow of the fire that engulfed the torn curtain. Soon all of the drapes would have burned and the illusion of different rooms would have vanished as well, revealing Cocteau's bizarre home for the sad creation it was, not some undersea kingdom but a lonely hiding place.

As she grabbed the nearest air tank, its mouthpiece already attached, she heard the wet, phlegmy bark of the skulker behind her. She spun the thumbwheel on top of the tank and the gauge danced up into the green, showing the flow of oxygen. With her free hand she grabbed a mask, but she could feel the skulker's eyes upon her and she started to turn, raising the tank to use as a weapon or a shield.

The skulker stood by the ragged concrete lip around the pool. Dr. Cocteau loomed a few feet behind it, his face contorted with all the madness and rage he had tried so hard to hide. His spectacles were gone and his white beard dripped with blood from his broken nose. The gas-men began to spread out, silently ominous, firelight flickering off the dark lenses of their masks.

"I tried to do this nicely," Dr. Cocteau sneered. "But now you're going to—"

Molly laughed, one hand coming up to hide half her smile. "You sound ridiculous with your nose all smashed up like that."

Her fist still ached, but it was a good ache. She wanted to hit Cocteau again. Instead she bolted for the pool, thinking she could slip on the mask once she was in the water. The gas-men didn't need oxygen, but she was willing to bet she could swim better than any of them . . . as long as they stayed in the suits. If they didn't, well, she knew she'd be in trouble then.

"Stop her!" Cocteau screamed.

The skulker launched himself at her. She hauled off and kicked him in the chest as hard as she could. It only staggered him, so she smashed him in the head with her air tank, clearing the way. But as she barreled toward the pool, about to dive in, she saw something huge and dark rushing up from beneath and she threw herself to one side to get out of the way.

The giant, needle-mouthed eel exploded from below, shattering the concrete walls of the pool. A wave of water thrown up by its emergence splashed down and soaked her, Cocteau, and the gas-men. Dr. Cocteau was screaming. The skulker screeched and ran around and banged his fists against his head as if this were a rational reaction to fear.

Molly stared at the eel, realizing that she had seen it before, only smaller. It had been one of the gas-men that Cocteau had sent after Joe. The two creatures had been released from their suits and lost their human form, reverting to this strange, almost larval shape. Cocteau had done something when he set them loose to make them grow—she had noted it at the time—but she had never imagined how huge they might become.

The eel thrashed, rising and slamming itself down on the floor over and over. It landed on top of the skulker, and Molly heard a sickening pop. A small cloud of yellow mist came out of the skulker's rubber suit and when the eel lifted up again, only a mess of rubber, blood, and greenish pus remained. Dr. Cocteau cried out in fury and panic and started to shout at the gas-men to take Molly, as if she had anything to do with the giant creature's return, when he was the one who had made it so huge and sent it out after Joe.

At last, the eel flopped one final time and went still, but that lasted only a moment before it began to twitch. They all saw the bulge in its middle, and saw that it was moving. The eel's slick flesh jumped and stretched and then it tore, a stench of death and rot wafting out.

The figure that stepped out had had most of its skin and clothing torn away, revealing living stone beneath. But the eyes were Joe's, even though they were now stone. And though it had sharper edges, she knew his face.

"Joe," she said. "What *happened* to you?"

He looked at her for a moment as if he didn't know her, and then those eyes lit with recognition.

Dr. Cocteau stared in surprise, his bloodstained face and beard making him look more like a madman than ever. The fire had leaped from curtain to curtain, spreading rapidly, and the blaze raged throughout the vast chamber. Smoke and heat began to churn around them, but Cocteau behaved as if the only crisis was the one right in front of him. He pointed a hand that shook with fury.

"Kill him!" he shouted. "But keep the girl alive."

The gas-men came at them as one. Joe stepped between them and Molly. She still held the air tank and breathing mask, but now she hesitated. Felix—the Felix she had known, the man who had been like a father to her—no longer existed. She still loved him, but the monstrosity he had become . . . the thing he was becoming . . . was not Felix anymore. The man she had known would have wanted her to escape, would have demanded that she run. Could she say the same of Joe? She barely knew him, but they had formed a strong bond in a handful of hours, and if she thought he could be saved, she couldn't bear to leave him behind. Had Cocteau done this to him? From the madman's reaction to his arrival, she didn't think so.

Again she glanced into the ruined pool. As the gas-men attacked Joe and he began to fight, tearing their suits and crushing the creatures inside, she started to slip the breathing mask over her face.

Something rumbled under her feet. Molly glanced into the pool and saw something huge and dark down in the water, and then she remembered that Dr. Cocteau had sent *two* monsters after Joe.

From the way the ground shook, she had a feeling this one must be even larger. If it tried to smash its way up through the opening to the pool, she didn't want to be there. With one more glance at Joe, she turned to run through the burning curtains and across the bizarre layout of the false home with its weirdly elegant furnishings, some of which were already on fire. The spiral staircase was still there, and she told herself there must be some way to get to the surface.

But as she ran, Dr. Cocteau emerged from the smoke to bar her way.

Beyond him, through the smoke, Molly could see the glass sphere. Water had begun to leak from its base, and suddenly she understood why. As Felix grew, the displaced water had to have somewhere to go. The thing inside, huge now, pressed its face against the glass and stared at her and Cocteau, and its eyes shifted like the Pentajulum, as if they existed both in this reality and another.

"Get out of my way," Molly warned Dr. Cocteau.

"Oh, no, Miss McHugh," he said, wiping a hand across the bloody wreckage of his nose. "I'm keeping you close.

"When I cross over, I'm going to make sure you're the first to die."

Chapter Twenty-one

As he fights, wreathed in smoke and chemical mist, Joe steals glances at the girl with the cinnamon red hair. She is so familiar, and yet trying to remember her name is like trying to force himself to wake from a dream. All he knows is that he has come here to help her, and these things in their slippery suits and their strange masks want to stop him. They aren't witches—or, at least, not like any witches he has ever seen—but they are tainted with sinister purpose.

Their master, however, is a man of evil and madness. Joe sees him menacing the girl and knows that he must be stopped. He punches his fist through the mask of the creature in front of him, shattering dark lenses and tearing straps loose, and then he tosses it aside, striding through the flaming remnants of curtains. The creatures clutch at him. They are inhumanly strong, but he is not human, either. He shrugs them off, hurrying toward the girl and the madman with his blood-matted beard. More hands drag at him, and then there are too many of them, and he must stop to fight them.

He glances up and sees the madman lifting the girl by the throat. She holds a metal cylinder in her hands and wears a strange black mask that covers her eyes and nose. Through that mask he can see her eyes, and she is looking at him. She screams a name. "Joe." It is his name, and not his name. This is a puzzle that he senses she can solve. Again he tears loose, dragging some of the creatures behind him as he tries to reach her.

But then the world trembles again, worse than before. It shakes, nearly knocking him over, and cracks splinter the floor. He hurls away two of the black-suited creatures that cling to him and twists around just in time to see the edges of the pool shatter. An eruption of slick black flesh explodes from the pool, accompanied by a wave of saltwater.

Joe killed one of the giant eels. The other has continued to grow, and when it hits the ground the entire vast chamber shakes. Some of the strange windows crack, and water sprays inward. The eel opens its maw, its teeth long needles almost as tall as the girl, and it begins to slither its huge bulk after him. The creatures restraining him release their grip and flee, but Joe will not. If the girl is to live, he must be alive to save her, and that means the monstrous eel must die.

It lunges toward him, huge mouth opening wide.

Joe can hear the girl screaming his name. . . .

Molly slammed the air tank into Dr. Cocteau's temple. He lost his grip on her and she staggered back, turned, and stared at Joe again. Her first thought had been astonishment that he was alive, but now, with the way the lamplight, firelight, and shadows played over his face and the contours of his body, she wondered if *alive* was even the right word.

"You little fool," Cocteau snarled.

"What did you do to him?" Molly demanded. "Those things you sent after him . . . what the hell did they *do*?"

Dr. Cocteau frowned, distracted by her fury, and glanced over at Joe. From the look of surprise on his face, Molly realized that whatever had happened to her friend, Cocteau wasn't responsible. But something *had* happened, and magic was involved. Joe no longer looked remotely human. He wore remnants of human skin like tattered clothes he had draped over himself as some kind of lunatic's disguise. She had seen his eyes and recognized them immediately, so she had no doubt this truly was Joe. As she watched him tear apart the gas-men with stone hands and saw the rough earth and rock surface revealed where his skin had torn away, she screamed his name again, not for help but in confusion and anguish.

"What *is* he?" Dr. Cocteau asked, a glimmer of sanity creeping back into his expression.

Molly didn't know how to answer. If this self-styled explorer, a man intimate with both science and the supernatural, and with things beyond the limits of human imagining, did not know what had happened to Joe, how could she begin to guess? Joe wasn't a man anymore, but was he a monster?

At length an answer came to her lips.

"He's my friend."

The gigantic eel creature lunged toward Joe. Molly watched it through the smoke and the flames. She called out to Joe again, but he ignored her, hurling himself at the eel and then dodging aside at the last possible moment. Joe slammed his fist through the eel's huge maw, snapping several swordlike teeth, and he hung on as it clamped its jaws on his arm. He pounded his free hand against its skull as it reared up, twisting, knocking over shelves and the rods that held up the burning curtains, which hissed as they struck the damp floor.

Dr. Cocteau started to shout, raging at the monstrous eel. For a moment, his anger at Molly had been forgotten. The eel coiled around Joe, trying to crush him to death. He got his feet under him and twisted the serpentine creature around, attempting to punch his way through its skull. Cocteau waved his arms, screaming, trying to get the eel's attention.

Joe and the eel crashed into the glass sphere holding the thing that had once been Felix Orlov. The many-armed beast spilled out of the globe in a wave of murky water, a confused mass of jointed limbs and writhing tentacles. Molly gasped at the sight of it, and suddenly the knowledge became too much for her. Her heart froze and shattered, knowing that the man who had taken care of her, whom she had loved as a father, might as well be dead. His humanity had come to an end, and she cried out, voice cracking with anguish. She shook, the air tank dangling in one hand, the mask over her face muffling the sound of her weeping.

Dr. Cocteau took out the Pentajulum, intoning a panicked chant as he raised it in front of him like an offering. It glowed warmly for a moment and then went dark, and the old man shook it like some ancient infant with a rattle, petulant over its refusal to do as he wished.

But Molly's eyes were locked on the view beyond Cocteau. What she'd thought of as the aquarium wall, with its many disparate windows, had sprung dozens of leaks. Water poured in around the frames or through cracks in the glass, and no matter how thick that glass was, water pressure would finish the job in moments. The river was coming in.

She spun, slipping the air tank onto her back, and bolted. Her boots squelched in the water that had spilled from the glass sphere, which made her feel a pang of regret at leaving Felix behind. But she did not allow herself to slow. Felix wouldn't be forgotten, but the man he'd been was a part of the past now, and she wanted to survive to have a future. He would have wanted that for her.

Unearthly cries filled the vast chamber of the old subway station, an eerie keening like the shriek of a badly tuned violin, poorly played. She thought it might be the thing Felix had become, but supposed it might have been the eel. Then she heard shouting and she knew that Dr. Cocteau had seen the leaking windows. He would be racing after her, knowing her destination, unless there was some other escape route.

With a glance over her shoulder, she saw one of the small windows give way, the river water rushing in. The eel had risen in a coil around Joe, and he pummeled at its eye and head, twenty feet above the flaming remnants of Cocteau's finery, as the old station began to flood. Dr. Cocteau and the gas-men had abandoned all pretense of controlling the situation. Some of the madman's servants dove into the ruined pool, making their escape that way, while others followed their master as he raced after Molly.

She bent into her run, ducking beneath a flaming arch of fabric. A colorful Arabic tapestry ignited as she passed it, and the fire leaped to a shelf full of books. But she knew that none of it would be burning much longer—not once the rest of those windows gave way.

Molly's chest ached, her heart thundering so loud she could barely hear the shouts and cries behind her any longer, or the roar of the flames. The fire's heat baked her skin, and panic clawed at her, but she forced herself to breathe evenly, not knowing if breathing quickly would mean she had less air. It seemed a waste, using it now, but the water could come in at any moment and sweep her away, and the thought frightened her too much to allow her to reason.

Something brushed her arm, and she glanced over her shoulder and saw one of the gas-men trying to catch up with her. Molly darted around a post and the gas-man had to slow a little, which gave her a moment to spare. She sprinted, wondering if she had gone the right direction, acting only on instinct. The gas-men had brought her in through a hatch that she thought must be straight ahead from the far wall with its failing aquarium windows.

And then she saw it. The smoke had begun to fill the vast chamber, and it clouded her vision. Without the air tank she might have suffered from smoke inhalation, might have been unable to make it. But she saw the door ahead and unleashed the hope she had kept tamped down inside her.

A roar filled her ears and she couldn't help glancing back, just in time to see several of the largest windows giving way. The water poured in, the whole river seeming to collapse into the room, surging across the floor. She caught a glimpse of Joe fighting the eel as it whipped through the water, still coiled around him, trying to crush him to death. Felix was there as well, his bulk gigantic, with open slits in his torso and thick, puckered tentacles. It was one of the most grotesque things she had ever seen.

She nearly slammed into the metal door. Her hands struggled with the hatch wheel, but she got it turning and spun it until she heard the clunk of the lock disengaging. As she tried to haul the heavy door open, she glanced back to see Dr. Cocteau bearing down on her with wide eyes, blood still smeared on his face and beard. With an effort that made her shout, she dragged the door open and threw herself across the threshold, thinking that she had to get it closed again, to keep all of it out—Cocteau and the water and the gas-men and the fire, and even Felix.

But then one of the gas-men stuck an arm through the gap and she slammed it on little more than gleaming rubber suit. She felt the door yanked from her grip and fell backward onto the metal landing as it opened. Through the gap she saw gas-men, and beyond them, water flooding the old station. Lamps and curtain posts were knocked over into the water and went out, and darkness began to spread as the wave crashed across the chamber toward her.

Dr. Cocteau shoved past the gas-men and through the door. He grabbed her by the arm and picked her up. Molly fought him, but only for an instant, because by then he was hauling her toward the spiral staircase, and that was the way she wanted to go. Apparently his fear of drowning was greater than his desire to kill her. The clang of the hatch slamming made her turn and look, and she saw the gas-men spinning the wheel, sealing it shut, even as a few inches of water washed across the landing.

The whole stairwell shook, but this was not the arrival of some new monster. It felt like a true earth tremor, and Molly cried out and held on to the railing, thinking about the last major earthquake in New York, and the result of that. If this was a real quake, what fresh havoc would it unleash?

Then they were running, boots banging on the metal stairs. The noise echoed off the stone walls along with Cocteau's labored breathing. As Molly raced upward, her hate for him festered and grew. For a handful of minutes she had given him the benefit of the doubt, thinking he might truly want to help Felix, but now she knew better. Dr. Cocteau might be some kind of genius, and if he wanted to explore primeval realities or parallel limbos or whatever he called the monstrous dark dimension Felix's "father" hailed from, she would never have stopped him. But he was a murderer who would use anyone to further his own ends, no matter the cost . . . even if that cost was the destruction of the world. The cataclysm he had predicted . . . she had no doubt that he wanted it to happen. The question now was whether or not it would. What would become of Felix and all of Dr. Cocteau's careful preparation?

The world shook around them again, dust and mortar sifting down from the walls and ceiling, the metal creaking underfoot. Dr. Cocteau let go of her arm to get a better grip on the iron railing. His breathing came hard and rasping, and she wondered if his heart would fail him. But every time she thought he might fall, he redoubled his effort and labored along behind her, wheezing and moaning. The stairs seemed to go up forever and her legs began to burn with the exertion, but she kept climbing. The gas-men weren't human, but how Dr. Cocteau kept up with her, she did not know.

At last he began to falter, and then paused to rest.

"Don't let her . . . get away," he rasped, practically choking on the words.

The gas-men stayed with her, not trying to stop or even hold on to her, but never letting her get more than a step or two above them.

Another tremor struck, this one so strong it threw her against the wall. From far below there came the high-pitched *skree* of weakening metal. Molly wondered how many stairs they had climbed, how many feet, how far they had to go before they reached the surface. Then a bang thundered up along the spiral stairs and the whole structure of the staircase shook from the sudden onslaught of water. The door had not held, and now the maelstrom would be rushing up beneath them.

Inside her air mask, Molly screamed in frustration and regret. She imagined the water surging upward, churning as it filled the spiral. Dr. Cocteau roared at his gas-men to hurry, commanded two of them to carry him, and Molly glanced back in horror to see that they had lifted him on a bucket made of their arms and were running upward. They slammed into her and she hit the railing before she fell backward, tumbling end over end down a dozen stairs, only catching herself on the railing because her body struck a turn in the spiral at a bad angle.

Hauling herself to her feet, Molly starting running again. Her ankle hurt, but it wasn't broken. Full of fear and anger, she chased Cocteau and his creatures, aware of the irony but unable to appreciate it through the storm of emotions already swirling inside of her. She heard the roar of water rushing up beneath her and she knew that the air mask would not be enough to save her.

And then she reached the landing. The metal hatchway door hung open ahead of her, but as she approached, the gas-men were beginning to close it. She hurled herself through the open door, slamming her shoulder against it as she forced her way past the gas-men. Dr. Cocteau screamed at them as they spun the wheel to seal the hatch.

The water struck it from below with such force that it squirted out around the rim of the door, even as the wheel was spun tight.

"I don't know if that's going to hold," Molly said.

Cocteau sneered at her but didn't reply. He turned and lumbered toward another door, this one entirely ordinary wood with a heavy latch handle. They were on a broader landing than in the spiral staircase. To the left a wall had been built, sealing this small space off from one she imagined to be much larger. It had been done with brick and mortar, but she had a feeling there was more to the wall than just masonry, like the huge wall erected down in Cocteau's lair, keeping the river out.

"Where are we?" she asked as she rushed to catch up.

Still he ignored her, tearing open the door, which opened on an ordinary set of granite steps that led upward. Molly followed, hurrying, and soon they were struggling up the last of four flights of stairs to a locked door. With a gesture from Dr. Cocteau, the gas-men threw themselves at the door, and it crashed open, letting a rush of night wind into the stairwell.

Chapter Twenty-two

Shaking with effort and relief, Molly emerged onto the roof of an old building and glanced around. She breathed in the salt air, looked up at the moon and starlight peeking through the clouds, and tried to figure out where they were. Somewhere way Downtown, she knew that much. The rain had stopped at last, but the thought filled her with a fresh wave of sadness, making her think of Joe, and then of Felix.

Lost in her own city, forever cut off from the only things in her past that had ever given her comfort, she nearly collapsed then. If she survived the night, what future lay ahead for her? She had friends and acquaintances, and there had been clients who had been kind to her when they came to see Felix, but she had no family except him, no home other than the one she had shared with him. Whatever future she might have, it would have to be of her own construction.

The building bucked and shook beneath her, a quaking that knocked her off her feet. She sprawled on her hands and knees on the roof, glancing around in terror, wondering if the old building would crumble and sink into the river, making her one more victim of the Drowning City. Gas-men toppled all over the roof. Dr. Cocteau had fallen to his knees but managed to stay there, propped up on one arm, the other hand frantically searching deep inside the pocket of his singed, bloodstained burgundy jacket.

Had he lost the Pentajulum? Molly hoped he had. The bastard could only do more harm with it.

A thunderous clamor reached her, and she turned toward it. Uptown quaked and buildings crashed together. A gleaming tower had given way, and she watched as it toppled. The upper floors of a landmark building imploded, windows vaporized. For generations the denizens of wealthy Uptown had turned their backs on the squalor and ruin to the south, pretending that no one would choose to live there, fancying themselves untouchable in their office spires and corporate battlements. Now they were crumbling, and Molly wondered if Upper Manhattan would sink the way that Lower Manhattan had so many years ago, if the streets would flood, making Uptown a part of the Drowning City. Part of her thought it served them right, the rich elitists who abandoned and ignored those less fortunate. But then she thought of the families, the children, the happiness devastated with every passing second, and she felt ashamed.

Yet ashamed or not, Uptown was falling. Soon, it would be drowning.

The roof she was on slammed upward, unbalancing her again, and she struck her head. Dazed, she tried to rise but succeeded only in tumbling a few feet closer to Dr. Cocteau. The roar of the earthquake filled the sky and drilled into her bones. From somewhere not far away she heard voices screaming and imagined them as frightened prayers that would go unanswered.

But in the midst of those screams, there came another sound—one she had heard before, only minutes ago. The eerie cry could only be the plaintive wail of the strange being that Felix Orlov had become. Now it grew louder and louder, and Molly scuttled toward the edge of the roof. A crack formed forty feet away from her and she hesitated, thinking the whole building would fall out from beneath her, but then the trembling began to subside.

A low wall ran around the edge of the roof. Molly edged toward it, gripped the top of the wall, and rose to her knees. If the quake worsened again, it might hurl her from the roof, but that awful, keening, sorrowful wail reached out to her, and she had to look. She had to see him.

Molly peered over the low wall, and what she saw paralyzed her. The water churned with the rumbling of the earth. The old City Hall had half collapsed into the river, and as she glanced at it, the water dragged more and more of the structure into its current. But in the intersection ahead, loomed over by half-submerged pieces of old New York, the thing that had been Felix Orlov thrust itself from the water and cried out its pain to the cosmos. The sound tore at Molly's heart, and she found herself weeping at the anguish in it. It didn't matter if the voice he spoke with had not been heard in her dimension since before time began; she could feel the sorrow and confusion in him, and it broke her heart. Some part of the creature was still the man who had cared for her so gently and with such warm humor.

"Felix!" she screamed. "It's all right! You'll be all right!"

And then she covered her mouth as if she had uttered some horrible profanity, because how stupid was that? Of course he wouldn't be all right. Even to suggest it was ridiculous. What she really wanted to tell him was that he wasn't alone, but that wasn't true, either, was it?

Molly pressed her face to the cold stone on top of the wall and peered down from the roof. The creature did not appear to be swimming so much as floating there in the river, half of his body above the waterline. The undulating waves and the current had no evident effect on him. The tentacles where his face should have been coiled and uncoiled, reaching skyward as if waiting for some un-dimensioned angels to come to its rescue. Felix had so many eyes now, and when Molly saw the strange collection of limbs moving under the water, she realized just how huge he had gotten. His reach beneath the river must have spanned the entire intersection, and she thought he might still be growing.

A voice rose above the chaos, a deep chanting baritone. Molly spun to see that Dr. Cocteau had risen from his knees and now stood by the edge of the roof thirty feet away, holding the Pentajulum up in both hands like an offering. His eyes were closed and despite the blood that matted his beard and the soot on his face and clothes, he looked radiant in his zeal.

Around him, the gas-men waited. Some of them were on their feet, but others had mimicked his kneeling posture before and now remained in that pose as if worshipping him—this monster who had taken men and twisted their flesh into something that should never have existed. One of them had transformed and its rubber suit lay empty, a yellow gas spreading out from it. A long, green-black leech slithered across the roof, moving away from the gas mask and leaking a trail of blood and viscous slime. It must have sustained damage in the ruckus down in Cocteau's lair, or during the quake as they ran up the stairs.

Taking a deep breath, Molly rose. She pounded the heels of her hands against her skull, trying to force herself to stop listening to Felix's anguished wail and to stop imagining the people dying all around them, the carnage of Uptown's collapse. But she could not scour any of these thoughts from her mind, and perhaps that was best, for they drove her forward. The building shook, but not so much that she couldn't stay on her feet.

"What have you done?" she screamed.

Dr. Cocteau faltered, glancing her way, and then he lowered the Pentajulum, holding it protectively, this artifact that had become the only thing in the world that was precious to him. She shoved past a couple of the gas-men, but his thuggish creations did nothing to stop her, little more than toy soldiers without orders from their master.

"Get away from me," Dr. Cocteau snarled. "You've ruined everything, you and Joe. It may not be too late, but if I can't get the Pentajulum working—"

"It doesn't work, you stupid son of a bitch!" she cried. "All of this is for nothing!" She swept one hand out to take in the catastrophe unfolding around them. "All of these people are dying, the city is being destroyed, because you set something in motion that you thought you could control, and you can't!"

Dr. Cocteau laughed, eyes sparkling with madness. "Weren't you listening? I never thought I could control what happens to this world. And I don't care. I'm going to be leaving it all behind. You can all drown as far as I'm concerned. But the young god is fully formed now, and once he hears me—"

The madman's eyes went wide with fear and wonder. A beatific smile spread across his features and tears of joy sprang to his eyes. His mouth hung open; he couldn't even form words anymore.

Molly turned to follow Cocteau's gaze and saw that he wasn't looking at the buildings behind her—he was looking at the sky above them. One of the gas-men was blocking her view, and she slipped around it, then stood and stared, her breath hitching in her chest.

There were slashes in the night sky, strips of blue-black void where there had been clouds, stars, and infinite space a moment ago. Molly thought of the curtains that had been hanging down in Dr. Cocteau's home and the way she had peered through them into the room beyond, but she did not want to see past these curtains. Through those rips in reality, even the darkness seemed different, and it went on forever, as though her whole world could fall through and be eternally lost in the void.

The crying of the thing Felix had become filled the city now, echoing off of buildings and churning with the rough river currents. It grew louder and louder, pleading and almost petulant.

But Molly barely noticed. Her skin began to crawl with the wrongness—the otherness—of the scene unfolding above her. Something had begun to manifest itself in the sky, a presence that seemed to have no definable shape, only coils that turned in upon themselves, or dangled down toward the city. Its tentacles, so much larger than those of its offspring, seemed to slither along the tops of buildings or to pass through them, solid one moment and ephemeral as a ghost the next.

"This isn't what you said was going to happen," Molly said, turning toward Dr. Cocteau even as she began to shudder with revulsion. The air itself felt like insects crawling all over her skin.

Dr. Cocteau shook his head, blissfully mesmerized. "I didn't know. But don't you understand what you are seeing? This is one of the old gods, a being from the other cosmos. You are seeing the face of God."

"Not *my* god," Molly said, glancing back at the thing whose very existence seemed uncertain. It shifted in and out of reality, edges blurring, its shape altering as though the physics of her world would not allow it to manifest its true self.

Dr. Cocteau lifted the Pentajulum in his hands and started pulling at it, first idly and then frantically. He pressed its coils and edges, held it between his hands and prayed to it, felt for some kind of trigger, and his expression went from joyous to helpless to frantic. Dr. Cocteau had run out of time to figure out how Lector's Pentajulum worked.

"Hey!" she shouted, but he ignored her, so she shouted again and punched him as hard as she could in the arm.

Two gas-men reacted, reaching for her. One got a good grip on her shoulder, but she squirmed away and they hesitated, waiting for orders.

Dr. Cocteau flinched and staggered away from her, still protecting the Pentajulum. He glared at her, and she remembered that he had promised to kill her. The gas-men would certainly murder her if he commanded it. Yet somehow she was not afraid. In the face of the anguish and the destruction all around them, her own life seemed such a small thing to risk.

"You are *not* going to figure this out in time to keep yourself from dying," she told him, shouting to be heard over the cacophony of the city's woes. "If you don't stop it, you're going to be killed with the rest of us!"

Dr. Cocteau stared at her, eyes wide, and a giddy laugh bubbled out of him. He turned from her to try to work the Pentajulum again. Molly reached for him, exploding with fear and grief, but Dr. Cocteau shoved her away. She slammed into the wall at the edge of the roof, pain shooting across her back, and nearly tumbled over the side.

Thirty-five feet below, in the turmoil of the river, Molly saw a flash of gleaming black and then the giant eel surged from the water. Coiled in its body, Joe battered at the creature's skull. Part of the eel's head had caved in, and slick blood and gray sludge dripped from within. The eel crashed back down into the river, taking Joe with it—or the stone man Joe had become, yet another thing she did not understand.

Molly turned to look at the gas-men, then at Dr. Cocteau. To her astonishment, the Pentajulum had begun to glow in his hands, light flashing along those strange coils and impossible angles. She looked up at the slits of darkness torn in the sky, at the eternity of nothing inside them, and the thing materializing there. Her skin crawled with its presence and she felt sick, but somehow she knew that whatever happened now, it would not go according to Dr. Cocteau's plan.

The thing that had been Felix still hovered half in and half out of the river, the tentacles on his face reaching up toward the old god in the sky, which she knew must be his father. He screamed his pain and sadness even more loudly, and Molly froze, staring at it, thinking of Felix, realizing that a part of him was still there, terrified.

He didn't want to go.

That was what had drawn the old god here. Felix didn't want to go. And as much as she didn't want him to go, she feared for the city—for her world—if the things that had abandoned this reality decided to inhabit it once again.

"Dr. Cocteau!" she shouted. "You've got to . . ."

But she never finished the sentence. He wouldn't listen to her. All he cared about was his own contact with this cosmic intelligence, as if he would attain some sort of godhood himself if it noticed him, as if he could even survive if his plan worked and he could travel between realities and explore the limbo of un-dimensioned space.

Molly darted up beside him. One of the gas-men noticed and tried to stop her, but not before she shot out a kick with all of her strength behind it. Cocteau's knee caved sideways, broken or torn, and the madman screamed in ferocious pain as he fell. Molly grabbed the Pentajulum from his hands. He tried to hang on, but she stomped on his arm and then danced beyond his reach as he shrieked in agony.

She knew that he deserved whatever pain she and the world could give him, and yet still she felt guilty. But now wasn't the time for guilt.

Molly spun, facing the intersection where the Felix-creature still wailed his sadness. She held the Pentajulum in front of her, running her fingers over its coils, wishing she could find some way to make it work. There were so many theories about this thing. Maybe it did amplify existing magic, in which case she would be out of luck, for she had none. But its coils felt like a tangle of hot and cold in her hands and it glowed a queer green and magenta, neither quite like any colors she had ever seen. The colors began to shift and undulate, and somehow she knew that what it reacted to was need. Desire. If it had worked for occultists in the past, it had responded to their yearning more than anything else.

Molly felt its awareness of her. It sensed her longing, and it knew the purity of her desire. She didn't want it as a weapon or a curse, or a tool to give her a fortune or a kingdom. She demanded nothing, but she needed to be understood. And as she felt something unlock within the Pentajulum, so she felt something unlock within herself.

"Felix!" she cried, leaning over the wall, holding the Pentajulum out over the river. "I love you." Her voice broke and tears streamed down her face. She shook with sobs but she forced the words out.

"You *were* my father. The only real one I ever had. But I'm going to be okay. I promise I'll be all right . . . but only if you *go*! I know you're afraid, but if you don't go, we're all going to die. You'll kill me, and you'll destroy every surviving piece of the city you loved."

Molly faltered, stunned to see that the Felix-creature had turned toward her, the tentacles of his face now stretching up toward the roof where she stood instead of toward the old god in the ruined sky. Dr. Cocteau had never understood the essence of the Pentajulum, but he

had been right about one thing . . . it could act as a conduit, a way to communicate.

She still didn't know the Pentajulum's secrets, but somehow it knew hers.

"Felix, please!" she cried.

The earth continued to rumble and the river to churn, but the creature had fallen silent, watching her expectantly.

"Give that to me, you bitch!" Dr. Cocteau roared.

She spun to see him propped up by two gas-men, left leg useless, fresh blood streaming from his nostrils. Molly started to shake her head, searching for a way to elude him. Dr. Cocteau lunged, tried to put weight on his left leg, and practically fell into her. Molly felt it happening as he collided with her, and she screamed. Dr. Cocteau tore at her hands, ripping the Pentajulum from her grasp even as they tumbled over the low wall together.

He grabbed her hair, clung to her, as they plummeted off the roof.

Molly screamed as the water rushed up toward them, and then they plunged into the maelstrom of the river and the currents tore them apart.

Chapter Twenty-three

The cold river churned around Molly, tumbled her end over end, and her chest burned for air. She hadn't had a chance to take a breath, and her brain cried out for oxygen as her hands clawed at the water and she kicked her feet. Panic drove her. The catastrophe taking place above meant nothing in those moments; the fate of the universe was a question for someone who wasn't drowning.

Her hand broke the surface first. She grasped at air and then her arm plunged into the water again, but now she knew which way was up. She stopped moving and got her bearings, even as her chest felt like it might collapse in upon itself.

Molly surfaced, fighting the current even as she gasped for air and blessed relief flooded her lungs. A rush of triumph and defiance filled her, and she glanced around for some purchase, anywhere she might drag herself from the river. The current in Manhattan was never like this, but this far south, with tremors in the earth below and whatever strange gravity working on the waters from the crumbling reality above, it had become a torrent.

The sound of the Felix-creature's cries filled the sky and echoed off of the faces of buildings. The deep grind and rumble of cracking earth and shifting foundations and the rush of the river filled her ears. A glimpse upward revealed the almost ghostly manifestation of the old god, a being whose shape and size seemed to be continually realigning itself. Long tentacles reached downward, rippling like holiday streamers in the breeze, but the god itself pulsed like something undulating in the deep currents of the sea. The sight of the ancient thing nearly made Molly surrender to the river, but she shook off that insidious temptation and struck out swimming toward a church on her right, a building hewn of rough brown stone. But even as she swam for it, the whole structure shook and began to crumble, and then the entire north side of it cracked away and slid into the water like a calving iceberg.

Exhausted, Molly spun in the water, beginning to despair, but then she spotted the familiar black metal of a fire escape to her left. Swimming hard, mustering all of her strength, she cut a path through the water. The current tore at her, and for several dire moments she feared she would be not reach it before the river swept her past, but she reached out and gave one final, fierce kick, and grabbed hold of the salt-rusted metal.

She held on, tightening her grip, and a moment later she hauled herself out of the water to stand on the fire escape. A tremor shook it, but she clutched the railing and would not be dislodged. At its far edge the fire escape had come partially free of its moorings, but for the moment it held, and as long as it did she would be all right.

Trying to get her bearings, she looking back upriver toward the intersection where the Felix-creature hovered half out of the water, even larger now. The tentacles on his face reached toward the tendrils snaking down from the manifestation of the old god appearing from the crack in the sky. Its body had become less solid, its angles less sure, and when she blinked it took on a strange, ephemeral aspect that it hadn't had before, as if from certain angles it did not fully exist in this world.

Molly leaned out and looked up at the roof from which she and Dr. Cocteau had fallen. The gas-men remained there, lined up on the edge of the roof like birds on a wire, gazing down through their emotionless lenses, their masks obscuring the horrors Cocteau had perpetrated upon them. She had half-expected them to jump into the river in pursuit when she and Cocteau had fallen, like lemmings following each other to their deaths.

Dr. Cocteau, she thought. *Where . . .*

She glanced downriver, thinking he might have been swept away, and then looked back toward the intersection. Only then did she see the haggard figure moving inside the relative safety of an arched and broken window, skulking like vermin in the ruin of a building where ordinary people had once lived or worked. The glass of the fourth-story window had been shattered, probably long ago, and little of its framework remained. Dr. Cocteau's beard and hair were matted, the white now gray with damp. His burgundy jacket had been discarded and his fine shirt was plastered to his rotund belly.

In his left hand, he held Lector's Pentajulum up toward the sky as though it might call down the lightning and put the power of the storm in his grasp. His mouth moved, and though his words were drowned out, Molly knew he was attempting the same weird ritual or incantation as before, trying to get the Pentajulum to work for him. Frustration and rage cut ugly lines into his face and after a moment he lowered his hand, paused, and then started to scream at the sky like a child in the throes of a tantrum. Whether he was trying to get the attention of the Felix-creature, or the old god that had slipped into this world, suffused with the menace and corruption of a reality where ruin and nothingness were natural, neither of them paid Cocteau the least bit of attention, and it had shattered something inside the lunatic.

As he screamed at the things from un-dimensioned space, he looked more like a fool than a madman. Then, abruptly, he seemed to feel the pressure of Molly's regard and spun in search of his observer. When he saw her, he pinned her with a look of murderous hatred. His mouth opened and he screamed something, but his voice had grown ragged and the chaos around them drowned him out.

Shaking, clutching the Pentajulum, he leaped from the shattered window and plunged into the water again. A moment later he bobbed up, swimming with one hand but mostly letting the current carry him through the turbulent water toward Molly's perch on the fire escape. She glanced up, thinking she could climb, try to escape him. But something shifted inside her, turning cold and hard. She refused to run.

Instead, she stood waiting, her whole body tensed with willing violence.

"Come on, then!" she shouted at him as he scaled the outside of the fire escape. "The whole city's falling apart! What're you going to do, kill me faster than I'm going to die anyway?"

With the same unnerving agility he'd shown before, Dr. Cocteau climbed over the railing and landed just a few feet from her. Despite his size there was something almost spiderlike about the way he had scrambled up from the water, and he hunched over slightly, staring at her, chest rising and falling with fury and exertion. He held out a hand, water dripping from his skin and his shirt, and the Pentajulum glowed softly, almost mockingly, in his grasp.

"Tell me how you did it, girl!" he shouted, his voice a wretched growl. "When you held it and you talked to Orlov, he listened to you! How did you do it? How do you make the goddamn thing work?"

Molly hesitated. She wasn't completely certain that the Felix-creature had understood her words. It had felt more like she had somehow touched whatever part of the monster was still Felix, that her voice had sparked something at his core. But the madness in Dr. Cocteau's eyes would be impossible to reason with.

"To hell with you," she said, hating him. "It isn't something I can teach you. Someone else, maybe, but *you* could never learn."

Molly didn't really know how the Pentajulum worked, but he didn't know that, and she wanted very much to hurt him.

Dr. Cocteau let out a ragged howl and reached out for her, his huge hand closing around her throat. She fought, clawing at his arm as he lifted her off her feet. Once again she could not breathe. He twisted her around and slammed her against the brick building.

"Tell me!" he screamed, spittle flying from his mouth, all reason having departed.

Beyond him, past the fire escape railing, something huge and slick bobbed to the surface of the river. The thick, green-black hide of the gigantic eel seemed to circle in the current, as though alive, and it took Molly a second to realize it was not. She slapped at Dr. Cocteau's arm, pointing toward the eel, trying to get through to him.

She squirmed from his grasp and landed painfully on her knees on the fire escape grating. As she struggled to rise, Dr. Cocteau noticed the giant eel at last and turned to stare at the huge corpse as it roiled and eddied in the river, sliding downstream and away from them.

"No," Dr. Cocteau said, his voice cracking. He shook his head, eyes wide with disbelief and madness, as if his dream had just died. "How can he still live?"

Coughing, clutching at her aching throat, Molly froze at the words, then thrust herself forward. She stood at the railing, staring in amazement at the sight of the stone man hanging on to the corpse of the giant eel.

"Joe," she whispered.

Dr. Cocteau stared, slack-jawed. Something inside of him had broken.

Joe pulled himself out of the river and crawled along the corpse of the huge eel, but only when the golem glanced up at them with that cracked, carved face, did she realize that he knew they were there, watching him.

His eyes were inhumanly bright in the darkness. Even though they were stone, they seemed almost to glow. It made Molly jerk back, still staring. And yet she knew those eyes, even at this distance. All of his skin had been torn away, leaving bare stone and hard-packed earth behind, but somehow this creature was still Joe. Still her friend. She remembered the stories he had told her about his dreams of a life centuries ago, when he had been a man of stone, and she realized that he had not really changed. What she saw now, dragging himself along the dead eel, was still just Joe.

Maybe not just *Joe,* she thought. That implied there was something ordinary or insignificant about him, something meager, and nothing could be further from the truth. She wondered for a moment if it was really possible for him to be the witch-killing stone man he had dreamed himself to be, and then she realized what a foolish thought it was. Reality was unraveling around her, and she was still thinking in terms of possible and impossible.

Dr. Cocteau bent over the railing. It shifted with his weight, giving way a bit, but it held to its moorings.

"Die, damn you!" Cocteau screamed at Joe, his voice mixing with the cry of the Felix-creature, the roar of the river, and the city's crumbling. "You can't be here! This is not the plan!"

As if by his command, Joe reached the part of the eel's corpse closest to them and slid off into the river, sinking out of sight. Molly felt her chest tighten as she pushed against the railing again, her gaze searching the water for some sign of him. Dr. Cocteau turned to her.

"It's an abomination, that thing," the madman said, eyes glittering. "If I'd known that Simon Church had a golem all this time, I would have tried much harder to kill it."

Molly frowned. *Golem.* She didn't know the word, but now she attached it to the thing Joe had become.

Dr. Cocteau watched the water as well, the Pentajulum clutched against his chest. Molly glanced at it, frowning. For a moment it almost seemed not to be there at all, and then to be half-embedded in Cocteau's chest, and now she saw it almost as fully solid as it had been when she and Joe had found it inside the cadaver of Andrew Golnik inside the trunk of that evil tree in Brooklyn Heights.

Another tremor hit, stronger than the last, and Molly let out a yelp and clutched the fire escape. Dr. Cocteau nearly toppled into the river, and he fell to his knees to keep from going over the railing. The building shook and Molly glanced around, watching the mortar dust and fragments of brick and glass raining down around them.

She looked Uptown and saw a tall spire—a building that looked as if it had been made entirely of crystal—begin to topple. The upper half of the crystal spire snapped off and tumbled out of sight, leaving a jagged stump of a building behind. Molly wondered how many people had died in that single moment, and how many other lives had been ruined. As she stared in horror, a gleaming black office tower began to implode, crumbling down into itself, shaken apart. Clouds of dust and ruin rose to the north, and she saw orange tongues of fire leaping toward the sky. How much of Uptown had fallen, she wondered. How much had flooded? How many people would have to learn to survive in ruin, just as the people of Lower Manhattan had been doing for half a century?

With every passing moment, the Drowning City was expanding its borders.

Still on his knees, Dr. Cocteau shouted in frustration. He thrust the Pentajulum upward, as if he were about to hurl it at the sky.

"You came for your child!" Dr. Cocteau screamed. "He's my brother. I helped him to embrace his true nature. I have earned a place at your side! I deserve to see your world with my own eyes. I belong there, and this is my key!"

He shook the Pentajulum. "Take it back where it belongs, and take me as well! But first . . . kill him!"

Molly flinched as Dr. Cocteau pointed south, realizing what had driven him over the edge. She leaned out and gaped at the sight of Joe—of the golem—holding on to the corner of the building. He punched a fist into the brick, then dug his fingers in, getting a handhold, and then he repeated the process. Brick by brick, he dragged himself back to the ledge of a shattered window and used its frame for purchase.

"He wanted to keep this from you!" Cocteau screamed shrilly at the torn and ravaged sky, its reality flickering, and at the undulating old god hanging from the clouds. "He wanted it for himself!"

But the old god did not seem to be listening.

The Felix-creature, however, had ceased its plaintive wailing again. A hundred yards ahead, in the churning water of the flooded intersection, he had turned toward them and watched with his many eyes.

Pushing stone fingers into brick and mortar, making his own crevices, Joe worked his way along the ledge toward the fire escape. Dr. Cocteau seemed to realize at last that his words had fallen on deaf ears, and he turned to run up the steps to the next level, shoes clanging on metal grating. But five steps up he seemed to realize his mistake, paused, and leaped back down to the landing. With a shriek, the far end of the fire escape popped free of the brick wall, but only the railing. The base stayed in place, even as the fire escape tilted toward the water.

Dr. Cocteau reached for Molly, and she could see the desperation in his eyes. But he had only one free hand, and she had two. She knocked his arm away and attacked, pummeling him so hard and so quickly that he had to defend himself or risk losing the Pentajulum. He screamed at her, uttering a stream of abuse and filth, but she ignored him, clawing at his arms and face, punching his throat, temples, and chest until at last he struck out, batting her away with such force that she banged into the railing, knocking the wind out of her.

As she collapsed on the landing, wheezing, heart pounding with fear and fury, she felt the fire escape tilt farther forward with a shriek of metal. Molly looked up to see Joe—the golem, Joe—standing above the kneeling Dr. Cocteau. Water ran in rivulets off his stone body, dripping from cracks and sharp edges. His eyes were alight with anger and intelligence as he reached for the Pentajulum.

Dr. Cocteau fell back on the metal stairs and tried to retreat upward, all of his cosmic ambitions forgotten in the face of this most solid of obstacles.

"No!" Dr. Cocteau shouted. "It's mine! It was always meant for—"

Joe snatched the Pentajulum from his grasp with a fast twist. The city had ceased its shaking for a moment, and with Felix quiet, Molly could hear Cocteau's fingers break even with the sound of the rushing river so near. The madman cried out in pain and held his broken hand and fingers against his chest.

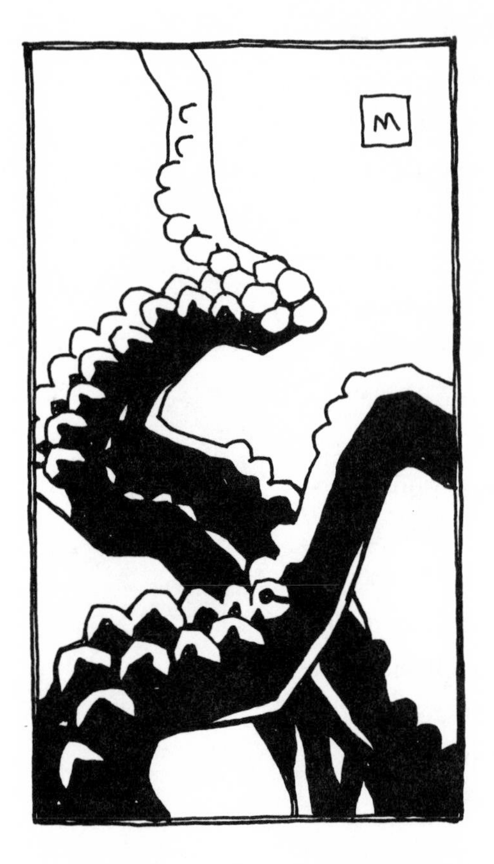

Turning away from Dr. Cocteau, Joe held the Pentajulum aloft. A hush seemed to fall across the city, and Molly felt sure that it was not only the Felix-creature, but also the ancient presence hanging above, that paused to see what the golem would do. The Pentajulum glowed brightly, its infinite colors throwing bright shadows on the brick, the fire escape, and the white tips of the churning current.

Joe crushed it in his hand, the Pentajulum going dark as it crumbled, as if it had had no more substance than an eggshell.

The whole city shifted violently, a massive yet momentary quake that slammed Molly against the railing. One half of the fire escape landing tore loose from the building and it swung out, twisting downward at an angle, dragged by its own weight. Molly screamed as she began to fall, but Joe was there, as he had been from the moment she had met him. He caught her by the wrist with one hand while he hung on to the next level of the fire escape with the other.

Buildings toppled. The remainder of the church across the river crumbled into the water. Another distant office tower simply gave way, crashing like felled timber into a smaller structure beside it. Molly closed her eyes and felt herself lifted, and she tried not to picture the devastation all through New York, both in the original Drowning City and in the newly flooded Uptown neighborhoods, where even more elegant spires and gleaming hotels were coming down.

"Climb," Joe said. One word, and only one.

Molly opened her eyes, forcing herself not to think about how many lives had been lost today. She put her arms around Joe's neck as if embracing him, the stone and earth of him rough on her skin, and then she climbed him as if he were just another edifice in the sprawling city in which she had spent her life clambering.

When she got hold of the next fire escape landing, she dragged herself up and over the railing. Joe followed, pulling himself up with a strength no man could ever have matched. Only after Joe stood next to her did she become aware of the soft whimpering from the stairs below them and look down to see Dr. Cocteau still nursing his shattered hand. He shook his head, whining and muttering to himself.

The world started to tremble again.

"Hang on!" Molly shouted, grabbing Joe's arm.

Then it stopped, as quickly as it had begun, and she stood there hanging on to him with no interest in letting go. Joe barely seemed to notice. His gaze was distant, and it took Molly a moment to realize he was not lost in some strange catatonia, but staring north at the intersection where the currents from side streets swept together.

"Oh my God," she whispered.

"No," Joe replied quietly. One word. But she understood his intent. The events unfolding in that intersection had nothing to do with any god she had ever known.

The Felix-creature had begun to rise from the river, tentacles dancing toward the sky even as his lower body undulated in the water. Floating, he began to emerge completely from the water, and this time when he cried out, the pain and sadness were gone from that keening wail. What remained felt to Molly like a song of yearning, and of home.

The old god reached down for its child, its form still shifting, never solid or definable to the human eye. Yet it lowered long, wavering tendrils downward as though pushing from one dimension into another. The lower it reached, the more substantial its tentacles became, until they began to twirl around those of its offspring, caressing and circling each other like elephants' trunks, gentle and loving.

Dr. Cocteau erupted from the stairs with a scream that Molly thought must have torn his throat to shreds. Still cradling his ruined hand, he rushed up to the landing where she stood with Joe. But he barely seemed to remember they were there, rushing past them, even bumping against Joe as he raced across the fire escape landing to the next set of stairs.

"Please!" Dr. Cocteau screamed, tears streaming down his face into his filthy white beard. "Please don't leave me!"

Molly looked at the old god and its offspring, and already they seemed to her to exist in another reality. The Felix-creature rose, curling himself in the vines of his father's affection. Jagged blades of light arced across the sky, but no thunder followed. Whatever storm brewed above the city, it was nothing of this dimension.

"Take me with you!" Dr. Cocteau screamed. "I did all of this! I dedicated my life to this—you can't just leave me here! Look at me, damn you! I am your brother! I know you see!"

He reached the top of the fire escape and hung halfway over the railing, one hand grasping pitifully at the sky, trapped in the human body into which he had been born, and that had now become his anchor.

"Don't leave me!" he cried, in a final, bloodcurdling shriek that ravaged his voice, so that afterward he could only open and close his mouth in a sad pantomime.

Molly watched in fascination as the old god and its child began to rise together, but they were not ascending into space. The slits in reality had begun to heal, and both creatures started to blur and run, as though they were simultaneously vanishing and slipping through a drain into the vast unknowable dimension where they belonged.

She saw Dr. Cocteau slump against the railing. He said something else, and she thought she could make out the words his lips had formed. *They're so beautiful.*

A single tendril from the Felix-creature drifted downward as if on an errant breeze. At first it seemed like the simple result of its swaying. But then, in an instant, it lengthened and straightened, reaching out so swiftly that it was only when Dr. Cocteau began to laugh that Molly looked up to see that tendril twining around the madman.

She held tightly to Joe, whose stone face remained impassive as they watched Dr. Cocteau lifted into the air, wearing an expression of utter bliss. The tendril coiled around him, hauling him gently but quickly into the sky, so that in a matter of seconds Molly could barely make him out among the fading, pulsing shapes of the old god and its child.

They slipped out of the world even faster then, their silhouettes running like mercury, draining back into un-dimensioned space. The city had fallen silent and still again, save for the voice of the river, and Dr. Cocteau's scream echoed out over the flooded wreckage like the piercing cry of some great bird of prey.

As the seams between dimensions were resealed and the creature that had once been Felix Orlov vanished from this reality forever, Dr. Cocteau broke into two pieces. Half of his corpse was tugged through the closing dimensional curtain, but the other half plummeted into the river at the same intersection where the Felix-creature had cried out his lonely misery.

Molly held a hand over her mouth and watched in horror as Dr. Cocteau's upper body floated past, bobbing in the water, white skin and hair glinting in the light from moon and stars that filtered through the remaining clouds. For just a moment, she caught sight of his face and saw the rapturous smile on his lips, and then she had to turn away. She pressed herself against Joe, but instead of human warmth, she had to take what meager comfort she could from the rough, stone embrace of the golem.

Chapter Twenty-four

As Molly held on to Joe, she heard the distant sounds of a city beginning to realize the worst was over. With a snort and a roar, an outboard motor coughed to life. Hundreds of boats would be plying the canals and waterways of Lower Manhattan within minutes, some people attempting to escape the ruin and others trying to rescue their friends and neighbors. Even the thieves and Water Rats looked out for one another at a time like this.

She wondered how many had died, how many buildings had fallen, and how many others were damaged in ways that were less visible. Molly had known entire neighborhoods by heart, every rope ladder and makeshift bridge, but now she would have to approach every structure that remained standing with great caution, every step wary. Everyone would.

And what of Uptown? The residents of Lower Manhattan—the

original Drowning City—would look after themselves, as they always had. But the people Uptown had existed for generations in a bubble of self-regard, an aura of imagined perfection and privilege. What would they do now that the towers had fallen and their utopian dream had been shattered? Molly figured that help would reach them swiftly from surrounding communities, places on the other side of bridges that had now likely been destroyed. They would be in shock and disarray, wondering why such a catastrophe had befallen them and how they could go on.

Most of the Uptowners had spent their lives pretending Lower Manhattan was a deserted shell, like some old haunted house, a place to be ignored except by children and the superstitious. But Molly had a feeling they would be paying attention now. If they wanted to recover and rebuild, if they wanted to survive in the Drowning City, the people would have to look south. Asking for help would mean acknowledging all the years that had gone by in which they had never offered it. Molly wondered if Manhattan would remain a splintered

city, or if this horror would bring Uptown and Downtown together again at last. Together in despair and hope.

Several blocks away, someone began to scream. There must have been other screams before, Molly presumed, but with the symphony of chaos around her, she had not heard them. This one cut across the evening sky as clear as a church bell, high and frantic. The voice belonged to a woman who fell silent after a handful of seconds. Molly could picture her, a wife or mother or lover crying out in grief at the loss of husband or child or cherished friend. But it wouldn't just be death that forced that scream from her—it would be the brutal intrusion of change, the knowledge that nothing would ever be the same again.

Molly shuddered at the thought, breath hitching in her chest. She pressed her cheek against the rough stone of Joe's body, felt her tears sticking against her skin where her face touched him. A small steamboat with pipes that whistled like teapots passed by no more than thirty feet away, moving upriver in relative quiet. The soft whistle was obliterated by a grinding, coughing noise as a longboat powered by with black smoke chugging out of the exhaust. The air suddenly filled with the stink of burning oil, and the smell made her think of Simon Church.

Molly pulled back from Joe, though they remained in a strange, awkward embrace. In the moonlight, when he cocked his head at a certain angle, he looked almost as he had before, and she could imagine he was still human. But the edges were too rough, and in the shadow of the building, the scars and fissures in his stone features picked up glints of light that showed what he really was.

She searched his eyes, finding a tiny spark of recognition amidst the confusion there. He seemed to know her, and then he cocked his head, as if he'd lost the memory somehow.

"You called me Joe," he said, his voice a grinding rumble.

"That's your name," she explained, trying to tighten her grip on his arm for emphasis. But he didn't seem to notice. His skin was cold stone. She doubted he could even feel her touch.

"Is it?" he asked, frowning.

Molly nodded. "Joe," she echoed, staring into his eyes, attempting somehow to reinforce the name.

"Thank you," he said. "I'll try not to forget."

Joe narrowed his eyes—stone, but somehow still human, with perhaps a hint of illumination from within—and studied her one final time, regarding Molly as if she were a puzzle he knew he ought to be able to solve. Then he took a step back and turned around, walking unhurriedly to the fire escape railing. He grabbed the underside of the iron grating above him and pulled himself up so that he was standing on the railing, about to jump.

"Wait!" Molly shouted, a rush of panic going through her. She had no idea where she would go next, or what she would do. "Where are you going?"

Joe frowned, as if it had been the most foolish question he'd ever heard.

"To hunt witches."

He dropped over the side of the fire escape and plunged into the river, water splashing high all around him. But the river rolled on, the current swirling, and in an instant he had left no trace. The water closed over him as if he had never been there at all.

Numb and lost, Molly stared down at the rushing water. She blinked and looked up, glancing around at the changed landscape of the Drowning City, and wondered where she would go. With Felix gone, she had no real home. If the theater hadn't been badly damaged, she could live there, but it would not feel like she belonged.

She looked downstream, watching the water flow out to the Atlantic, and realized that more than anything what she wanted was to go with Joe. Something had happened to his mind along with his body. His memories were a mess. Even if he wasn't the Joe she had first met, he was still going to need someone, a friend. Maybe more than ever.

A friend, she thought. And then she swore softly, realizing where she had to go.

The fire escape below her was too damaged for her to descend, but that was all right. She would go over rooftops or through the interiors of buildings, begin mapping the new layout of the Drowning City. She climbed the metal steps, her boots ringing on the iron grates. Whatever it took, she would make her way to her destination. She owed Joe that much, at least.

Mr. Church's ghost was waiting for her in his study when Molly entered the room. Working and living with a medium meant she had seen ghosts before, but never like this. The specter loomed over the dusty bones that were all that remained of its corpse, head hung in regret so powerful that it filled the room. With only the light from the moon and stars to illuminate the darkness of the study, the spirit had all the substance of morning mist, ready to burn off at any moment. After her first glimpse of Church's ghost, Molly moved from side to side, hoping to get a better look, but it seemed to become even less solid instead of more. It had no lower body, and where its hands hung down, its fingers drifted in and out of view as though lost in a cloud.

The specter did not look like the Mr. Church she had known. Its facial features were still dour but much younger, and the haunting silhouette showed no sign of having been tampered with. Church's spirit revealed him in his prime, before the need for magic and mechanisms to prolong his life. Molly found herself less shocked at the fact of his death than she had been at the knowledge of his long life.

A shiver went up her back, icy fingers creeping along her neck. She took a step backward, intending to depart. She had come here to tell Mr. Church what had become of Joe, but no one remained for her to tell except the ghost, and she didn't much want to talk to the dead. That had been Felix's trick, not hers.

Yes, the ghost said, his voice a whisper in her ears, like a soft breeze rustling her hair. It seemed to come from everywhere in the room and nowhere, all at once. *You should go.*

Molly agreed. Fear rippled through her as she took another step back. She could hear the grief in the voice of Church's ghost, but she was afraid to spend even another moment in that room. When she had first seen the ghost, she had felt only sadness. But now fear embraced her, and she no longer cared about putting either Joe or Mr. Church to rest.

Then the ghost looked up at her, and the depth of the sadness in his eyes drew her in.

I think now that I was selfish, the ghost whispered. Phantom tears touched the edges of his bottomless eyes. *I had lived so long and bid farewell to so many friends and associates that I had decided I couldn't bear to have another partner. I had resigned myself to a lonely life, but I'd begun to grow tired of it. Of living such a solitary life, but also simply of living.*

Molly stared, heart pounding in her ears. Her body wanted to run, but her heart would not allow it. She had to hear the rest. The ghost drifted nearer, eyes imploring her to understand.

When the golem came to life, I thought that somehow it must be a reward for both of us. The universe had given me a brother or a son, grateful for all that I had done to fight suffering in the world. And the golem—Joe—like Pinoc-

chio, he had become a real boy, with an opportunity to learn what it meant to be human. He had waited hundreds of years, standing in a box, but now he could live and die as a man.

Molly stood in the midst of the dust and the strange books and artifacts that Mr. Church had acquired during his long life, and she could not help thinking that Joe had been one of those things. The thought troubled her deeply.

"He *did* die," she said. "In Brooklyn Heights, at the cemetery. They shot him so many times . . . he *must* have died."

Again, Church's ghost hung his head, but now she saw the shame in his posture, the regret that weighed so heavily on him.

I had no choice but to bring him back. Someone had to stop Dr. Cocteau.

Molly stared at Church's ghost, gooseflesh prickling her skin. As the words sank in, she raised a hand, afraid for a moment that she might be sick.

"You . . . you did it to him on purpose?" she asked. "You're saying God, or the universe, gave him this gift of being human, and *you* took it away?"

Church's ghost lifted its cold gaze and stared at her. *You would be dead now, otherwise. And if Dr. Cocteau had somehow learned to use the Pentajulum . . . reality itself was in danger. If I had asked Joe, he would have willingly sacrificed his humanity for the lives of so many others.*

"Cocteau would *never* have learned," Molly protested.

He was . . . he was my best friend, Molly. If there had been any other way . . .

Molly exhaled, closing her eyes for a moment as grief settled even more heavily upon her.

"So, what now?" she said, staring at the ghost. "You're still here. Is this you now? You're going to just keep lingering however you can, holding on to the world until it gives up spinning?"

Not at all, the ghost whispered. Its voice remained the tiniest breath upon her ear, but now it had diminished further, Mr. Church's regret quiet and yet overpowering. *My soul will pass from the world now, and you will be the only person alive who knows the true story of Joe Golem. He's out there wandering now. You must find him, Molly, and remind him who he is.*

"He knows who he is," Molly said.

He knows what he was. You need to help him remember what he can *be.*

"Me?" Molly asked, incredulous, shaking her head. "How the hell am I supposed to do that?"

Church's ghost stared down at the withered husk of his own mortal remains. *You have to help him recapture his humanity, so that one day he can truly, finally, die as a man.*

A hundred thoughts filled her head, a hundred reasons why she could not possibly do as Church had asked. But before she could summon a word in reply, the ghost faded from the world, leaving Molly McHugh alive but alone in the Drowning City.

Outside, the water had calmed, as if New York was holding its breath. But soon the current would strengthen again, the river churning toward the sea. The tide had shifted, and it was headed out.